seven kinds of ordinary catastrophes

seven
kinds of
ordinary
catastrophes

amber kizer

delacorte press

Text copyright © 2008 by Amber Kizer
Jacket art copyright © 2011 by Getty Images
(cracked mirror; green lips; girl in neck brace; ice cream cone)
and Veer (girl in boots; broken heart; red pantyhose)

All rights reserved. Published in the United States by Delacorte Press, an imprint of Random House Children's Books, a division of Random House, Inc., New York.

Delacorte Press is a registered trademark and the colophon is a trademark of Random House, Inc.

Visit us on the Web! www.randomhouse.com/teens

Educators and librarians, for a variety of teaching tools, visit us at www.randomhouse.com/teachers

Library of Congress Cataloging-in-Publication Data is available upon request.

ISBN 978-0-385-73432-5 (trade)
ISBN 978-0-375-89124-3 (ebook)

The text of this book is set in 11-point Goudy.

Book design by Kenny Holcomb

Printed in the United States of America

10 9 8 7 6 5 4 3 2 1

First Edition

Random House Children's Books supports the First Amendment and celebrates the right to read.

To Connie Wick, my justice-seeking, speak-her-mind, leave-the-world-a-better-place, bring-it-on grandmother.

Thank you for the love and lessons.

And to Dr. Joe Wick, the king of storytellers, who after hearing the title of book one told me he'd practice twitching his cheeks one at a time. How's that technique coming in heaven, PawPaw? Got everyone trying it yet?

acknowledgments

Thank you to Lynne Malecki, who asked the most important question. To the ladies of the book club, who are unceasingly enthusiastic and interested in every detail: Mary Bakeman, Judy Burnett, Chris Fitz, Kathy Hein, Rachel Kizer, Lynn James, Lynne Malecki, Miriam Raabe, Joyce Veatch, Sarah Diers, and Susan Kofkin. To Sarah LaMar for being the best intern ever! Katie Taylor for her joy and belief in me—BFF since five years old and until one hundred, I'm sure! Tara Kelly, the world's most supportive friend, who understands when movies and vegetating may be the best my legs can offer. To Barney Wick for his unconditional love and support. *Semper Fi.* To Judy B for her professional excellence. Brenda George for her amazing favors and willingness to share her expertise with me, thank you. To Rosemary Stimola, agent extraordinaire, who is right there every step and who gets me even when I boggle myself. To Stephanie Lane Elliott, crème de la crème of editors—I couldn't ask for more. To Diane João, thank you for your work. To Noreen Marchisi and the fabulous PR department at Delacorte Press and Random House, thank you.

seven
kinds of
ordinary
catastrophes

 one

Oh, Holy-Mother-of-High-Heels-and-Dropping-Balls, what does a girl wear to a New Year's Eve party?

Stephen and I have been dating for about eight weeks. We don't really go anywhere. Mostly we talk on the phone, sit together at lunch and meet at the movies. I'm not supposed to drive boys and he rarely gets the car. Correction: according to my mom, who watches way too many judge shows, I'm not supposed to drive any life-forms, including amoebas, who might be endangered by my skills. Fab skills, if I do say so myself. But she sees lawsuits and cardboard boxes in her future with me behind the wheel.

Tangent: sorry.

They don't believe me when I say the mailbox had it coming.

Back to Stephen: to hear him talk, our great-grandkids will be showing up soon. We've been dating eight weeks. Ish. Does that sound fast to anyone else? Seriously. That's like two months. I don't really know how it got to be eight weeks so fast. I mean, time flies when you're dating. Or seeing a guy. Or hanging out. Or whatever we're doing.

I. Have. Nothing. To. Wear. I move a pile of clothes off my bed so I can sit down and contemplate the disaster that is my closet.

Here's the deal: he wants to go to this party, and I'm sure the guy is hoping to get me drunk and take full advantage of me. I saw that on an after-school special. Those boys are all CIA operatives when it comes to planting the flag on virgin earth.

And if he's not planning on trying to get somewhere, I will be crushed. What's not to love about me? I'd want to do me.

I tug on an off-the-shoulder old-school sweater. I look like my mother's favorite throw pillow.

"Mom!" I scream out my bedroom door. I'm desperate. I need assistance.

She comes barreling up the stairs. "What? What happened? Are you bleeding?"

"No—"

She presses her hand against her heart and glances around. "I told you not to light candles in your room. The curtains caught on fire, didn't they? Where's the fire extinguisher I put in here?" She pushes past me into my room. "Gert, what have you done?"

Why did I call for my mom? What demon possession caused that brief and deadly miscalculation? There's nothing I can say that will get me out of a two-hour lecture about respecting my belongings and taking care of things that children all over the world, and down the street, would, and do, kill for.

"I don't have anything—" I stop myself. Not a good idea to be honest. Really bad idea.

"What is it?" She turns and looks at me. "I like that sweater on you. It's very grown-up and it reminds me of something."

Your throw pillows?

I think fast. "Um, my period started and I don't have enough stuff—"

"I'm going to the store in a few minutes, I can pick up whatever you need."

"Thanks." Crisis averted.

"But, Gertie, this is no way to treat things we've spent good money on." She starts picking up and folding my clothes.

"I know, Mom." Inspiration strikes. "I'm cleaning out my closet for a fund-raiser."

"Oh, that's lovely. What's the cause?" She beams at me, all expectant.

Cause? Crap. Think. Think. "Teen pregnancy."

"Good for you. I like my girl interested in making the world a better place."

"Yeah." I should feel bad about lying.

"When is your young man's father coming to pick you up? Should you nap before the party, dear?"

"I'll be okay."

She shuffles back down the stairs. We don't celebrate New Year's Eve in my family. My parents may have clinked glasses one time before 1960, but we go to bed early around here. Geriatric early. Then, religiously, they get up to watch the parade the next morning. They wake me up to see horses and flowers, and horses made out of flowers, at an ungodly hour. I'm told I love seeing it every year. That's good to know, considering how much I love sleep.

I have no clothes. None. They are all wool, plaid, strangely middle-aged. What happened on the hangers between the store and my closet? They morphed. Sex kitten to roadkill.

Must call Adam. He'll have an idea. Plus, he got a fun new cell phone for Christmas. Of course, I'm not speed dial one. His boyfriend Tim is. That's wrong. Really, really wrong. As the official best friend, I should be number one. Not two. Not six. One. Someday soon we'll have to discuss my sucky speed-dial position. Now, must put clothes on for party so Stephen can drool and forget what we're talking about.

"Yes, Gert?" Adam sounds like he has something more important to do.

"Why are you answering the phone like a snobby British receptionist?" He's too cute for his own good.

"Because I knew it was you. I gave you a ring tone."

Shakira? Rihanna? I won't ask. I'll be cool.

" 'Wild Thing.' " Adam barely gets the words out before cackling.

There's a loud thump. I hope the roof caved in. I am not a "Wild Thing" ring tone. I will not dignify that with a response.

He huffs back into the phone. "Sorry, I fell off the couch."

Break much? "Sure hope you didn't get hurt." I don't even fool myself.

"What's up, Gertie?"

"I said yes to the party."

"Good, you only live once."

"Oh, so you're coming to make out with your boyfriend in public?" Two can play this Hallmark movie moment.

"Nope, staying here." He doesn't even sound insecure about his choice.

Hypocrite. "What do I wear?" Please, I don't want to discuss Tim's assets again. I really don't want to have to—

"What do you want to say?" Adam must be doing crunches while we talk. There's grunting in the background.

"I can converse just fine—help me with clothing."

"Your clothes. What do you want them to say?" He acts like I'm the slow one.

"I am not writing on my clothes."

He snorts. "Gert, hello, wake up, anyone home?"

If I wasn't so desperate, I would hang up on his homo fashionista ass and pretend I'm starting a new fashion trend with whatever I pull out. *Queer Eye* need not apply. "My clothes must make a statement?"

"Yeah. Sexy? Party girl? Crazed sociopath? Cute? 'Do me'?"

"No sex tonight." Even the thought of sex with Stephen starts me shaking. I've seen the guy handle a stick shift; he's not a soft and gentle lover. I read that tip in *Cosmo*.

"Cute?"

I consider. "Cute is fine."

"Brows tweezed?"

"Yes, and I found out about this great new thing called deodorant. I thought maybe I'd try that, too."

"No need to get bitchy. Just trying to get your back."

"Cute. Yes. Fine." How hard does this have to be? Clothing. Put on. Go. Voilà!

"Pay attention. You might want to write this down."

"I think I can manage." He knows me too well. I have pen in hand with a stick-figure diagram, who looks nothing like me, drawn on a pink Post-it.

"The dark denim, the tank from the lime green sweater set and your black velvet bolero jacket. Bangles. Go big on the jewelry, and flashy."

Not what I would have chosen in a million years.

"Oh, and the strappy heels you wore to homecoming."

"With jeans?" Am I channeling mid-eighties Madonna?

"Trust me."

Hmm . . . "Perhaps." Need I point out I couldn't dress myself? Obviously, I trust him.

"Go dark and smoky on the eyes. Gloss on lips."

Who am I—New Year's Eve Barbie? "Yes, makeup maven. Anything else, maven?"

"What are you doing with your hair?"

Shaving it? "Kate Beckinsale in her last movie."

"Chase scene or the party scene?"

As if there's a choice. "Party."

"Works. Tim's here. I've got to go play host." Adam doesn't even try to make me feel as important as his boy toy.

"Your parents okay with this?" I'm dubious at best. They're into coldly ignoring Adam's gayness unless his mother decides to randomly slap him.

"They're at the casino for an all-night bash."

"They know Tim's coming over?"

"Do I seem stupid to you?"

"Just asking."

"I promised I wouldn't have a party or drink and drive," he says.

I understand. "And one person over doesn't constitute a party. Gotcha." Dealing with parentals requires omission. Don't ask, don't tell. Be honest, but only up to a point. Survival of the fittest.

"Right."

I have seen less and less of Adam since Tim became numero uno. "Thanks." I try very hard not to be jealous. Rarely do I succeed.

"Call me tomorrow."

"Sure." Maybe. Must ready self for sociality. I didn't even ask

Stephen where the party is. Maybe I should have. Maybe Stephen's parents are at the casino and he defines "party" more intimately than I do.

I wonder what Lucas is doing tonight? Lucas is Tim's twin brother and the most deliciousness boy in the world. I drool at the sound of his name. Like Pavlov's bell with pecs and amazing shoulders.

Clothes on. Made up. Where's Sephora when you need its specialists?

Hair is so not Kate Beckinsale party scene. More like hostage on the twelfth day.

"Gert, Stephen is here," Mom yells up the stairs.

I spray on a last bit of hold-till-the-end-of-the-world hair spray. Tug. Tuck. Pinch. Heels. Must walk in heels like floating ballerina, not hippo.

Concentrate on stairs. Don't trip. Don't trip.

"Oh, hi." I try to act nonchalant yet completely put together. I think he buys it.

Oh, Holy-Mother-of-Old-Spice, somebody got cologne for Christmas.

"Ready?"

"Sure." I pick up my purse, which I've preplaced for optimal suave factor.

"Not too late, Gert." I can tell Mom's fighting the urge to scrapbook this moment.

And then there we are at the empty, parental-less car. Where's his father? I thought his parental was driving us?

"Where's the party?" I try to sound casual and slide into the car like Audrey Hepburn.

Stephen shuts the door and pretends he doesn't hear me. As

soon as he turns on the ignition, the bass makes conversation impossible. How can he think with this much reverberation?

"Got new speakers from my brother," he screams in my direction. "Parents are out; Dad gave me the keys. No parents." He has the smarmiest look on his face. Does he think parents are the only reason we're not doing it like bunnies?

Good thing I'm adept at reading lips. I smile. Are we trying to break the speakers before MLK Day? 'Cause they're maxed out.

I buckle my seat belt while trying not to vomit. The boy pulls more Gs in this rusty heap-o'-metal than the space shuttle. I don't think cars are designed to do this. I hold on and pray. And try to look cute while keeping the vomit at the back of my throat.

Please tell me the party isn't too far away. I can't handle road-trip Stephen.

He's slowing down. Thank God. I wonder if I can roll down my window without him thinking it's because the entire bottle of cologne is asphyxiating me.

This looks like Jenny's neighborhood.

I roll down the foggy window. I don't care if it's cold, I need the view.

This *is* Jenny's neighborhood.

There are a ton of cars parked outside. It could be complete coincidence.

No. No, we cannot be pulling up here. He's kidding.

"You're joking, right? Messing with me?" I ask, but he motions he can't hear me over Fluffy Pete's acoustic rapping.

He brakes. Turns off the car. "This CD rocks. Did you say something?"

"Yeah, this isn't the party, right?" Please tell me you're really a serial killer. That works better for me.

He has the audacity to look perplexed. "So?" Now he's going to act all oblivious to the undertones of bringing me here.

"This is Jenny's house," I try to point out without screeching.

"So?"

Must I paint him a mural? "This is the party?"

He doesn't get it. "Yep. Let's go."

Is my reaction that hard to read? Could he possibly not know Jenny and I hate each other? Didn't I tell him before we ever started dating? I mean, I wouldn't put him up for a Mensa membership, but isn't it clearly defined in the school handbook that Jenny Cohen and I cannot abide each other? Stephen was in a group project with us; he knows.

I close my eyes and try to inhale.

"Come on, Gert." He acts like I'm the one with the problem. All he needs to do is tap his toes and he could be my father.

"Fine." I'm sure there will be lots of people and I won't have to face her at all. She'll never know I voluntarily spent time at her abode on a holiday.

Stephen opens Jenny's front door. Most of the school is here. Good. Lots of people. The stench of sugar syrup, cheap candles and alcohol blasts me in the face. Is that cigarette smoke? Pot?

Buttocks. Jenny, two o'clock.

"Hey, Jenny, thanks for the invite." Stephen taps her shoulder like they're on the offensive line together.

"Gert." She nods at me.

I smile back. My brittle I-can't-believe-I-have-to-play-nice-and-not-kick-you-in-the-shins smile. "Jenny."

"Drinks are in the kitchen. Movies are on in the den and upstairs in the film room. Dancing in the living and dining area. A bunch of people are skinny-dipping in the pool. It's heated."

Skinny-dipping? I must be hallucinating. She did not just suggest naked swimming on December thirty-first. Stephen has the nerve to wink at me. If he thinks he's getting me naked in front of half the school, he is so not even worth oxygen.

"Great." I take Stephen's hand and wander toward the kitchen.

"You want beer?" Stephen pulls the keg spout like he's done it before.

"Not yet." Disgusting. I don't find fizzy horse urine that appealing. "Coke's good."

"Want rum in it?"

When did my boyfriend turn into the bartender?

"I see Maggie. I must go say hey." I grab the Coke and move toward the dining area. I glance back to see if Stephen's following me. Nope, he's talking to some guys. Beer bonding.

"Drive your boy away already?"

Dear Lord, is she everywhere? It's unholy. "Jenny, how nice to see you again." Twice in five minutes must be a record.

rant #14
the word "orchard"

What is the etymology of the word "date"? Who looked at a wizened piece of brown fruit and thought, "Perfect. Girls and boys getting together can be called dates. What an inspired idea!"

Did cavemen growl about fire and then decide tup-ping was fruity? And what's with the fruity thing being gay? If heteros go on dates, then aren't we fruity too? Who of dating age isn't fruity?

And if we're going for obscure fruits for naming get-togethers, why not a hot fig? Or a spicy kumquat? Or a durian?

The obvious would be to call them bananas—or if we want to be biblical, we could call them apples.

To Australians, "date" means "anus." So what do they call a date? And do you have to be really care-ful around Aussies and clarify that you're using the other meaning? And seriously, how did that evolve? Did someone get focused on anal sex and start a whole word revolution? Can you imagine being the first person who said yes to a date and got a surprise at the end of the night? That makes my toes, and my date, curl.

Personally, I think I'd like a kumquat. Can't be nearly as confusing as dating. Although now that I consider it, what exactly is a kumquat?

 **two**

"Great party," I say. Lying is a necessary skill for high school.

"Isn't it." Jenny's eyes glow red.

I wish I had my camera with me; no one will believe me when I say she's a demon. "So?" Why isn't she moving on to the next victim? Don't I look paralyzed enough?

"So. Stephen?" She quirks a brow at me. I'm not sure if that's a precursor to the deathblow or if she's trying to be chummy.

I stick with noncommittal. "Uh-huh." Has she forgotten we're not friends? We will never be friends again. Ever. She killed my favorite stuffed animal at a sleepover in fifth grade. Drowned him in urine. I will neither forget nor forgive.

She crosses her arms. "He's cute."

Why do I feel like I'm dating her boyfriend? She seems like she's trying to make me feel guilty. I don't even understand why. "Yes, he is."

She nods, never breaking eye contact. "He's nice, too."

What's with the catalog of Stephen's assets? "Oh, look, there's Maggie. I should—"

"I don't see her." Jenny must have demon eyes in the back of her head, since her front set is still piercing my brain.

"I do. And I promised I would say hello immediately. So thanks. Great talking to you." I walk away slowly, waiting for her fangs to sink into the back of my shoulder. Talk about an angry cobra. I am mongoose.

Too bad I have no idea where Maggie is. My saying yes to this darn party was all her fault. She thought I should spend New Year's with my boyfriend instead of her. I didn't want to, but she made me. She got this sad face and said, "I wish I had a boyfriend to spend New Year's with." Well, then what do you say? *Too bad—want to borrow mine?* I'm sure I should feel more possessive about him. I mean, I'm not likely to slit my wrists if he doesn't call me—isn't *that* real love? The melodramatic, kill-myself-on-theatrical-cue kind of love? I so don't love him up to that standard.

Of course, I think secretly Maggie was thinking about this guy Jesse who started new this year and whom she casually brought to my surprise sixteenth birthday party. She gets all dreamy talking about him but then flatly refuses the idea that she might want to date him.

I move around a pile of bodies playing naked Twister. I'm not old enough for this party. I will never be old enough for this party.

What is that smell? "I'll take Dead Beer for six hundred, Alex."

I step in something sticky and crunchy. It oozes over the toe of my shoe before I can step away. It's between my toes. I hate these shoes. I will back the car over these shoes, after I put different ones on; I'm not going to back the car over these shoes with my feet in them. I don't think that's possible. Plus, it'd be painful.

Smiling at guys with Cheetos stuck in their braces. Avoiding groping hands and almost avoiding pinching fingers. I rub my butt

cheek. That hurt. I shoot a glare over my shoulder, but the perpe-
trator could be one of many guffawing baboons. Forced chuckling
at jokes I can't catch completely. Probably for the best that I can't
hear much over the bass and amped-out guitars. Cats in heat,
anyone?

I am so over acting like I want to be here. Whose idea was this?
And why was I persuaded that I'd have a good time? Momentary
lapse in my otherwise stellar judgment.

There must be someone here to talk to. I swivel, trying to manage the cool-vibe-photoshoot-in-Paris twirl. Nicely done. Still no
one up to par.

Someone. Anyone?

I catch a glimpse of hair. A curl over the collar of a black polo
shirt.

Could it be?

Lucas. Lucas is here. My heart races. My toes tingle.

He's here. That hair. That mouth. I push through a few random hookups and almost slip on a puddle of—God, I hope that
was beer—trying to get a better look.

Those shoulders. My breath hitches as my gaze follows the way
the shirt caresses his lean muscles. Long strong arms. Those un-
believably manly hands that are on another girl's butt. What?

Quick. Close eyes.

Reopen. Crapping buttocks! Same butt.

Oh, Lucas, why do you do this to yourself? With Sophie? Senior Sophie? Rumor has it she has three kids in a Swiss preschool
high in the Alps. Sophie has the body of Angelina Jolie with the
face of America's Next Top Model. However, since this is her fifth
year as a senior, I take comfort in knowing I probably outscored her
on the PSAT. Very cold comfort.

Lucas obviously doesn't know how important brains are to a relationship. I should enlighten him. I should bring him up to speed. Yep, I'm going to march over there. As soon as he and Sophie unmeld their tongues, I'll explain it real slow.

"Watch it! I'm walking here." Thing with a keg of beer on board beefy back bumps into me; it'd be a swishy piggyback ride if the keg had legs. How charming.

I can't help pointing out, "You're weaving. It's a whole other sport."

"Bitch." The shade of green tingeing his cheekbones isn't attractive. Though I'm guessing he doesn't care if I find him sexy. Neither is the stench: vomit-filled ficus tree. Wonder if that makes good fertilizer, or can plants get alcohol poisoning?

Lucas and Sophie have disappeared. Just as well. I'd hate to vomit without the benefit of being drunk first.

Stephen. I should find Stephen. I look around, hoping to spot him without having to wander through the downstairs again. And here I was thinking he's clingy. He wants to talk all the time.

Are there right answers to his questions? I always feel like I'm in an interview for the role of girlfriend and at any moment I can be fired for not measuring up.

No Stephen, so I'm wandering. Drunk people are so drunk. Do you start with fewer brain cells to want to get that way, or is it a cumulative effect of parties like this? I mean, a good buzz I can see. Haven't ever touched the stuff, but I can appreciate the appeal. The beer bong, pass-out-in-less-than-five-minutes approach to responsible drinking? Not so much. I am no one's mother, but I'll just keep my eye on that chick over there whose chest is barely rising and falling. Maybe I should call 911. Maybe not. How do I know if she's dangerously drunk? I didn't hand her plastic cups of fun. And frankly, do I want to be the-chick-who-called-911-on-the-sober-sleeping-girl? I'd never live that down.

Where's Maggie? She promised to come. Where's Clarice? She thought she might come. Where's my bestest friend, Adam? He is at home smooching his honey and I'm here trying not to get vomit on my sexy bare toes. I'm fairly certain I have someone's Cheetos and Cuervo as nail polish on my left foot.

Oh, I see Stephen. Relief abounds. He's talking to a bunch of guys I don't really know. Relief is replaced with panic.

"Hey, Gert!" Stephen yells, waving at me. He wants me to come over. I can tell this from my fabulous powers of deduction. "Get over here so I can introduce you."

Or perhaps he just thinks I'm stupid and don't know what the waving means.

"Hi." I do a girly simper and three-finger twiddle.

Stephen puts his arms around me from behind and smashes his chin against my very complicated and now flat hairstyle. "This is Gert. My girl."

Your girl? Are you an ape now? But I manage to keep my cool and simply smile pithily in the general direction of the rest of the silverbacks.

"You in high school?"

Nope, just graduated med school. I'm a neurosurgeon; can I drill into your skull right now? "Sophomore."

A rather cute dark swarthy type asks, "You play football?"

Do I look like I play football? Diet Coke, here I come.

Stephen laughs at my expression. "Ricardo is from Colombia. He means soccer."

That explains the funky, though slightly erotic accent. "No." Soccer? Me?

Stephen tries to whisper in my ear. "You want another drink?" But it comes out sounding like a loud demand.

The fumes on his breath alone could kill roaches.

"No, I'm good." *And I won't be driving anywhere with you tonight.*

He wiggles against my butt. Oh my God, he actually rubs an erection against me. What am I, Aunt Irene's ottoman? Are you a shih tzu on Viagra?

"Be right back."

"Take your time." The crowd of he-men thins. I'm stuck staring at Mr. Exchange Student. At least he's an attractive diversion.

"You like it here?" I ask.

"Party is good." He nods.

Where is he from again? "You like the U.S.?"

"Party is good."

Okay then. I can adjust the conversation. "Good party, huh?"

"Yes. You know football?" he asks.

I know nothing about football, but dear God don't make me mingle anymore. "It's a great sport." I try to appear interested and, more importantly, interesting.

"I like." The relief on his face is blinding and frankly, I'm not sure if he's saying he likes me or that he likes soccer, but I'm in party hell, so I'll take either one.

"Who do you like to watch play?" I smile encouragement.

He lets out a torrent of Spanish (I think). Could be Portuguese, or Russian. It's unclear.

Nodding and smiling seems to do the trick to keep him going. I throw in a few "*Sí, sí*'s," which about sums up my *Sesame Street* bilinguality. At least I can ask for *agua* if I get desperate. Foreign languages aren't my thing.

I tune back in to the conversation, hoping I haven't missed

anything I can understand. Ricardo seems to be waiting for me to respond. I try widening my eyes. No dice. Who was he talking about? Who, who, who? I dive in. "Jaime is a good player."

Ricardo bristles. He even starts to turn a daring shade of red. I've said something wrong. I thought we were talking about how good Jaime is. Obviously not. I laugh and wave my hands around like I've made a big joke. "Sometimes. But mostly Jaime is a bad player." I wrinkle my brow and put my hands around my own throat like I'm choking myself. Maybe overkill, but his face lightens back up.

Better. Much better. I should be a UN ambassador. This multicultural stuff is easy.

Crapping buttocks, I know that look. Ricardo is waiting for me to take over the conversation. Now he thinks I have as much to say as he does. I grab at any foreign-sounding name with the hope he might think I'm mispronouncing something familiar. "Personally, I really like Sephora. This side of heaven. Really."

He gives me the confused you-stupid-American look. I guess Sephora doesn't come from wherever he's from. I try to broaden our discussion. Other popular names . . . think, think, think. "Jesus?"

He smiles, a quick show of teeth; then he's off to the races again. "Jesus." Another torrent of fast coolness I completely don't understand.

I nod and smile. I answer a question. "Yes, Jesus made a big impression on history, didn't he? All blessings and healings and stuff." I don't think we're discussing the same guy.

"Gert. It's almost midnight." Stephen grabs my waist and leans into me. Thank the Holy-Mother-of-Boyfriends, there are no bulging parts this time. I don't really know what to do with those yet.

"Sorry." I give Ricardo my best apology face. The one I've practiced in the mirror in case a cute cop pulls me over for speeding.

"This is the best party," Stephen gushes while pulling me down a long hallway. *Sure, drunk boy, whatever you say.*

"Yeah." Here's the deal, I didn't think lying was part of the whole dating thing. Aren't we supposed to be completely, totally honest with each other? Isn't that what a healthy relationship is? Holy-Mother-of-the-Self-Help-Section, am I sabotaging this relationship? Do I want to end up alone, wearing housedresses and talking to parakeets? Must fix. I open my mouth to tell the truth when I hear—

"Jenny is so cool. Great chick." Stephen doesn't even turn around while delivering this info.

Okay, we'll start the honesty stuff tomorrow.

He keeps dragging me along the world's longest hallway. "They've got five big screens set up in here to watch the new year come in all over the world."

It's a technology shrine. I am doomed.

To add to the technological haze, the only lighting comes from the sets themselves. Which is probably more light than you'd think, but still not enough to sober anybody up. I need a spotlight to shine in Stephen's pupils.

Stephen's had a few too many. I can tell because the fumes are overpowering the cologne he got for Christmas. The combination could be a WMD, as it's making my eyes burn.

He's nuzzling my neck like I'm his favorite pillow.

Bodies are intertwined all throughout the room, and I'm busy trying to figure out how Jacquie is able to hold that position. Doesn't she have a neck cramp or something? I catch a glimpse of flesh as she sits up. Was that a—Holy-Mother-of-the-Cartoon-Network, is that a penis?

I slap at Stephen's hands and turn my face back toward his. I'm not done here. Dude's all zipped up now. Jacquie is downing a beer like she's been in the Sahara for weeks. Interesting. Must file this info.

But Stephen's hands are everywhere.

Everywhere. Good God, he's grown more hands. I swear there are four distinct palms groping. None of which has heard the term "tender love."

Stephen breathes across my face. "It's almost midnight, Gert. You know what that means?"

I gulp air and try to shove myself over toward the wall as more people pile into the room. "It's a new year?" This has to be against fire codes.

"Ten!" everyone but me screams.

Oh, Holy-Mother-of-Stopwatches, we have to count down now? The house actually reverberates. "Nine!"

Stephen looks really happy as he finds my butt cheeks with the palms of his hands.

"Eight!" I'm too stunned to move.

Decidedly, deliriously happy as he squeezes like he's found a new toy.

"Seven!"

Goofy, but at least he has let go of my butt; it can breathe now. Where are his hands going? Tell me he's not going to grab my boobs. Please don't grab, please don't grab.

His hands keep moving up, past my breasts. "Six!" he yells like he's howling at the moon.

He gazes back at me while cupping the cheeks on my face. Why is he bracketing my face like I'm in trouble? Like Aunt CiCi used to do when she babysat and I swiped a cookie.

"Five!" He is so strong.

Eye contact. We have eye contact.

I anticipate the next number. "Four!"

Thank God, he lets go of my face. That's my butt. Again. "Three."

He smashes his face against my ear. "You have the best butt. I am so into you."

"Two." The crowd keeps pressing around us. What do you say to that?

"I'm into—" I start to say.

Stephen smooshes his face against mine. He has super-tongue, all big and strong, pushing past my lips. The shock makes my jaw drop. Big mistake.

His tongue is in my mouth. If I had tonsils, he'd be fondling them.

Is this it? French kissing? This isn't romantic; it's revolting.

Swallow. I have to swallow spit or I'm going to drown. I so don't like the taste of beer, which is why I didn't drink any. I had no idea I'd have to taste it anyway.

I can't retract my tongue any farther. I'm trying to stay out of his way, but I feel like someone's got a tongue depressor in my mouth fit for an elephant.

Where's the sound track? Where are the gooey feelings? Where's the liking this?

He pulls back. His hands are still on my butt. Squeezing like I'm taffy.

"Wow. Happy New Year!" Stephen smiles at me. He appears to think that was a fine first French. Was it?

I think my first French kiss just sucked. Does it get better? Or, oh my God, am I gay?

 three

"You're not gay." Clarice shakes her head. I can hear her shaking her head, even over the phone at two a.m.

"How do you know?" Now I'm panicked. I thought I was supposed to know from birth or something. Shouldn't I be really into home improvement stores and rugby?

Maggie, always the voice of reason in three-way calls, says, "Gert, instead of Stephen, picture a really hot chick doing that slobbering-conquering-choke-with-tongue thing."

Hot chick? Who's my type? "Who?"

Maggie hmphs. "Jennifer."

"Which one?" There's Aniston, Garner, Lopez, Love Hewitt— how do I know which is my type?

Clarice doesn't let me waffle long. "Pick one."

They don't have to sound so exasperated. This could be a defining moment in my life. "Just asking." I'm visualizing. Yuck. Still feels like I'm the beaches of Normandy being stormed by Enormotongue. I must gag out loud because Maggie and Clarice both jump in and break my visualization.

"So?" Clarice asks. "Do anything for you?"

"No." Not really. Short of wondering how Jennifer gets her hair to stay like that, it sucked.

"Sucked?" Maggie clarifies.

"Still," I add. Sucked once, sucked twice. I think it's safe to say it's not a gay thing.

"Then it's simply a bad kiss." Clarice sounds so confident.

"You think?" I'm still not convinced. Do bad kisses exist? All kisses are good kisses, or aren't they? I'm stuck just a little on the gay thing. I like looking at the Victoria's Secret catalog. I even sticky-note pages for exercise motivation. Seriously, what's the diff between wanting to be that body and wanting to do that body?

"Have plans tomorrow night?" Maggie asks.

"No." Both Clarice and I answer.

"Come over. I'll rent all the best-kiss movies and we'll figure it out," Maggie says.

Exhale. "I'll bring junk food." Screw the waifish models with SUV headlights on their chests, this calls for Reese's Cups and Twizzlers.

"I'll bring tunes and gossip mags." Clarice hangs up.

"Don't worry, Gert. He's just a really bad kisser." Maggie sounds so sure. I wonder if she's ever kissed him. I hear a click.

"Happy New Year," I say to dead air. Happy Freakin' New Year.

"Rise and shine, porcupine!" Mom thinks she's so clever.

"Time?" It's not even light out. Have they no courtesy?

"Almost time for the parade. Your brother and Heather will be here soon. I made eggs Benedict."

Oh, Holy-Mother-of-Food-Poisoning, doesn't she remember last New Year's? Does she think we all happened to get sick and fight over porcelain thrones on a whim?

"Great."

"Mike's also bringing Krispy Kremes—at his insistence—and I think Heather made her family's special breakfast casserole." Mom fluffs the pillow that's still warm from the head she pulled it out from under.

Thank God Mike has told Heather the truth about this family's cuisine. When in Rome, bring a picnic. I will surreptitiously throw away my eggs Benedict, make lots of yummy noises and eat donuts instead.

I wander down the stairs. I got about two hours of sleep. Every time I closed my eyes, tongues attacked. I'd wake up gagging and then panic that not only might I not be hetero, I'm anti-tongue. I don't want to be anti-tongue. That leads to other anti things that will leave me alone and talking to parakeets.

"About time." Dad thrusts a mug at me. For some reason his idea of me celebrating the new year is drinking coffee with milk and sugar in it. I don't have the heart to tell him I've been going to Starbucks since I was in first grade. Maybe the caffeine and sugar will burn off the haze of spit clouding my vision.

He peers at my face and I briefly wonder if I have an enormous zit somewhere. "Okay night?"

"Fine."

He grunts and turns back to the TV.

I hear a car. "I'll get it." Mike and donuts to the rescue!

"Hi!" I'm involuntarily loud as I throw open the door. Buttocks! Mustn't appear too eager to avoid Mom's cooking.

"Hiya, Gertie." Mike hands me three large boxes of assorted. "I

brought lots of extras, since we get to leave later and you don't."
He says this last bit under his breath. "Heather's family is having
us over for dinner."

"Thanks." I inhale all sorts of artificial molecules and feel
slightly more human, thank Goddess. "Hi, Heather."

She smiles at me and kisses my mom on the cheek. "Thanks for
letting me make my family's traditional breakfast. It means a lot."

She's good. Laying it on, but not too thick to be unbelievable.
I wonder if she picked a recipe out of the cookbook last night or if
she actually planned ahead.

"It smells lovely, dear. And we always love trying something
new."

We do? Have my parents tried anything new in the last decade?
Must consider at length later after I swallow half a box of Boston
crèmes.

"The parade's starting." Dad doesn't get up from his chair but
instead growls in our general vicinity.

I'd love to report scintillating conversation about world issues,
or in-depth discussion about the latest bestselling novel, but alas,
we all sit, watch the floats and the horses and listen to the same
John Williams medley played, with varying degrees of success, by
marching bands from all over the country.

I pass out extra paper napkins and put a garbage bag between
me and Heather while Mom serves up plates of edible and highly
inedible glop. I figure with Heather's help, we'll avoid serious puking for dinner.

Who designs band uniforms? It's an insult to the blind, deaf
and mentally disabled to suggest that there's a commune full of
rejects designing band gear to get back at the society that displaced
them, but is there any other explanation? No one looks good in

triple-ply poly and ten-gallon hats with pom-poms or feathers. I mean, not even the remotely cool drum majors can pull it off. I just spend time feeling sorry for them all.

Tangent: sorry.

Why doesn't someone stick banders in jeans and white T-shirts? Maybe baseball caps and sunglasses if it's necessary to accessorize? Go wild and put everyone in matching sneakers, but please not uniforms that get recycled each year to the freshmen. That's just cruel and unusual, especially since kids are getting bigger and bigger and poly only stretches so far. And yes, I have seen just how far poly can go several times today.

"So, Gert, what are your plans for the rest of break?" Heather doesn't understand the no-talking thing yet.

I turn my head and speak out of the side of my mouth in a low almost-whisper. "I have a sleepover with some friends and then it's back to school."

"That sounds fun." She smiles and doesn't lower her volume. Poor girl will need the rules spelled out for her after all. Must e-mail her later and bring her up to speed. Obviously, her boy toy isn't good on family prep.

As the last horse craps on the parade route, I stand and stretch. "Later, people." I'm going back to bed. I have serious sleep to make up for. I only feel a teensy bit bad about leaving Mike and Heather to escape on their own. I take the last box of donuts with me—they will be safest in my room, where I can devour them later.

I'm thoroughly enjoying my sleeping emptiness when Mom knocks and pokes her head in. "Gert, honey, your phone keeps ringing. Is it important?"

Don't you think I'd have answered it if it was important? How stupid do you think I am? I can't ignore the damn phone to sleep instead?

Is there some rule that says the phone must always be answered? I say, revolt, people! Rebel! Let the phones ring!

"Okay, I'll get it." I turn over and grope for the phone. " 'Ello?"

"Gert? It's two. Why do you sound funny?" Stephen has the gall to act all perky and chipper.

I clear my throat and lie. "Getting sick." I have no makeup on and I'm sure I'd stink if I were to smell myself.

"Sorry. Sucks."

There's a long pause. I've momentarily forgotten my script.

"How are you?" I ask, blinking the sugar coating out of my eyes. Fell asleep on the box of donuts.

"Good. Good. You have a good time at the party?"

"Yeah." Lie numero *dos*. Oh, Holy-Mother-of-Long-term-Relationshipage, I am doomed. "Lots of people."

"Jenny's pretty cool. The guys really liked you," he says, like I passed the major exam.

"Yeah, liked them." Ricardo was cool; the rest were a little too drunk to apply adjectives to.

"Ricardo kept going on about you after you left. Should have heard him saying your name. Hilarious."

Sure. That sounds rocking funny. Apparently, my boyfriend thinks I'm an object of humor and the exchango-mano enjoyed my company. Funny. Real funny. This is why I got a ride home from Maggie's NYU sister—that and the fact that I was so not riding in a vehicle with drunk Stevie behind the wheel.

"So?" Stephen draws it out.

"So? Family good?" I really should be more attentive. I'm sure I'm not being a good girlfriend.

"They are. Crazy. You see that show this morning?"

"We had to watch the parade."

"Rose Parade? That's cool. We were treated to Dr. Phil's Holiday Family Makeover. My mom TiVo'd it so she could stop it and make us all do the exercises."

That's hideous. I thought my mom was the only one who watched bad talk show reruns. "Wow."

"Yeah. Look, I really like you."

"I like you, too."

"I feel all, you know, safe with you, like I could tell you anything."

Wow, um, really? Because I don't think I feel that way at all. "Me too," I say, since the silence kinda demands it.

"So I'm not sure how to say this—"

Oh, Lord, he's breaking up with me. I sit up and blink in the dark. I'm getting dumped on New Year's Day. I was a ball-dropping kiss and nothing more.

"I have a small dick."

What? He did not just say that.

"I'm sorry?" The bacteria on the eggs must be replicating in my brain, causing all sorts of irrevocable brain damage. And ear damage.

"My penis. It's small," he says again.

Good God, what the hell do I say? I have to say something. *Your tongue makes up for it.* I try to laugh a little to break the tension. That makes it worse. Are we really in the place in the relationship where you can fart freely and overshare insecurities? God, that was quick. I thought you had to have sex half a dozen times and do holidays at the other family's house before you got to be this free.

Must say something supportive and not totally mortified. "I'm sorry." Think. Think. Is there anything worse for a guy? I don't know. Think. "Maybe it's not. I think my boobs are small." Not really, but I'm so not using the V-word on the phone with a guy I've been dating for a couple of months. Besides, I'd be lying if I mentioned my vagina. I have no idea if it's small or humongous. I'd like to keep the lying to a minimum.

"You think your boobs are small?" he asks.

"Yep." Brain hemorrhage right now, please. Quick death.

He's grunting and breathing. "Well, they are a little small. Have you thought about getting a boob job?"

Have you thought about getting your dick expanded? "No, they're still growing."

"Oh." He sounds deflated.

I feel the need to soften my last comment. "I'm sure yours is, too."

"What?"

"Growing. Your penis. Is still growing." I'm almost whispering this, hoping my mother isn't listening for the first time ever at my door. She'll never believe I'm as shocked as she is. We are not having this conversation. I'm in an E. coli–induced nightmare. I will wake up in a hospital surrounded by balloons and flowers.

"Sometimes, but I don't think it stays that way."

This could not get worse. Couldn't. Must get off the phone. "I have to go. My dad is yelling for me."

"Oh. Okay. I'll talk to you later."

"Sure. Later." *Like when I know what to say to you.* I just can't get the image of a teeny-tiny dick out of my head. I don't want this picture in here. Get it out. Get it out!

I hang up the phone and stare at the ceiling. Did that really happen? Let me be hallucinating.

Please. I am not that lucky.

"How was your New Year's?" Adam's much-needed call breaks my small-penis-am-I-gay-inflicted trance.

"Uh." Language is beyond me.

"What's that mean?"

"Uh." The idea of Stephen's small dick is just painfully mortifying—so is that proof I'm gay? Although frankly, if Stevie was a girl I'd have to kill myself. What does this mean?

Adam waits a second to launch. "Whenever you're ready, but in the meantime we had a fabulous time. Incredible. Love cuddling. He's so cute and smells so—"

"I—I—gay?" I stammer.

"What?"

I try again. "Am I gay?" I have to move the phone away or risk the laughter damaging my eardrum.

Adam calms down long enough to ask again, "What?"

"I am not repeating myself." He so heard me the first time.

"No." He sounds adamant.

"You're sure?" Don't gay people have a sixth sense about these things? *I smell gay people* or something?

"Why do you ask?"

"Cuz," I hedge.

"He's a bad kisser?"

"I don't know, that's what I'm trying to figure out."

"One has nothing to do with the other."

"Huh?"

"If you're gay, a kiss can be nice but take-it-or-leave-it. Don

Juan could kiss you with a millennium of knowledge and you'd ask him to pass the salt."

"Oh."

"But if you're with a bad kisser, your orientation is so not the issue."

"Oh." Really? Could it simply be a case of badness? Thank Goddess, or God—the devil even. I'm just happy.

"Stephen lack chops?" Adam wants details.

"His tongue seems abnormally large."

The cough can't conceal a laugh. "I'm sure his tongue isn't setting records for size." For Adam's sake, I'm glad he's not eating right now, because he'd so be needing a long-distance Heimlich.

"And that's the other thing."

"What?"

"Size." I can't even bring myself to repeat this. It sounds like bad reality TV even in my head.

"Of his tongue?" Adam sounds confused and frustrated. Not that I blame him. I'm not Miss Articulate at the moment.

"Are you happy with your size?"

"Of my tongue?"

"Your codpiece," I clarify with what little dignity I have left.

"My what?"

"Your dick." Oh my Lord, I am reverting to a nine-year-old wannabe Pops language.

"My dick? Am I happy with the size of my penis? You want to know—"

"No. Forget I asked. I don't really want to know. But are you?" My face is burning. I hate being a girl. We are so unprepared for genital insecurity. We're too covert for this.

"I'm not throwing myself on any swords."

"Meaning what?" Please, now he gets all cryptic. Spell it out for me.

"I'm about average, I guess. Maybe a little more. Nice size when erect. Nothing I'm worried about. Where does this come from?"

"Stephen called me."

"And said what?"

"He's uncomfortable with his . . . size." And I know I'm totally perverse, but all I can think about is the baby boy I babysat whose teeny-tiny didn't seem to matter when he peed all over me. Never change a boy's diaper. Let them sit in it. Or bring a change of shirt for when they decide to engage in water sports.

"He did not. I am not falling for this crap. You have to be joking."

"Have I ever in my life joked about penis size?" Knock-knock jokes, an occasional ironic comment, sarcasm, yes. But a shtick about sticks? Not my style. "I'm not kidding. Honestly."

"Swear on the Barbie you mutilated."

"I swear on Barbie's double mastectomy, I am not kidding."

"Oh my God."

There's a long uncomfortable silence.

"Adam?"

"Yeah."

"You there?"

"Hmm. Trying to figure out what to say." He sounds as blown away as I feel.

"Is it as weird as I think it is?"

Adam hmphs. "How long have you been going out?"

"Almost two months."

"Yeah, it's a little odd."

"I mean, do guys talk like that? I thought you were supposed to be all silent and hard to figure out even after years of marriage."

"Well."

"I mean, first he makes me wonder if I'm gay and then he drops that one. And what do I say? What in the world did he want to hear? That I think his dick is just right for my inadequate vagina? How does he know? I have no idea if I need to add that to my list of things I should have therapy for, so how does he know? And why does he think this is something I want to hear about? What in the world was he thinking? That I want to know his every secret and fear?"

"Breathe, Gert, breathe."

I gasp for air, but with a little oxygen, I get going again. "We've kissed. Once his tongue touched my spleen, but that's it. Shouldn't we date long enough to, I don't know, meet each other's families before the issue of dick size is even raised? Isn't that something that should be talked about in marriage counseling before the divorce? I bring up how small it is, and how he can't use it, and he makes cracks about size not mattering, but then when it gets down to it, he's been ashamed of the small size all his life?"

"You've been watching too much Lifetime Television."

"I have not."

"I guess it's good to know now." Obviously Adam is reaching.

"How so?"

"Well, if dating a horse is something you aspire to, then you need to look in a different stable. Saves time." He's chuckling. I can't believe it. He's finding humor in this.

This is not funny. "This is not funny."

"Yes, it is."

"No, it's not." Okay, it's a little funny. I swallow a chortle.

"Yeah, it is. Very." Adam giggles.

I giggle. I hate growing up. I am not prepared for this crap.

Adam says something and then repeats it. "Did you"—pause for gasp of air—"did you reassure him?"

Tears stream down my face. I'm laughing so hard my stomach hurts. "I don't remember. Isn't that horrible? I don't know what I said." I am the worst girlfriend in the world.

"Maybe he wanted you to convince him. You know, check it out and pronounce it worthy."

"That's as likely as me having sex in a room full of people."

"He doesn't know that. Maybe it's a new line."

"Maybe he thinks dating means actually being honest about all that."

"That's a possibility."

"I don't want to know. I want to kiss and cuddle and have someone to go to dances with. It was nice having a guy on New Year's."

"Hear you on that."

"But I don't think he's the one who's going to eclipse my moon."

"Tell me you haven't been reading Hallmark love cards again."

"Some are very poetic."

"Sick. You are ill. No one looks for romance in the romance section, honey."

"I like them."

"He's not going to buy a card for you."

"You never know." It's my secret fantasy for a guy to hand me one of those huge smooshy-squishy, lovely-dovey Hallmark cards for no reason other than because he saw it and thought of me.

"Not going to happen. Why don't you bring the fantasies back down to earth. Hope for an orgasm the first time you have sex. Something at least possible in the known universe."

"You're not helping."

"Yes, I am. I'm being the voice of reason."

Change the subject. "Tim's good?"

"We're good."

"Good." I really want to ask about his proportions, but, well, that could be construed as invasive.

"You okay?"

"Yeah, I am. Maggie and Clarice are having a sleepover later."

"Good. Let's have burgers on Saturday night?"

"Yeah, it's been a while. That'd be good."

"And Gert?"

"Hmm?"

"You're not gay. Maybe you're just not that into him?"

That's something to consider.

rant #15
and
rave #6
twin peaks

This is both a rant and a rave because frankly, I can't decide how I feel about them. My boobs took the idea "reach for the stars" seriously. Lying on my back, I've got twin launchpads with shuttles. Any minute now, I'm going to hear the NASA voice counting down to liftoff.

My bras aren't fitting right. I'm kinda spilling over the top and out the sides. I haven't gained weight, since my jeans still fit, but my boobs are getting ginormous. Slight exaggeration, perhaps, but who tells them to grow? And more important, who tells them to stop? Has a woman ever had boobs that didn't stop growing? She's probably stuck facedown somewhere, her throat hoarse from calling for help because all of a sudden her boobs went from having their own zip code to dry-docking her right where she stood.

Seriously, where's the reboot function? Where's the off switch? Who do I have to say nice things to to get them to stop? If I sleep on my stomach, will that slow the rate of growth?

 four

Clarice pulls out a bag full of candles and begins setting them around Maggie's room. We're starting to look like the candle store at the Plaza—the one with eighty discreetly placed fire extinguishers and no overhead lights.

"What's with the candles?" I ask.

"My sister says you must have the correct ambience when discussing kissing and kissing techniques," Clarice answers, intently positioning pillars and votives.

Maggie moves behind her with one of those foot-long lighters, setting every wick aglow. The lit candles begin filling the room with a mosh pit of scents.

"Didn't she mean actual kissing ambience?" The room smells like a yummy brothel in Turkey.

"No. It's a ritual thing in our family. You get Frenched, you light smelly candles." Clarice sets the empty shopping bag aside.

Uh-huh. And when do you sacrifice the chicken and smear frog intestines on your face? I glance at Maggie, hoping I'm not the only one feeling empty of understanding. She smiles at me. I hesitate, then venture in. "I don't get it."

Maggie shakes her head in minute agreement.

"There's nothing to get." Clarice is oblivious to the look Maggie and I shoot each other.

"Okay." I don't get it. But I really like the fruity coffee-cream candle wafting to my left.

Maggie pulls out a file folder from under her bed and shuffles through computer printouts. "I did a little research."

Okay, here's the deal, I've never understood how much I need and want girlfriends until this moment. I'm not going to get all gooey and gushy, but I have to say that watching Clarice light candles to purify my kissing karma and Maggie pull out her file-o'-technique, I realize that I'm blessed. I have to wonder why it took so long.

Maggie shuffles the papers and pauses like she's gathering her thoughts before starting the lecture. "I'm impressed by the sheer number of techniques! I'm not sure we can cover the spectrum in a single sleepover."

"Whatever. What are they?" Clarice waves her hands and jingles several very goth charm bracelets.

"Soft. Hard. Biting. Sucking. Breathing. They all have weird names."

"Maybe we should watch the movies first, then decide which is which?" While I'm a serious fan of book learning, I'm thinking visual aids may be much more helpful. And more fun. Fun is good.

"Fine." Maggie reaches for a stack of DVDs while Clarice pops the tab on a Diet Coke and rips the bag of Ruffles.

I pull out the Twizzlers, gummy bears and Doritos. Quite a

delicious combo when eaten together. The salty, the sweet, the artificial chemical haze of the twenty-first century.

"What's first on the list?" I ask, grabbing a full-calorie beverage.

"*From Here to Eternity*." Maggie puts in the DVD and stacks more pillows for better viewing.

The beginning credits roll. Either there's something wrong with Maggie's HDTV or the movie is really old, like precolor.

"What's that?" Clarice licks her fingers. "It's black-and-white. Who makes black-and-white movies anymore? Seriously retro."

Maggie shushes her. "It's voted the best kiss ever on-screen," she says.

"It's in black-and-white." Apparently, Clarice only lives in Technicolor.

"I'm just the librarian here," Maggie offers.

I prepare to be blown away by the mind-blowingness of the most perfect kiss ever to grace the silver screen.

Clarice can't just give herself up to the experience. "Are we watching these chronologically?"

Maggie presses pause. "Nope, 'best kiss' is how they're listed." She waves her stack of papers around.

Clarice motions to the television. "Who are these people? They're old."

"Yeah, so?" Maggie shrugs with disdain and pauses the movie.

I try to break the tension. "Frank Sinatra is in it. I recognize him." This must be the original.

"Oh." Clarice shuts up as Maggie presses play again.

"What's it about?" I ask, thinking there could be more action to the best kiss ever.

"Barracks life in Hawaii in 1941." Maggie hands me the DVD case so I can read the back.

"World War One?" Clarice asks, munching on more chips.

"Two. One was in the teens," I answer. What number are we on now? Four?

"He's hot," Maggie says.

I look up. Not bad for a colorless man. "Where are the women?" This is way too old to be the first gay kiss, so where are our counterparts?

Clarice says exactly what I'm thinking. "Okay, I'm bored. Can we fast-forward?"

Maggie turns to me. "Do you think that affects the kiss rating? If we don't know the whole story?"

I compromise. Isn't a kiss a kiss no matter what the rest of the story is? Would porn be so popular if the story was important? "Well, go to where we see a girl come in."

Clarice screeches "Stop!" when a woman comes on-screen. This woman's got a reputation. She's married. Is she giving him "the look"? They're making eyes at each other. Is that allowed? How old is this movie? She smokes.

We glance at each other, hoping we're not the only one unsure of the content. Is this movie about unhappily married people? "How is this a great kiss? They haven't even shaken hands," I ask as minutes click by.

"He likes her," Maggie says.

"Who?"

"The sergeant guy," Clarice answers.

"How can you tell?" I ask, still dubious.

"He's ogling the pic on the guy's desk," Maggie says, zooming forward a little more.

"Do they like each other or hate each other?" Clarice asks.

"I can't tell," I say. "Can you tell?" I shrug, pointing to Maggie.

"Not really. But isn't that what great love is all about? Not liking each other, alternating with liking?" She doesn't take her fingers off the remote.

We skip more. Sandy beaches and bizarre swimming attire. "This could be it." I have a vague recollection of my mother having watched this movie before. Ooo, they kiss. In the sand and covered in salt water.

"Can you see anything?" Clarice turns her head to the side like she's the camera and controls the scene.

"His head is in the way." Maggie shifts too.

I'm not any closer to knowing anything. "Is that the kiss? *The* kiss?"

"I don't know. The list just has the title of the movie, not a specific kiss." Maggie peers at the papers like the answer is there, waiting to be deciphered.

"She gets around. They're dating? I thought she's married. Is she a tramp? He's yelling at her and she finds this attractive. Chick needs therapy." Clarice starts narrating the film.

"Go faster, this sucks."

"Is he going to die?"

"Yeah, think so."

"Then the kiss wasn't that good, was it? Why'd it make the list? Pearl Harbor? We're almost two hours into the movie and now they bomb Pearl Harbor?"

Maggie skips the rest in superspeed.

"So what did we learn? Boys die. Girls sail away and no one lives happily ever after. Why was this a great kiss movie?"

"I don't know." Maggie has a crestfallen expression on her face. Her good idea could turn out to be a very bad one.

"What's next?" I ask.

41

"*Gone with the Wind*," Maggie replies.

"It's like four hours long," Clarice complains.

"We'll skip the unimportant stuff," says Maggie.

Forty minutes of fast-forwarding and one pee break later, we're looking at THE END.

"Huh."

" 'Kay."

"Aside from a bunch of bigots, did you get anything from that?" Clarice shakes her head. "Me either."

"What's next?" I can barely ask.

"*Cruel Intentions* and *Wild Things* are the girl-on-girl best kisses."

"I thought we decided I'm not gay."

"*We* did, but this is just clarification. Besides, I'm pretty sure a kiss is a kiss is a kiss. And frankly, don't girls do everything better?"

"Wasn't that in a song somewhere?" And true. So freakin' true.

"Maybe."

"Aren't we too young to be this cynical?" Clarice asks. A good point.

"This coming from the world's hugest femme rock fan?" I say. She blushes. "I am not."

"But cynical you are."

"At least we're not bitter." Maggie pops open another can of Dr Pepper.

"Bitter comes in the twenties," Clarice adds.

"Says who?" I don't want to be bitter. A survivor's pointed perspective is not bitter.

"My sister."

"Miss French-kiss-candle-girl says the twenties are bitter?"

"She did just break up with the love of her life."

"Oh."

"Her fourth soul mate in six years."

"Do we really have that many?" Is it possible that we all have multiple soul mates? People who could be the ONE but aren't the ONLY?

"She hasn't exactly been in a long-term relationship with any of them, so I hesitate to say yes."

"Point." Maggie pauses the movie. "Don't you think if we have a soul mate, the divorce rate should be lower? I mean, we must have more than one since people keep looking.

"Or are they impossible to see? Like everyone's soul mate is on the other side of the world and unless you join the Peace Corps, or backpack through Europe, you're destined to never find him."

Clarice swallows, then says, "Let's say there's always a soul mate somewhere near you."

"What do you mean?" I ask.

"What if there's always a soul mate around and you only have to recognize him?"

Lucas? Yeah, my soul ain't that pretty. But maybe he's my beautiful half and I'm the smart half. That would make me ugly and him stupid. Not quite the halves divided equally.

"Who's yours?" Clarice pins me with a dare-you expression.

Mine? Like I'm going to say it out loud. Am I an idiot? You say these things out loud and one way or another something irreversibly bad happens. Like he vomits on you, or you move to Florida, or it's printed in the school paper in the editorial section under the title "Get Real."

"Mine's Spenser," Clarice says.

Shocking. "No, really?" I laugh.

"Come on. I know it's obvious. I'm making progress, though."

Uh-huh. What is progress, exactly? The boy doesn't run away, he walks?

"Maggie, who's yours?"

"I don't know." Maggie looks about to cry.

"Is it a girl?" I'd never gotten the lesbian vibe from Maggie, but I could be wrong.

She doesn't even seem offended. "No. I'm just not really interested."

"Really?" Is she a freak? Is it normal to not be crazy about the idea of penises on the premises? I mean, if guys think about sex every three seconds, then we must think about it almost as often, or more, since our brains are bigger and more efficient.

"I'm a freak." Maggie pulls at the carpet with her fingers.

"No, you're not." Clarice hands her a tissue and a box of Runts.

"I think maybe I am."

I'd tend to agree, but that doesn't seem helpful at the moment. Maggie doesn't seem freakish to me, but then, I'm dating a guy who thinks sharing his insecurity is a necessity for a good relationship. Maybe I'm the freak of nature.

"Why?" I ask. Seems the safest question.

Maggie shrugs. "I mean, I like looking at men. I really do get all Jell-O-ey over biceps and washboard abs, but the idea of dating feels far-fetched and too soon. I like Jesse, but I can't even imagine it going anywhere beyond smiling."

"My sister says her college roommate had never been on a date until her senior year when she met her senior advisor."

Dare I ask? Clarice's stories don't always have a happy, pointy reason for the addition to the conversation. "And?" I can't help myself.

"And they have like six kids and are so blissfully happy my sister had to stop speaking to her because it was disgusting."

"Your sister has issues," I say, feeling the need to point this out.

"Tell me about it." Clarice bites into a chip and noncommittally licks the salt from her lips. She doesn't seem to care what she looks like with her tongue all gyrating to get the salt crystals only she seems to be aware of. Gross.

"So, maybe you just haven't met him. I mean, really, Maggie, you have an amazing brain, and you're so good with computers. Here's the deal: you have to be complete yourself before anyone else can make you more."

Both of them stare at me like I've just turned into Oprah and Dr. Phil's love child. That's a picture.

"Thank you, Dr. Gert." Clarice snorts chips out her nose, and it's so gross we all roll on the floor laughing.

"Onward, Kissing Soldiers! Push play and let's educate the masses." I wave my hand in the general direction of appliance-dom. "Next?"

"*Body Heat* and *9½ Weeks*."

"Okay. Are these in color?"

"Yes."

And hours later? Our necks hurt from watching other people kiss and pretty much what we all know now is what we knew before watching the movies. At least it was a fun way to come to grips with the truth about the kiss. And I'm definitely not gay.

I hesitate to say this out loud and give it power, but what the hell. "I think Stephen sucks."

"Yeah. That's my conclusion," Clarice says with a belch. " 'Scuse me."

I'm disappointed and utterly confused.

Maggie, good ol' bookworm Maggie, asks, "Can he be taught?"

"I don't know. Can he?" Can you teach a thing like kissing? Or is it divine knowledge shared with a few privileged souls at birth and the rest of us are destined for bad kissing?

"Yes, he can. My sister says most guys have to be taught everything." Clarice throws a bunch of wrappers and soda cans in the trash.

"Everything?"

"Sex-wise. They're pretty dense."

This is comforting? How does the species propagate if boys are so bad? I guess pleasure doesn't babies make.

"Maybe that's it," Maggie says.

"What?"

"Is he a virgin? Are you his first kiss?"

"I don't know." Talk about pressure. "I don't think so." Holy-Mother-of-the-Breath-Mint, I hope not.

"Stephanie and Ruth in my English class say they've seen him at some pretty wild parties and he's so not a virgin." Clarice shakes her head, shooting the idea out of the clouds.

What's that mean? "I'm dating a man-ho?" How do I feel about that?

Maggie hands me a box of Junior Mints. "I don't know about that, but he's not monkish."

"A monkfish?" Clarice asks, looking up from the diagrams of kama sutra positions Maggie printed out.

I can't eat Junior Mints right now. They are the first food I ate with Stephen.

"How is this possible?" Clarice holds up a particularly acrobatic pose.

Here I am worrying about kissing and she's showing me Rubik's Cube position number eight. "I don't know. Who's who?"

"I can't tell."

"So, Stephen isn't a virgin." That is news. "Why did you wait until now to tell me this?" I must reel us back on topic.

"I didn't know if it was important to you or not. Are you a virgin?"

"I'm watching black-and-white movies to find out if I'm a sucky kisser. I'm thinking the odds are good." I don't try to keep the ire down.

"Point."

"Hey, you didn't say who you think your soul mate is," Clarice says.

And here I was hoping we'd all forgotten that little bit of conversation. Moment of truth. I will find out if I can truly trust these girls, or if I'm going to have to move to Florida. "Lucas," I say.

"Lucas?"

"Soccer-playing girl magnet of the junior class?"

"That's him."

"Wow."

"He's your soul mate?"

Why do they look so incredulous?

"He's hot."

"Yes, even my frigidness thaws in his direction." Maggie smiles.

"I know I don't stand a chance, but a girl must have dreams." Why do I need to defend my soul-mate choice? As if I have anything to say about it.

"True."

"Point."

"Confession time." Clarice chews on her lips like they're part of the menu.

"Shoot." I'm ready. Confess away. My heart will stop popping anytime now. At least they didn't laugh. They could have laughed. I would have laughed at me.

"Spenser wants to be benefriends."

"Benefriends?" Oh, Holy-Mother-of-Euphemisms, what is she talking about?

Clarice raises her eyebrows and does a little shoulder seizure. "You know."

"Of course I know." What the hell are benefriends?

"What do you think?"

Maggie starts making clucking sounds.

"You have something stuck? Need me to practice the TV hindlick maneuver?" Clarice waggles her tongue in Maggie's direction.

When the laughter dies down, we all keep giggling.

Clarice picks at her blanket. "I'm serious here."

"I know you are." Best to reassure and tell her I'm in agreement. Oh, and ask questions. "What do you want?"

"I'm asking you guys."

Bad, bad idea.

Maggie clucks again.

"What is your problem?" I try my most potent fake glare.

"Well . . ."

"What?" Clarice yanks a strip of red licorice from the bag sitting next to her and chews furiously.

"My grandmother always talks about cows and milk when this comes up," says Maggie.

"Huh?" Now I'm really lost. Benefriends is a farm animal thing? "What is Spenser into?"

"Kissing and stuff." Clarice waves her hands. She obviously doesn't know either. "Your grandmother knows what friends with benefits are?"

"Oh!" I blurt out my comprehension, but they ignore me. *That's* what benefriends are. Who knew? Obviously not me.

"Yeah, she watches all those *Dateline/Primetime/48 Hours/ Access Hollywood* shows on teens. She wants to stay with the times and speak my lingo." Maggie sighs.

"Uh-huh. And she mentions cows?"

"She likes them. They always come up in conversation. You should see her bedroom. Spots and udders everywhere."

That explains a lot.

Maggie shrugs. "But can you? Really not get emotionally attached, I mean? What did he say exactly?"

Clarice turns over onto her back and stares at the ceiling. "He said he likes me, but he's not ready for a relationship and wouldn't it be great to kiss and stuff without the pressure of dating."

"The pressure of dating? Was he high?"

"No, he doesn't do that kind of thing. I don't think."

Clearly, Clarice and Spenser are completely honest about every aspect of their lives. Two more perfectly attuned human beings would be difficult to find.

"And you *want* to be benefriends?" I need some adultish guidance here on what to say. If I asked my mom, she'd wonder how friends could qualify for health insurance or 401(k) plans.

"I—well, he said he's not ready for a relationship now, right?" Clarice asks.

"Apparently."

"So he didn't say he didn't want to have a relationship with me."

"True." I'm having a hard time not shaking her back into one of Earth's orbits.

"So doesn't that mean that eventually he'll want to be my boyfriend?"

"Maybe." Is there a correct answer to this one?

Her face falls all the way back to terra firma.

I change my answer. "Of course he wants to be your boyfriend."

She brightens. "It'll take some time, but how could he not want to be together? Especially when we fall madly in love. Then we'll be exclusive, and so this is like a warm-up for that."

Maggie clears her throat. I wonder if she has weird nasal allergies or something. "What if he doesn't—" She breaks off when Clarice's eyes well with tears.

"Why wouldn't he want to be my boyfriend? Am I that repulsive?"

"Clarice, of course not. You're not repulsive. If I was gay, I'd totally want to date you," I say.

"Really?" She seems to find comfort in this.

"Honestly." In the friends-sometimes-have-to-lie-to-each-other sense of the word "honestly."

"Thanks."

Maggie pats Clarice's shoulder. "So when are you officially benefriends?"

"I think we are already. We kissed in the back of the gym last week. And he put his hands on my waist."

"That's good, then." Would it work? Could she change him by easing him into the whole idea of togetherness? I thought you were supposed to wait for someone you didn't want to change. Like Lucas. Lucas is perfect.

rant #16
Facial Faux Pas

Didn't anyone get a new razor for Christma-nukahzaa? What is it with guys and shaving? We're out of school for two weeks and they all revert to caveman-gorilla antics. I mean, it's like they forget the truth, and the truth is—boys can't grow beards.

I have never in my life seen so many spotty Brillo pads. And not nice, even Brillo pads, but the kind Aunt Erma used for thirty years and couldn't bear to part with, so it's all sparse in sections and blotchy in others.

There isn't a single manly-boy in our school who can successfully grow any facial hair without looking like an armadillo in a Spider-Man costume. Okay, maybe that's a bad example, but can you imagine how bad that armadillo looks?

What's with the fuzzy cheeks and single strands on chins? Just because they don't shave doesn't mean it belongs there. It's like us not shaving a section of our calves and calling it fashion. It's not sexy, it's inept.

And what's with the soul patch thing? Who thinks that's attractive? It just looks like he missed a spot. And what's with touching the hair all the time? Is it the same primordial instinct that has them grabbing their penises just to make sure they're still attached? Scratch the chin, pull the peter and it's all good.

 five

Don't mind me. I'm just in the crappiest mood ever. It's the Monday after Christmas break. Which means we're no longer counting down to vacation, but instead starting back at square one. Summer's too far away to count down to and spring break doesn't count because it's close to summer.

I have official post-vacation traumatic syndrome. I am a victim of the system. Oh, there's Adam. We have Introduction to Ceramics and Photography this semester. Thank Holy-Mother-Registrar for that one. At least I have a chance to see him without Tim around. Though want to bet I will be their official Pony Express for notes they don't feel like texting?

"Gertie."

"Addy." I hate that nickname, Gertie. Sounds like something your grandmother buys to keep her boobs from dragging on the ground. We walk to class together and get seats next to each other.

He laughs. "So, I heard the first couple of weeks are yoga."

"In art?" Maybe this isn't such a miraculous event.

"It's to get our Shakira all flowing smoothly."

"You mean chakra?" I clarify.

"Whatever. It's weird."

"Why are we taking this class?"

"It's a graduation requirement."

"That's right."

"Maybe graduation isn't so important," Adam whispers as silence falls in the classroom.

Ms. DaVoe glides in wearing black Lycra shorts with an ancient tube top, draped in one hundred colored polyester scarves and wearing earrings that qualify for landmass proportions. Her hair is three different shades of boxed reds with jet-black roots and a black swath down the middle of her head like a roadkill skunk. Her wrists are covered with silver bangles and each finger sports at least one ring, most with stones the size of boulders. Her feet are tucked into striped socks that have been darned several times and Birkenstocks that must have actually been at Woodstock. Have I mentioned she's like a hundred and three? And she emits an aroma seriously resembling pot. There's an almost visible haze surrounding her. How did she get this job?

"Children of my heart. Welcome to this sacred space. We are going to have a beautiful time together." Her voice is raspy and deep, like she's obliterated her vocal cords inhaling one too many times.

"Kill me now." I'm not really a beautiful, sacred-space kind of person. I'm more a glass-and-chrome, wire-me-and-leave-me-alone, I-like-my-personal-space kind of girl.

"Suicide pact." Adam looks as horrified as I feel.

"We'll get to expressing ourselves using the media of your choice, but first we must release the creative spirits in each of us. Let's push the desks back and make a circle in the middle of the room." She snaps her fingers and we all jump. "Hearts, please trust me."

I am so screwed. I have trust issues with doped-up grannies who use words like "spirits" and "hearts." I should work on that.

I walk into history ready to have Ms. Whoptommy kick the dope smoke out of my brain. There's no way I didn't inhale for the entire period of art. I think the drug dog must be dealing on the side not to notice Ms. DaVoe's digs.

My glance settles on my usual desk. There's a rose on it. My feet slow. Wrong desk? And then it hits me. It's the right desk.

Stephen's sitting in his seat, turned toward me, trying to sneak a peek at my face without being obvious.

He did not. Oh my Goddess, you have to be kidding me. Holy-Mother-of-a-Young-Girl's fantasy, there is a red rose on my desk. I can't believe it.

"Congratulations." Ms. Whoptommy twitches in the general direction of the rose like it pains her for me to receive any tokens of affection.

"For me?" Of course I have to say that. "Thank you." On our eight-week anniversary and everything. Maybe the bad kissing can be balanced out by gift giving. No. Not really.

Stephen blushes. I've never seen him blush. It could be the glare Ms. Whoptommy is shooting at him. "You—well, you know, eight weeks," he stammers. Then he mouths "anniversary" to me, like clearly I read lips better than I understand spoken word.

Anniversary. Wow. I have an anniversary. Maybe I should have given him something. But how was I supposed to know that we celebrated weeks? I mean, who celebrates weeks? I didn't think guys could handle remembering wedding dates, let alone serious-dating-exclusivity-hanging-out-hooking-up dates. What to say? What to say?

"Hi."

"Hi."

"Thanks." I'm not supposed to say "I love you," am I? I mean, am I? What if I am? Do I love him? How do you know?

How in the world am I supposed to know?

Can't breathe.

Can't breathe.

Must breathe.

Air. Need air.

Love. Do I love him?

No, I don't. I don't think I do.

Here's the deal. I don't believe I could fall in love with such a bad kisser. Oh, wouldn't that be the best? It's so me. I fall in love with the world's worst lover and he'll be my soul mate. I will be destined to lots of time on my back without any moaning.

At least, not real moaning. Maybe that's what they mean by faking it.

What if good lovers are rare and the bad ones are ubiquitous? Can you learn how to be a good lover like learning how to play the piano? Is it an acquired skill, or is it heredity? Like blue eyes or left-handedness. Why don't they teach us the useful crap?

He's waiting. Looking at me. Expecting something. What does he want from me? "How are you today?"

"Good. You?" Again with the peering. My dentist spends less time staring at my mouth.

"Real good." *Real good?* What am I, the Dairy Council's new campaign? *Got good? Real good.*

"Okay, students. Focus, please. Some of us came here today to learn something." Ms. Whoptommy pauses to give me a scathing glare. She's insanely good at glaring.

"Someone didn't eat her oat bran this morning." I don't actually say that out loud. Only think it. Wait. No. I look around. The shock and awe on everyone's face pretty much confirm that I said it out loud. Ms. Whoptommy is ruining my rosy moment.

"See me after class." She clicks her wicked-fake orange fingernails on my desk.

My anniversary will also be known as the day I got expelled from high school.

I wait until the class empties, clutching my rose like it's a magical ward against evil.

"Ms. Garibaldi, do you have anything to say before we get started?"

"Sorry?" Sorry is always a good place to start and since I'm sure she's going to make me say it eventually, maybe I'll just get it over with now.

"You sound unsure." She presses her lips together until they're just a white slit.

"I'm not. I'm sure. I'm sorry," I grovel. I'm not proud of it.

"Hmm. Ms. Garibaldi, you have the potential to be one of my best students. But it's potential you seem eager to waste."

I open my mouth.

She flicks a hand to stop me. "Let me finish, you've had your say today. You need to seriously consider where you want to end up in two years. At the college of your dreams? With a career? Or pregnant with your second child and married to your baby daddy?"

I'm horrified I just heard the words "baby daddy" come out of Ms. Whoptommy's mouth. "I—"

"I think it serves your interests to discuss your apology with Principal Jenkins, don't you?" She turns back to her desk.

I don't move.

"That's all." She doesn't even look at me when she says it.

Clarice is determined to ignore Spenser by violently eating carrot sticks while turned in my direction. "You have any interest in soccer?" she asks me.

My mind is still on Ms. Whoptommy's dressing-down. "Why?" Am I going to have to move to Bolivia to complete my high school education?

Clarice's eyes roll back in her head like she's trying to see Spenser without actually turning around to get a good look. "They're starting a girls' team."

"So?" I'm still not following. Though I am fascinated by the things her eyeballs can do. I wonder if mine do that.

"It's a Title Nine thing. Some parent got pissed because there's a boys' chess club." She's scary intent today, chomping on the carrots like they're Al Qaeda carotene.

I ask the obvious. "Then why don't they open a girls' chess club?"

She shrugs. "Quid pro something legal." She says each word in between Spenser's like she's eavesdropping, then speaking.

"Oh." This makes less sense than her usual.

There's a pause in the action as Spenser grabs his stuff and stomps away. Clarice can't converse well with me and focus every atom on a guy, not that I blame her. I haven't mastered the art of multitasking either.

Her whole body relaxes when he's out of earshot. "So, they're having tryouts. Word is anyone who shows up will get on the team." She throws the carrots back in her bag. I'm pretty sure she consumed more vegetable matter than is grown in California in the six minutes Spenser sat behind her.

She's still talking about soccer? Here I thought we were just making stupid small talk until he left. Huh. She's serious. I say, "Which means that hypothetical try-ees will actually have to run around after a ball, right?" This doesn't work for me.

"Well, yeah." She drinks the end of her green tea juice thingy.

The drawbacks are obvious to me. Running, and oh yeah, running.

"Maggie said she'd do it, if you did it." Clarice puts on her best diplomat face. "I'm not saying this because I think it will influence your decision, but in the interest of full disclosure, you should know Lucas is the assistant coach."

"Oh." I'm dating Stephen. I repeat that out loud. "I'm dating Stephen."

"Right. Which is why I'm sure that bit of information will have no bearing on your decision at all whatsoever. I just didn't want you to think I'm keeping secrets or anything." Her eyes twinkle maniacally.

"About the soccer team?" Why would I think she's keeping secrets about the soccer team?

"I believe in honesty." She's so full of shit. She knows damn well I can't resist the idea of hot and sweaty Lucas. Even running sounds appealing.

Of course, the odds that I'll be able to stay beautiful and not really run around getting nasty are slim, but I'll think of something. Maybe I can have bad ankles and turn them often. "Ouch." I practice.

"Are you okay?" Clarice looks at me like I've ruptured my appendix.

"Fine." Yes, this could work. "I'm in. As long as Princi-Pal doesn't expel me." After he talks to Ms. Whoptommy I may be packing for Bolivia.

"The freshmen are all talking about how amazingly brave you were saying that out loud."

How do the freshmen know? "Great. I'm infamous. Just think how much they'll talk when I'm no longer a student at this school." I might even make the local news.

"You are not going to get expelled. Danny brought meth to school and sold it, and all he had to do was pick up trash after school for a week." She waves her hands like that's the epitome of punishment.

She may have a point. "Oh." Maybe it's not that dire. Meth does not equal oat bran. I don't think. Does it? Maybe for the bowel-impaired it does.

"Don't worry. Just give him the whole having-PMS thing, and mention you're thinking about going out for soccer to be part of the school spirit. They're afraid none of us will try out."

My face lights up. Okay, now I really do care. Sweaty, sexy Lucas and getting out of Brangate. I like. "I'm in."

"Good." Her expression has "gotcha" all over it.

I sigh. I hate running. "Give me the details tonight."

"Sure." She bites into a rather nasty-looking peach and spits out the bite.

I so could have told her peaches aren't in season. But then it occurs to me I don't know why she wants to play soccer. "Clarice, why do you want to do this?"

"I don't know. It feels important." She actually looks serious.

I guess I can live with that, at least until I can drag the real reason out of her. "Do you know anything about soccer?"

"Not a thing. Other than all the exchange students are mad about it. And Lucas, of course." She shakes her head and bats her eyelashes in an effective manner.

"Of course." I slug her shoulder.

"I've got a couple of DVDs with Mia Hamm on them. We'll watch them."

Somehow, I'm fairly certain watching the soccer will lead to playing the soccer. Oh, Holy-Mother-of-Shin-Guards-and-Grass-Stains, what have I gotten myself into?

"Ms. Garibaldi, I have to say I'm surprised to see you in my office." Princi-Pal Jenkins leans back in his throne, trying to be all pally and stuff.

I've been in his office many times to pick up the Brain quarterly awards. He's conveniently forgetting all those times. "Me too." Seems safest to agree with him and feed the delusions.

"I have spoken with Ms. Whoptommy and she's given me her side of the story." He throws his hands in the air. "I know, hey, there are always two sides to a pancake. I mean, hey, I'm cool." He stands up and moves closer to me.

What in Holy-Mother's-Name-of-the-Elderly is he talking about? He wants something from me. Is this when kids start crying? Cuz I could try that. I pinch my outer thigh really hard to work up some wet.

"Gert." He leans on his desk all casual-chummy. "Tell me your side of the pancake."

"Oh." I really don't think Ms. Whoptommy got it wrong. I mean, there are only so many ways to say it. "Here's the deal. I really didn't mean to say it out loud. Really, I'm shocked it came out at all, because I respect Ms. Whoptommy." I'm trying to get my cues from his facial expression. Can't beat them, join them in the delusion. "I—really, so, I have really bad PMS." I can't believe I just said that. Who uses PMS as an excuse anymore? I feel dirty.

His eyes glaze over. He's wearing his discomfort like a new tie— all choked up and turning red. What is it about men not getting the bleeding thing? It's not like we have a choice.

I continue. "I just really don't know how that happened and I assure you it won't happen again, because I will wear duct tape over my mouth once a month to ensure it doesn't happen again." I frantically blink, hoping to give the appearance of tears. I wonder if I can poke myself with the pencil without his noticing. That would make me cry.

Can you believe this drivel I'm making up? Who knew I'm this quick on my feet? I should maybe think about a career where I'm all off-the-cuff all the time. I'm good at it. Passing this authoritative moment with surfing colors.

He pats me on the shoulder. "That won't be necessary. We don't like students to hurt themselves as part of self-expression, or in this case, self-unexpression. It's against board policy. So please, don't use the duct tape, I'd hate to see you back here."

"Okay, no tape. But I will be supercareful about what comes out of my mouth." *Super?* I used the word "super."

He nods, all serious. "There is the need to make sure you understand the gravity of the situation. Now, I think you did have a point and I really appreciate you being so candid and taking responsibility for your actions. That ranks highly for me."

Goody. I nod, try to smile.

He doesn't seem to notice. "I want to talk with you anyway about a high school exchange program we submit student applications to each year." He picks a thick packet off his desk. "I'm sure a girl like you is very interested in the world around her."

He's waiting for a response. "Of course." I nod vigorously.

"Good. Some years the competition is very stiff, and rarely do we have multiple teachers suggest the same sophomore, but this year your name came up several times."

"Really?" I fail to see how I popped out at people when the words "international" and "travel" were batted around.

"It's a confidentiality issue that I can't tell you exactly which of your teachers think this would be an exceptional opportunity for you."

Why the hell not?

"So if it's all right with you, I'll have the school's guidance office work on the paperwork from our end, and all you need to do is fill out these forms and essay and submit them by the deadline."

He hands the packet to me. I open my backpack and shove it in as politely and nicely as I can. I sense he has more to say that I may not like to hear. "Okay. I will fill it out and send it in. Sure." What are the odds, really?

"Good. Good. Also, here's the information on soccer tryouts.

I think this might also be a very good venue for your creative and unique approach to the world."

I think he just called me a freak. Ah, one of the grown-up crossroads. He is offering me an olive branch of compromise. I pretend interest in soccer and he pretends he influenced my life in a healthy direction. "My friends and I were just discussing the tryouts." I try to look all perky.

"Really?" He's pleased.

Like I'd lie about that? Of course I would, but I don't have to, thanks to Clarice.

"Really."

"Well then, I'll expect to see you at tryouts and we'll just consider this conversation concluded." He pats my shoulder.

"Great." I try to sound all TV Land.

He scribbles on a pass. "Here's a tardy slip. Better get to class."

I practice my inflection. "Great."

"I'm glad we had this talk." He actually looks glad. Odd. Silly, silly man.

Slater. Aka Mr. Butt-Twitcher. "Nice of you to join us, Garibaldi."

I slink into a desk near the front. No one likes sitting in the front of this class. We're all afraid the twitching could be a contagious African disease he picked up in the Peace Corps.

"Richards, explain to the class what we've been discussing."

Andrew sits taller in his desk. "Our term project, sir."

"Sir"? *Suck-up.*

"Which is what?" Slater slaps the eraser against the board.

"A twenty-five-page paper about us." Drew is going to slip a disk sitting that tall. No one has posture like that.

"Specifically about?" Slater doesn't bother to turn around.

"Who we are specifically in the world around us, and who we are in comparison to a historical figure at our age." Now Drew doesn't sound so sure. Slater isn't throwing him any cookies.

"Such as?"

"Christ, Gandhi, Abraham Lincoln?"

"Any women on that list?"

Andrew swallows and looks down. "Helen Keller, Queen Victoria, Cleopatra?"

Slater taps the board with chalk. "Yours is called?"

" 'Who Is Drew Richards Compared to Christ?' " There's a distinct question at the end of that.

We all twitter. It can't be helped. Drew as Christ is such a miscast.

"And in this paper you will answer that question in twenty-five double-spaced pages. Your historical data will be accurate. Your comparisons will be inspired, illuminating and thought-provoking. You may use quotations from literature or popular music. Anything is game if it illuminates your character. However, you may not use more than fifty words from any one work or source. I will count, so don't test me, people."

This is the assignment that gets whispered to eighth graders when they tour for orientation and registration, the one seniors use to terrify the little squirts. It's the world's hardest paper to get a passing grade on. Mr. Slater loves failing people because they were inane and uninspired. Basically, he uses this paper to tell each kid they suck and will never amount to anything important.

We've all heard stories about flunking out because people didn't know themselves well enough to prove they existed in Slater's mind. He's brutal. Supposedly Jenny Oppenheimer drove off a bridge after turning in a blank piece of paper. That was in the nineties, way before our time. But instead of being convinced the assignment was a bad thing, Slater took her death as validation he was pushing us in the right direction.

Tangent: sorry.

Who is Gert Garibaldi?

I wish I knew.

 **six**

The parentals are out at a charity thing, so I light a bunch of candles and turn out the harsh overhead fixture. Everyone looks better by candlelight, right? Even my fuzzy pink lamp isn't soft enough light. I strip down to nothing. Just me. Naked me. I open my eyes and stare at the reflection.

Where did I go?

I wasn't too tall or too short, fairly straight no matter what angle I looked at. No disfiguring humps or scars or fins. What happened?

I'm still average height. Not so straight. When did my thighs get pudgy? Last week?

My bottom lip hurts from biting down too hard.

I have curves on my hips and curves from my butt, and boobs—all of a sudden I have boobs. I can't cross my arms like I used to. I have to go under flesh, or put my hands up on my shoulders.

I half turn to the right and keep on inspecting. There are bumps on my upper arms and there's a zit on my right butt cheek. The backs of my knees stick out; they don't curve in like they're supposed to.

My neck is too short. I don't have a swan neck, I have a chick-adee no-neck thing going on.

Where have I been?

My tummy pooches out, rounded like it wants to try out for a geometry class prop.

Where's my waist supposed to be? Is it the dip under my ribs or right before my hips take center stage?

I want to know. Have I been sleepwalking? I don't recognize myself. I don't know this person. I pinch my side just to make sure I can still feel pain.

I have fur between my legs and, even though I shave daily, incorrigible wannabe Chia Pets under each arm.

I face away from the mirror but peer back over my shoulder, trying to see what other people witness when I walk away. *Oh my God. Shoot me now.* I'm so hoping to find those twin dimples at the base of my spine. Hope is overrated. No backless gowns for me. Hefty garbage bags with armholes.

Snap out of it, Gert. I tell myself to get a grip.

You're not hideous, just not gorgeous. There are worse things than homely. Right? I could be stupid, or dense, or incapable of honest emotion.

But here's the hideous deal: I would trade my brains for the bod of any A-list actress. Maybe being beautiful would get old.

Eventually.

No, it wouldn't. Who are those people who think the inside is so much more important than the outside? No one gets past the outside to get to the inside unless they like the packaging. When was the last time you bought the horridly packaged hot dogs with the little flying pigs on them because you thought the inside had to make up for the piglet motif?

Tangent: sorry.

I shut the closet door, effectively bringing the curtain down on the mirror.

It's not me in that mirror. She's almost adult and I'm seriously missing the mutant gene that makes me deep and unshallow. Maybe it's my problem. Maybe someday I'll be happy with my lumps and bumps and trunk, but that day is not today.

I'm no closer to feeling at one with my body than I am to speaking fluent Swahili. It's possible, but not highly probable. And please, no breath-holding.

Buttocks!

I throw my naked self against my pillows and navy-puke bedspread.

How come every time I try to visualize myself comfortable and at home in my skin, somehow I'm a size two, with perfect breasts, white sparkly teeth, the hair of a goddess and golden skin? Seriously, what happened to being okay with reality? I was a happy kindergartner focused on crayons, not flaws. I colored outside the lines and I was creative. Now I grow outside the lines and I'm a mutant. I don't get it.

"You okay?" Clarice asks me on our way to lunch the next day. "You look sick."

"Just school and stuff." I can't shake the post-vacation blahs. I try, but I get bogged down in odd weepiness.

"Whatever, I get it." Clarice pats me on the back. "When's the big family dinner?"

I'm having dinner with Stephen's family tonight. Maybe that's why I feel like I'm going to puke at any second. And here I'm thinking it was the shrimp I didn't eat last night. "Tonight." *Breathe, Gert. Breathe.*

"Wow. You nervous?" she asks, all guru.

"Maybe." I swallow bile.

"I think I'd be puking."

"Hadn't occurred to me," I lie.

"That's a big step, you know. They'll be all microscoping you and judging you. And you'll never be good enough for little Stevie." She speaks as one who knows.

"Not helping." *I'm going to go find a cliff to jump off, thank you.*

"Sorry. That's just what I've heard."

The Oracle, aka older sister. "Older sister, right?"

"Yeah," Clarice says almost apologetically. "She has doozy stories about weird relatives. She pretty much says it's the determining factor about your future together."

"Future together?" Are we kidding? I thought it was food and talking and maybe seeing where he sleeps—a chaperoned tour, of course. Can it really be about the future? "We're not getting married."

"You're certainly not getting married if his mother doesn't like you."

"What are you talking about?" I stumble over a perfectly flat floor. "She's met me. Driven me." Granted, it was terribly dark and we didn't speak in the car.

"My sister. Head over heels with this guy, and he was great to her. Perfect. His mother still did his laundry and grocery shopping, even though he lived on the other side of town. The mother hated my sister. Venom. He never called her again. Not that she was too upset because the dude's boxers were always starched and she didn't understand that until—"

I must stop the flow. "I get it."

"I'm just saying—"

"I know. But we're sophomores." Like this mitigates the relative horrors.

"Never too early to be stealing away the little prince."

Holy-Mother-of-Small-Boys, what have you done to us? Could we just have a drive-by? I can stand on the curb and Stephen's mom can peer out the window at me and tally up all the reasons I'm not good enough to date her son and we could all move on. Do I really have to eat food while we're at it? I'm liable to snort it out my nose.

"I wouldn't worry, though. Really." Clarice tries to soothe me.

The panicked horse-near-a-rattler feeling must actually be an expression on my face, not just a lump in my gut. I have nothing to say. I'm afraid to open my mouth.

Clarice's concern bubbles out her mouth. "My sister is a lunatic. I'm sure she's exaggerated those stories so I won't date until I'm thirty or something." Clarice waves her hands around and pushes her hair out of her eyes.

"Right." I nod. Here's what I've learned about Clarice's older sister stories: rarely are they exaggerated. I'm not that lucky.

I glance down at the skirt my mother made me change into. I will never admit this, but I'm kinda grateful she gets all forceful and tells me what to wear occasionally. A plain pale pink blouse and a black wool skirt that hits my calves. I'm even wearing ballet flats I don't remember having.

I brush a hand over the bracelet Mike gave me, which I'm wearing for luck, and lick my pink-glossed lips. I look like a girl. A nice girl. I'd want my son to date me. I don't have the Eve-the-seducer look about me at all.

Stephen insists on talking the whole ride over. I think he thinks he's making things better by giving me the rundown. He's so not. "Just ignore my grandmother, her glass eye is wonky and she's nuts." That's encouraging. "She lives with us; otherwise, I wouldn't make you meet her."

"She can't be that bad." Everyone exaggerates how terribly wacky their relatives are, right? To listen, we're lucky we evolved past rocks and spears.

"She gave me a box of Depends for Christmas." Stephen sets the parking brake and half turns in the seat to look at me.

"Oh." How do I react to that?

He doesn't find my reticence off-putting. "Wrapped in shelf paper."

What the hell is that? I nod, then give in and ask, "What's shelf paper?"

"The ugly wallpaper that goes on shelves in the pantry and dresser drawers. She had some extra from my dad's childhood."

"Oh." That's what that's called. Mom has rolls and rolls of it in the basement. I can't recall ever seeing it on any shelves or in any drawers, though. *Snap out of it, he's waiting for a response.* "That's pretty bad."

"You're not kidding. She gave my brother a letter that willed him her dentures. She wants him prepared for the future." Stephen is playing with my hair. Why is he playing with my hair?

"Your parents cool?" I'm just plain scared. I try to pass off the shiver of fear as sophistication. That so did not work.

"They're okay." His parents could look like Attila the Hun and his horse named Ray.

Again with the lack of comfort. This should be a fun evening. Why did I agree to this? Because I want to see his bedroom. Do you know how much a personal space says about a person? More than any book ever could. But now I'm calculating that the odds of seeing his room without an escort are nil to none.

Not that I really want to be with him in a room that has a bed. I so don't want him to be thinking I came to dinner so he could jump my bones with Daddy's approval.

"Ready?" He's already shutting his door and moving. My answer obviously isn't too important here.

I smile. I should have put gloss on my teeth like Miss America so my lips slide easily. They're kinda sticking. He doesn't open my door but walks up the walk without me. I scramble to catch up.

"Hey!" Stephen calls as he throws open the front door and grabs my hand, dragging me in. Or rather, I follow, because I'm afraid he's going to dislocate my fingers if I stop the forward momentum.

"You're late."

"Sorry, Dad, traffic was nuts," Stephen replies.

Traffic? What traffic? And hello—not a great start to the evening.

"We're at the table. Come in, come in." His mom is wearing a black suit that looks like it was sewn on. Can she breathe in that? Her hair is a reddish brown I've only ever seen on television actresses or news anchors. And it doesn't move.

"I'm Ms. Hudson, Stephen's mother, but you remember me as homecoming chauffeur, I'm sure." She shakes my hand like she's trying to crack walnuts.

"Gert. Garibaldi. Stephen's . . ." I trail off. I glance wildly around, hoping he'll help me, but he's already sitting down.

"We know. That's my husband, Mr. Blasko. And his mother, Mrs. Blasko. Stephen's brother, Walt, is at a Boy Scout event. He's going to be an Eagle Scout." She head-bobs around the table. Never once losing the smile. Her smile is terribly unnerving. "Sit."

I do, because holy buttocks, I don't want to know what happens if I refuse. I've seen South American dictators with less commanding personas than Ms. Hudson.

Stephen isn't looking at me. It's like we've never even met.

His dad is reading the *Wall Street Journal*. "Dammit, cattle is up again."

"Not at the table. We have a guest." Ms. Hudson glares at him. Mr. Blasko puts down the paper and returns her glare.

"I hope you don't mind takeout. We rarely cook in this house." He directs this comment to me, but I have a feeling I'm not the intended recipient.

"I love takeout." I feel the need to bond with Ms. Hudson. Besides, I know what home cooking can taste like, and it's overrated.

"So, Gert, our boy here hasn't told us much about you," Ms. Hudson says, passing me the container of General Tso's chicken.

"I want sardines. Where are the sardines?" Mrs. Blasko yells across the table at me, making me jump. I'm the only one who seems surprised by the outburst.

"They're coming, Grandma," Stephen answers without even looking at her.

Ms. Hudson is still looking at me, with her eyebrows up above her bangs and her smile gleaming. She's being too nice. A little odd. I feel like she's a talent scout I need to impress.

I put a spoonful of noodles on my plate. "Oh, there's not much to tell."

"Dear, don't flirt with the truth. Tell us everything." She puts some iceberg lettuce on her plate and drizzles it with vinegar. She keeps handing me containers but never puts any on her plate.

Am I not supposed to eat anything? What's the expectation?

"So you and Stephen have been dating officially for a few weeks?" she continues.

"Yes."

"How'd you meet?" She uses a knife and fork to eat the lettuce.

"Mom, school." Stephen takes a breath from inhaling egg rolls and noodles. He's not a very pretty eater.

"School," I reiterate.

"Where are the sardines? Joan, I told you I wanted sardines." Mrs. Blasko shouts.

Everyone just ignores her, so I shrug and avert my eyes apologetically.

Stephen's dad picks up the paper again and mutters under his breath between bites. His mom's cell phone rings.

"Not at dinner," Stephen's dad huffs over a dirty look.

I really want to go home. Now. Forget seeing his room. I just want mine.

"Work. Sorry." She flips open the phone and moves away from the table. I think she must work for the State Department or something.

"She's a reporter at Channel Six," Stephen whispers.

That's why she looks so familiar.

74

"Gotta go. Gert, it was nice seeing you." She grabs her keys and dumps the lettuce in the garbage in one motion.

"When are you coming back?"

"Late." She slams the door.

"I want sardines." Mrs. Blasko sounds like a three-year-old.

I stare at my plate.

"And then she kept yelling she wanted sardines and his dad just mumbled about cattle fixtures or futures or something weird." I try to finish my story over the ever-increasing volume of Adam's mirth.

"Stevie didn't say anything?" Adam asks once he gets his breath back.

"Noooo," I squeal into the phone. I'm staring at my ceiling in utter awe of how horrible that was.

"I'm so sorry, Gertie. Swear I had no idea his mother was Moany Joany from Channel Six."

Apparently Joan Hudson is a local celebrity. I guess I would have known that if my boyfriend had told me, or I ever watched the evening news. She's an investigative reporter whose delivery is the stuff of *Penthouse* breathiness.

"Was it as bad as I think it was?" I ask. Perhaps I'm being too harsh. Perhaps if I squint really hard at a lightbulb, the memory will get fuzzy and warm.

"Uh-huh."

"Yeah, what was I thinking?" Of course it was that bad. And then it just got worse.

"He dragged you up to his bedroom?"

"Yes." I don't even really remember the décor because I was so focused on evading the tongue of death. "And he tasted like cheap Chinese takeout and kept shoving his tongue into my mouth like he was some tentacle-man from outer space." Let's not even talk about the hello erection rubbing on my thigh.

"What'd you do?" Adam gulps air. I can hear it.

"I kept asking him about the model airplanes hanging from his ceiling like I cared." Stephen's taller than me, so about all I could see while his tongue was in my mouth was the ceiling. The angle was brutal.

"Uh-huh. And you weren't into kissing him back?" Adam asks like he's afraid of my answer.

"That was not kissing. That was carpet cleaning."

"Huh?"

"It was uncomfortable and boring. For buttocks' sake, I was having juicy conversations about P-3s."

"What are P-3s?"

"Planes. Very old planes," I snap.

"Oh. How'd you get home?"

"I made a big deal about my neck hurting, which was actually true, but I pretty much lost it when he started to pull me toward the bed. No way was I leaving my feet." Visions of having appendages or breasts sucked into the Hoover mouth are going to haunt me for years.

"So, you were into him," Adam says.

Do I sound into him? I want to be into him. "Not then."

"Then he brought you home?"

"Yes, and he wanted to make out in the driveway like we hadn't been doing that for an hour. And it's a good thing I didn't eat any food, I would have thrown up all over him when his tongue got my gag reflex. Still, I was hungry."

"You have a bowl of ice cream?"

I clink my spoon into Chocolate Chip Cookie Dough. "Yes, comfort food."

"Are you going to break up with him?"

The sixty-four-million-dollar question: Am I going to dump him? "Maybe he's special."

"Special?"

"Like I wouldn't dump a guy in a wheelchair if he popped a wheelie, so why would I dump Stephen for popping a boner?"

"We're not talking about his dick here. His dick wasn't in your throat, was it?"

I shiver. I can't even imagine the alternate reality where that might have happened. "No."

"Let's recap. He tells you his grandmother is nuts but leaves out the part about his mother being on television and, oh, by the way, anorexic from the sound of it. He doesn't talk to you at all during dinner. Doesn't let you finish eating before pulling you up to his bedroom so he can shove his unwanted tongue down your throat—"

"Wait, I don't know that it was unwanted." I have to be fair. I like the idea of French-kissing. I just hope it's not all like this.

"Okay, but he doesn't check in to make sure you're having a good time, right?"

"Well, no."

"Then he gets huffy when you say your neck hurts and you need to go home and you won't make out with him in front of the prying eyes of your parents. Right?"

"That's close, yes."

"And you think there's something wrong with you, right?" Adam hits the nail on the doorjamb.

"Is there?" I have this terrible sinking feeling that this is the best my dating life will ever be. It will all be downhill from here, until I have fifty cats and wear Lycra on my massive butt.

"There's nothing wrong with you. Really."

"Really?"

"Really. If I put it to a vote right now—no, we all agree, there's nothing wrong with you."

"Thanks."

"And Gertie, the tongue thing is great with the right person."

"You're sure?"

"Yes, someday there will be a boy whose tongue you want in your throat. Not to mention his—"

I cut him off. "That's strangely comforting."

"Go eat more ice cream." Adam hangs up.

He always makes me feel better.

rave #7
lip-locking, tongue-tangoing, smoochey-woochey

Kissing. I'm talking good kissing. Ice-cream-melting, toe-curling, tingling, don't-want-to-stop kissing. I want some of that.

There are whole websites devoted to the healing properties of kissing. It's been known to cure cancer and at the very least brighten a clinical depression.

It's a hobby. It brings people together. I want it. I want the kiss that lasts forever. Okay, I'd like bathroom breaks and neck-sprain breaks and probably occasionally might want to do something else, but mostly I just want the feeling of a kiss that could last me a lifetime. That lost, dreamy, creamy feeling of being in the moment with one other person. With a manly-boy.

I don't think that's asking too much. Is it?

 **seven**

"I'm . . . going . . . to die. . . ." My face is so hot it's melting off my skull. I can hardly breathe. I lean against the auxiliary gym wall like a gargoyle in heat. I don't care how pathetic I look. I don't. I'm sure I won't survive these tryouts and then people will never say a bad thing about me again. Because you don't say bad things about dead people. Unless they're serial killers or something. And I'm not.

Tangent: sorry.

"Gert, we just walked over here." Clarice is looking at me like I've lost my mind.

"I'm practicing." Okay, so I'm not on my deathbed yet, but it's out there. I can see it coming. "Why are we doing this, again?"

"It's our only opportunity to be jocks." Maggie keeps picking at her shorts and T-shirt like she's never worn anything with fewer than five layers.

"Winter sports, ladies?" What was I thinking? I don't care about being a jock. I want to ride the away bus with Lucas. I've heard things about the away bus. "It's outdoor soccer in January."

"Technically this is just tryouts."

"Maybe we're not destined to be jocks. Has it occurred to any of us that we aren't genetically equipped for this activity? Do you even know what a soccer ball looks like?" I ask my compatriots quasi-seriously.

"It's black and white, right? With shapes on it?" Panic blooms on Maggie's face for a minute before she quite stoically brings herself back under control.

"Listen up, people." A lanky guy with calves the size of Montana loops a whistle around his neck. "This is tryouts for girls' soccer. This is the first year it's been offered, but that doesn't mean it'll be easy to make the team." He puffs up his chest like we're an incoming class of wannabe Navy SEALs. "We have a freshman squad, which will also be the junior varsity squad, and then room for the varsity ladies. My name is Mack. I'm going to be your head coach, but just call me Mack. No mister. Mack. Got it?"

I'm still looking at his knees. They have amazing definition. All sinew and muscle. I will have to take the magnetizing mirror to my knees when I get home. I don't think mine look like that.

"Where are my student coaches?" Mack asks.

I straighten. This is where Lucas comes in. I begin to panic when I can't locate him casually. He's the entire reason I am doing this. He must be around here somewhere.

"Mack. We're over here." Lucas and three other guys I've never seen in my life part the crowd like Moses and the Red Sea. I swear a collective sigh and hair toss moves across the girls like a wave at a football game.

The guys all slap hands and thump each other with their shoulders. A bigger display of masculine preening you've never seen—not even on Animal Planet. Not to say I'm immune. I'm not. Look at that smile. That hair. Those shoulders.

"Good to see you." Mack repeats this strange dance of slap and thump with each of them. It's that odd hello ritual guys do.

"Who are the other guys?" Clarice whispers to me. We both sneak a glance at Maggie, hoping she'll have done some research.

Her blank look is not comforting. The guys are skinny. Muscular, but, well, there's no fat on their legs. On anywhere.

I swallow, doing the math. Unless they're all brothers, which I know they're not—the rippling muscle thing must not be genetic. Five guys, not related, plus soccer equals no fat.

"We're going to die," I stage-whisper.

"Uh-huh." Clarice finally makes eye contact with me. She's figuring out there will be pain.

"Can we sneak out?" Maggie tugs at the oversized cotton covering her dainty proportions like a crescent roll on a toothpick.

Mack turns back to us. He's smiling. A really big smile. "Now, we're going to work you today. Don't worry if your soccer skills aren't up to World Cup level, we'll get there later."

I have a mental flash: I think I kicked a soccer ball once in PE, in the fifth grade. It hurt my big toe. Why have I blocked this memory until now?

Mack continues. "We need to get a feel for your conditioning, put you through some basic drills, and then tomorrow we'll get out the balls."

Oh goody, I will collapse before even touching the soccer ball. That'll be humiliating.

"We'll start each practice by running a couple of miles to warm up. The red line is an eighth of a mile. This gym is your new home. We'll live in here for tryouts. Any questions?"

Do I want to be buried or cremated? Bagpipes or boy band?

I look around at the group of about fifty girls. Some faces I know but most I don't. I pull Maggie into a huddle with Clarice. "How hard can it be to get cut the first day?"

Relief blooms on their faces. "You're right. There are lots of girls here. Odds are we're the least skilled," Maggie says.

"There's no shame in giving it a try and being ousted because we suck," Clarice adds.

Mack announces, "People, let's do a mile to start. Eight laps, people. Look alive." He nods to one of the guys, who presses a remote button. Supernova's latest riff fills the gym with reverberating chords. "Run, run, run." Mack herds the group in a clockwise motion.

It's either run or be trampled. I am so not about to die by trampling.

"I'm so sorry!" Clarice screams at us.

"You'll pay later." I put my hands around my throat in a mock choke.

We run. In straight lines. Around cones. From line to line. We dodge balls thrown at our heads at alarming speed.

Two girls drop because of turned ankles. Another is sent to the nurse because she doesn't dodge the ball quite fast enough. Someone else slips on sweat and hits her nose on the floor, which means we get a five-minute break while the janitor cleans up the blood.

"I can't feel my feet." Maggie pokes her toes with her finger.

"I have blisters on blisters. These shoes are cute, but they suck for support." Clarice's sneakers are so trendy they're never actually supposed to be worn.

"Am I dead yet?" I haven't sweat this much since—let me think about this—never.

Maggie looks at the clock and groans. "We're only half done."

"Okay, people. Mess is cleaned up. On your feet. Don't want to stiffen up." Mack smacks the clipboard and blows his whistle in a jaunty little jig.

I've been too preoccupied to even notice Lucas until hands appear from heaven to pull us up. I look up, knowing my hair is standing up sticky with sweat and rehydrating product. Let this be a lesson: no gel or spray until after practice.

"Gert, good to see you." He smiles at me, then at Clarice and finally at Maggie. "You guys are hanging in there. Good spirit."

I grimace a smile. "Thanks." I'm too tired to care that my sweat and his sweat have blended on my palm. I'd love to say I'll never wash this hand, but all I want is a shower, so I'd be totally lying. He jogs away toward other heaps of girls, pulling them to their feet as well.

"Has Mack even broken a sweat?" Clarice leans in.

"He glows like a good mist, I guess." I squint, trying to find one rivulet on his brow. Just one drop of perspiration.

Maggie rolls her eyes.

"Now for some fun, people." Mack wheels out an ancient television screen. "This is an unorthodox practice, but Manchester United is rumored to use it for mental acuity, balance and body control. The Chinese have used it for centuries to focus and calm the mind."

"Math puzzles?" I ask quietly, hoping no one hears.

"Tai chi." Mack smiles at all of us like we know what that is.

Maggie leans over. "No running." She twitches her lips like she'd like to smile but doesn't have the energy.

I smile at her and at Mack. Okay, I can do no running for a while.

"We'll start easy, learn the movements, then speed it up as practices continue." Mack and the five horsemen take places around the gym so they can see us and the TV. "Don't feel like you have to perfect the movement immediately. Just go with the motion."

"That sounds bad," I say to Clarice as we spread out.

We do lots of inhaling and exhaling. I like the breathing thing; I wasn't sure that was a high priority around here.

"People, pay attention: this is embracing the moon!" Mack shouts. A few of the girls giggle.

Lucas is perfectly and completely engrossed in the screen. I've never seen such concentration on a manly-boy before.

"Part the wild horse's mane, people!" Mack shouts.

I try, I really do, but I'm just not horse-mane-parting talented. In fact, I think I'm more like braiding horse's tail. I'm tempted to find a pen to put eyes on my hands so I can do a puppet show while we breathe and flail.

"I suck," Clarice says.

"So not," I say. She's even lunging in the right place. I could hate her.

"Back to embracing the moon." Mack doesn't have to yell any-more. Most of the girls are just swaying to an unknown pop tune. It's like VH1 in slo-mo.

I so am not kidding: I almost think I'll jinx myself if I say this out loud, but I don't suck as bad as some.

"It's kinda fun, isn't it?" I ask Maggie when Mack calls us to a stop.

"The running?" She collapses on the ground.

"No, the dancing." I heave a sigh next to her.

"Dancing?"

"The moony horsey thing."

"The tai chi." Clarice gulps from a water bottle.

"Are we done yet?" Maggie asks.

"We're supposed to stretch while Mack and the other coaches cut ten people from tryouts."

"What are we supposed to stretch?" I ask, watching the contortionists contort around me.

"Beats me." Maggie doesn't move off the ground.

I start counting spit wads on the ceiling while Clarice does some flailing of her own.

I raise an eyebrow at her.

"What? My mom does yoga all the time," she says.

"Oh."

"Thanks to all of you for coming out for the soccer team. However, we only have a few places, and based on injuries today, we'll be cutting ten of you. If your name is not crossed off this list, please show up tomorrow as scheduled for round two."

"I can't move," Maggie mumbles.

"Clarice, go see if we're done, please?" I ask Miss Perky Yoga Girl.

Clarice wanders over to the crowd.

A couple of girls actually look like they're going to cry.

Clarice pushes in and reads down the list, then comes back over with a glum expression on her face.

I applaud. "Good acting. That way no one will know we want to be cut."

"We're not."

"We're not what?" Maggie sits up, groaning.

"Cut."

"There must be a mistake!" I cry out. Way too loudly because Lucas comes over to us.

"You guys don't want to stiffen up. You'd better stretch it out or tomorrow you'll hurt like hell."

"Tomorrow?" Maggie squeaks.

"At practice." He waves and walks toward the locker room.

"It'll be harder to stay in tomorrow, right? We'll be cut for sure."
We hobble toward the locker room. "Right?"

No one answers me.

I can barely move my arm to reach the ringing phone. I am
dying. There's no explanation for the pain and the more pain. I
tried the WebMD symptom checklist. Right now it looks like I
have early-onset Ebola, or a skin-freezing thing that'll kill me
slowly. If I start bleeding from my eyes and pores like I'm in a horror film, I have Ebola. "What's up?" I ask Adam.

"You sound terrible."

"I'm dying."

"Oh. Didn't you have soccer tryouts today?"

"Yes, and I didn't get cut."

"That's bad?"

"Did you know there's running involved?"

He laughs. "I'd heard that rumor. But why are you dying?"

"I'm in terrible pain, my skin is all itchy and with every breath
it gets harder to move."

"I can cure you."

"How? Ebola has no cure."

"I guess not, but you don't have Ebola."

"No, it might be this other one."

"Gertie, it's called exercise. You've heard of it before."

"I thought fat killed you, exercise made you live forever. Those
asses! I'm having a cheeseburger with extra fries on Saturday. If
I'm still alive."

"You'll live."

"If it's not deadly, why is it so—" I moan instead of scratching an itch on my thigh.

"Painful?" Adam finishes my thought. He's such a good friend.

"Why do people do it? You have an in with jocks, what gives?" I'm truly curious why this is supposedly addictive.

"It gets easier the more you do it."

"So does puking, but you don't see me all bulimic."

"It doesn't hurt as you build muscle up. Trust me, by the end of the season you won't even remember how this feels."

"That's right, because they'll be cutting me at practice tomorrow."

"They will?"

"Yes, there are only so many slots and we've figured out we have to be part of the seriously uncoordinated group to get cut."

"Really?" He says this like he knows something.

My antennae try to stand up, but they don't get past flaccid interest. "Why? What have you heard?"

"Well, I don't know if you want to know this or not."

"I do. I swear I do."

"Tim said Lucas came home all happy because the coach was talking about seeing so much potential in the girls."

"So? I'm sure there are a few good ones." I don't think I've seen them show up to tryouts, but they had to be out there. Of course, the sweat stinging my eyes made seeing anything fairly impossible.

"He distinctly mentioned your name."

My antennae jump. "As in, she'll make the team? Or as in, I'm sad she's seeing someone else because I want to date her?"

Adam doesn't even try to soothe my ego. "He was talking about the team, Gertie."

"No dating, huh?"

"Not in this conversation."

Reality dawns. "Oh my God, so that means he thinks I'll make the team?"

"Uh-huh. Isn't that good?" Adam trails off to an almost-whisper.

I have to think about this. Well, yes, I don't like sucking at anything, and yes, this means away game bus rides in the vicinity of Lucas, but . . . "There's a lot of running."

"Gert, did you think you were trying out for shuffleboard?"

"No, but how much running can there possibly be?"

"I'm fairly certain marathoners run more than soccer players."

"Only fairly certain?"

"Yeah, it's not really a sport of standing around."

"Well, it's going to be if I make the team."

"That's the sporting attitude I love."

"Just being honest," I huff.

"I need to ask you something." Adam sounds uncertain and confused.

"Okay, I'm all ears." Damn, I wish my legs would work. Who needs working legs anyway?

"What do you know about nipples?"

Huh? He's kidding, right?

"I'm not kidding," Adam rushes to add.

"I think maybe I misheard you."

"No, you didn't. I'm asking about your nipple knowledge."

"I have a pair."

"Are they sensitive?"

What are we really talking about here? My nipples? I don't think so. "What's going on? Give—"

"You have to promise not to say anything, but—"

"I'm dying—"

"It's Tim." Adam goes quiet.

Oh, no. I know what this is about. "You know it's perfectly natural to have three nip—" I don't even get to finish the thought before he cuts me off.

"Gert! He has two."

"Oh." That is the only nipple issue I'm aware of. "Go on."

"We were making out and he took off his shirt."

Ooo, this is getting good. "And?"

"And he has a really killer body."

"So what happened?"

"We're making out and I start playing with his chest."

Sure, I know what that's like. Happens to me all the time.

"And I touched his nipples. He started moaning and his breathing changed, so I started kissing his chest and I licked his nipple and he came unglued."

"As in he came?" Do I really want to know this?

Adam growls. "No, as in freaked out."

"Why? Did you have nails in your mouth or something?"

"No, he just freaked out that I was playing with his nipples. Total mood killer."

"Oh." I so do not know what to say.

"The thing is, I'm sure he liked it. I'm positive he liked it." Adam sounds sad and clueless.

"Okay, supposing he did like it, could you get him to tell you what happened?"

"No, he kinda shut down and didn't want to talk about it."

"Oh."

"Are guys' nipples different than girls' nipples?"

"I don't know. Maybe. Man boobs and all that."

"But are they different?"

"As in what?"

"Girls like their nipples sucked, right?"

He's asking *me*? Queen of the bad French kissing? I don't know the answer to this. I will rely on movie knowledge. "I think so."

"Do you?"

I'm just going to assume he doesn't care who is doing the touching—because when it's just me with Maya and the parentals are gone, I do like a little nipple action. "Um, yeah."

"Me too. But, like, maybe there are differences. Maybe I hurt him and I just think he liked it."

"Don't get all worked up. Let me do a little research and I'll call you back. See if he'll talk to you and tell you what the problem is."

"I'll try."

"I'll call you back," I say, and hang up. Are boy nips different? Aren't they the same from development? It's just that they don't get all boobish unless you do steroids or hit puberty with the X-chromosome cocktail.

I dial Stephen. This is something boyfriends are around for, right? If we're being honest with each other, then I should be able to ask him about this.

"Hi, gorgeous." Stephen sounds like I woke him up. "What's up?"

"I have a question for you."

"Shoot. Anything."

"How do you feel about nipples?"

"I like them. Really. Like them. Want to come over? My parents are out. Grandma's upstairs and won't bother us."

Crap, he thinks I'm asking him to play with mine. "Thanks, but I'm not, you know, angling for a make-out invite. I just, um, am doing research for a health class project and asking guys I know about their nipples."

"Mine?" He sounds deflated in more ways than one.

"Yep, how do you feel about yours?"

"I don't know."

"Well, do you like to play with them?"

He snorts. "I'm not a girl." His tone is offended.

"I don't think you are." I roll my eyes. "At all," I add, hoping to soften the offense. "I didn't mean anything. I'm just asking the question. I'll note it down as a no."

"You do that. I gotta go. Grandma's calling."

"Okay, sorry. I'll see you tomorrow." I hang up quick. That was useless. I ticked off my boyfriend and got no information. I call Clarice. "Hang on. I'm hooking Maggie on here."

"Maggie, Clarice is on too." I switch us all to the conference calling that the parentals are now paying for. "I have a nipple question."

"You have extras?"

"No! Do guys' and girls' nipples behave the same way?"

"Oh, you mean are they sensitive and stuff?" Clarice asks.

"I think so," Maggie says.

I ask, "Clarice, what's your older sister say?"

"Guys are total freaks about their nipples. I don't know why, but some guys won't let her touch them and some guys like it way more to have her suck theirs than she likes them to work hers."

"We're talking nipples here?"

"Yes, nipples. There's a variance in sensitivity, but it's not a girl/guy thing. Depends on the person."

I'm almost astounded by Clarice's knowledge of this subject. I choose not to dwell. "So, why would a guy freak out if he liked tongue action on his chest?"

"Maybe he doesn't think he should?"

The light comes on. "Oh, that makes sense."

Maggie adds, "Maybe he thinks it's cuz he's a guy and only girls like their boobs played with."

"Do you really like that?" Clarice asks.

"Why?" I ask, deflecting the idea that I have any experience with this. Which I don't.

"Well, I just always get the feeling Spenser is trying to open a jar of pickles when he's touching my boobs. It doesn't do anything for me."

"Have you told him?" I ask, all sex-therapisty.

I can hear Clarice shrug. "Told him what? Maybe it's just me."

"If he's twisting and stuff, maybe he thinks you like it, but doesn't know what else to do," Maggie says.

I am about to ask Clarice why she hasn't shared this with her older sister when Maggie jumps back in. "What's the guide say?"

Of course. With it hiding under my bed, I tend to forget I have it. "Good idea. I'll bring it to school tomorrow and we can check it out at lunchtime."

"Maybe you could make a copy of the breast section and drop it in Spenser's locker," Maggie suggests.

"Nah, that'd be too clingy. We're not having a relationship."

"Why is that clingy?" I ask.

"Cuz it presupposes he'll be touching my boobs again, and benefriends don't make that kind of commitment."

"But won't he?" I ask.

"I don't want to stop making out. But who knows."

"Like he's going to give up the opportunity to practice opening pickle jars!" Maggie snorts.

I bite back a snort of my own.

"Ha, ha!" Clarice doesn't seem to find the humor. "Does this mean you've been playing with Stevie's nips?"

"No, it doesn't." The idea makes me slightly nauseated because of his reaction to my question.

"Oh."

I can hear their wheels turning. "What?"

"It's Tim, then." Maggie all but nods over the phone.

"Adam having boy trouble?" Clarice sounds cheered by this.

"Just breast trouble," I say.

"I thought being gay he got out of the whole breast issue."

"I think that's the problem."

We chat a little more, then hang up. I root around under my bed to find the guide's hiding place. Mike gave me *The Guide to Getting It On* for my sixteenth birthday. It's the best book ever. But I don't want my parents to see it accidentally. I think it might cause a coronary in one of us.

I dial Adam, pull out the guide and flip to the breast section.

"He says it's because only girls like their nipples sucked and he's gay, not a girl."

"Okay, I'm so making a copy of this chapter for you."

"Why? It says he's not a girl?"

"Kind of. Basically it says some girls don't feel anything when their nipples are messed with, some it hurts and some like it. Same with guys. It's all the same nerve endings."

"Really?"

"Really. That's what it says."

"So he's not a girl."

"No, he's just blessed with good nerves."

"Well."

"Maybe you should volunteer to have him suck yours next time so he can be assured you don't have to be a girl to like it."

"In the name of science, of course."

"Of course."

"Thanks, Gertie. Oh, and if you tell anyone we had this conversation, I'll have to kill you."

"So I shouldn't send this e-mail to the whole student body?"

"Ha, ha!"

"Bye."

"Gert, can you come down here, please?" Mom calls up the stairs.

What does she want now? "Coming," I yell back in her general direction.

I meander down the stairs, taking my time. Must not appear too eager to please. I look from one face to the other. Both my parents are seated and perky in the living room. Uh-oh. My stomach clenches and I feel slightly nauseated. Though that could have a direct correlation to moving my body, which resents me fiercely for it now. My mom and dad have that we-need-to-have-a-conversation look about them.

"Dinner ready?" I try not to hobble too much. Stairs are tough.

Mom waves her hand at a chair. "Not quite. We wanted to talk to you first."

Dad turns the game on to mute. "We like that you're playing soccer for your school." He's all scary intent, like this is the first thing I've ever done he can understand.

I blink and it takes a minute for his words to sink in fully. Oh, oh no, back up. "I'm only trying out. We won't know until after tomorrow who makes the team."

Mom bobs her head. "Right. But we want you to know how much we appreciate this new interest of yours and we want to offer you—"

"A deal," Dad finishes for her. "We pay your car insurance and gas until the end of the season."

"In case you make the team, we didn't want you to worry about having to hold a job down too." She must sense my panic. It's not the work idea that panics me; it's the running.

Dad flicks a finger toward me. "Your grades can't slip."

"Right, we don't want your GPA to fall, because we're so proud of you." Mom tries to soften his dictum.

I can skip working if I make the team? Are they serious? Apparently, by the looks on their faces.

"If I make the team, I don't have to work and you guys will pay the car stuff?"

"Until you're done with the season and can get a job, yes, we'll cover your car expenses." Mom and Dad both nod like they've brokered a cease-fire.

I'm stunned. "Wow. Thanks." Now I understand why jocks do what they do. There are benefits to this so-called exercise.

Now I have to decide whether or not I can survive running for the next couple of months. Must make list. Pros and cons. I think the cons might be a longer list if I mention every body part that is screaming at me individually. "Okay, thanks. I don't know if I'll make the team. There are really good athletes going out for it and I'm not so coordinated." I try to ease them into the realization that I'm not jock material.

"You'll make it," Dad decrees, defying my perspective on reality.

a guide to groups (continued)

Oscars: Oscars are those kids who have been in every school play, musical and talent show. Students who are never happier than when they get to pretend they are someone else and not have to be themselves. These kids banter the words "stage direction," "cue me" and "what's my line?" like the rest of us use swearwords. They can memorize whole books of poetry and Shakespeare without getting nauseated. Some have parents who wanted to be on the stage or screen but mostly they're kids that came out of the womb like chameleons, searching for the part that will change their lives.

Emmys: Emmys are the kids who work really hard to have life imitate art and want their lives to re-semble the fantastical reality shows called soap operas. They think <u>General Hospital</u> and <u>Gossip Girl</u> are docu-dramas and work to steal boyfriends from their so-called best friends and cry on cue. In the feminine form, they tend to be daddy's girls and thus control his credit card. In the masculine form, they tend to be extremely popular, suave and sophisticated, frequent- ing clubs and attending events usually reserved for those actually old enough to drink. There is a bright- ness to their smiles, like the toothpaste ads, and theme music accompanies any entrance and exit.

   Banders: Students who think arriving at school in the dark all year is fun because they get to play jazz, or who carry around instrument cases rather than set- ting them down and risking said black plastic hulk wandering off. Students who have a nice array of white shirts and black pants/bottoms for each and every special concert event.

 # eight

I am a pile of goo. I am a husk of my former self. Dehydrated like a raisin. I gasp for breath. "We made the team."

Maggie groans. Wipes the sweat out of her eyes. "We did."

She sounds as bad as I feel.

Clarice bends down to untie her shoe. Her mouth emits noises like she's trying to climb a rock wall with only her fingernails. "How is that possible? I crawled through some of the push-up-crab-walk things," she moans, trying to sit on the bench. "On my butt."

I hate to point out that we all crawled on our butts. It seems mean.

"Varsity?"

I try to turn my head to check out the rest of our team but think better of it as an ice pick rips down my back.

"I'm changing my name," I mention to Mom as she bustles into the kitchen with her arms full of binders.

"Why's that, dear?"

Because Gertrude is an old lady's name. I don't actually say that out loud, though I want to. Think of my maturosity. "Because I'm baking a cake for Dad's dinner tomorrow and chefs all have fabulous names."

"Oh." Mom looks at once impressed and horrified. "Do you think that's a good idea?"

As opposed to letting you *make the cake? Hovels in India are more edible than your cakes.* "Well—" I put down the *Gourmet* magazine I picked up on the way home. Perhaps starting with a five-tiered meringue and marzipan concoction is a bit beyond my skill set.

"I see." She opens a cabinet and pulls out a few big books. "These were your grandmother's. I'm sure there's a nice simple cake in one of these that we have the ingredients for." The unspoken statement is *that you can handle making.*

"Thanks," I say.

"And what does your name have to do with this project?"

"I need a sexy name." Like Jean-George, Colette or Gigi.

"Gert, you don't need to use language like that." Mom is shocked.

"What? Sexy?"

"Yes, exactly. You're not old enough for a sexy name."

"Mom, it doesn't mean what you think it means."

"I've heard that before."

"It just means groovy."

She hmphs.

"Seriously, 'sexy' has nothing to do with sex."

She looks up at the clock. "I'm late for my meeting."

"What's today's?" I ask, trying to keep the rancor out of my voice. It's not her fault she has meetings about her meetings about nothing at all important.

"Bunko tournament for baby seal protection."

"Oh."

"I'll be back for dinner." She air-kisses my cheek from five yards away.

Whatever. I rummage around in the books until I find a cake that sounds good. "Devil's food with marshmallow cream frosting," I say to no one. I really need to get a goldfish to keep me company.

I get out the beaters. It's harder than you might think inserting the ends into the holes and getting them to stay. I fumble around. I wonder if I can go ask Dad to do it—is it cheating to attach the beaters for your own birthday cake?

I put the butter into a big bowl and turn the beaters on high. Butter splots shoot everywhere, including in my left eye. Just as quickly I turn off the beaters. I glance around the kitchen, hoping no one is secretly Webcasting. I toss another stick of butter into the bowl because it really doesn't seem like there's much left. I turn the beaters back on low speed.

Where are the measuring cups? I can't find anything remotely resembling what I think a measuring cup should look like. What's the diff between a measuring cup and a drinking cup? I use a water glass to measure out the sugar and flour.

Then I add the eggs. I try to suavely one-hand-crack the eggs like I've seen them do on the Food Network. Part of a shell falls in, and just as I'm about to shut off the machine to fish it out, the beaters crunch it up. I'm hoping no one will notice.

Is cocoa powder different than hot cocoa? I think there must be a slight difference, maybe the country of origin, but since we don't have Dutch-processed cocoa powder, I'm going to use Swiss Miss. I'll pick out the mini-marshmallows later.

Grease the pans. With what? Oil? Butter? WD-40? Huh. Skip it.

Oops, didn't preheat. I wonder if I should turn up the oven to compensate? Is there an average oven temperature?

I more or less evenly distribute the batter.

Reread the recipe to make sure I didn't miss anything important. Baking soda? Buttocks!

I search out the box and sprinkle the top of each batter layer with a small handful of baking soda and use my index finger to mix it together. Close enough.

I squeeze the two pans into the oven and set the timer. I think I set the timer. I'm not sure. Maybe I should just wait here until they're finished baking. Just in case.

Piece of cake, if I do say so myself.

The phone rings in my bedroom. I race up the stairs. It could be Stephen. I think I'm starting to really like him. My day doesn't seem complete unless I've had a conversation with him. Even just a little one.

It's him. "Hello, handsome."

It's our new thing. I'm gorgeous and he's handsome. Maybe that's kinda obvious. "How's it goin'?"

"Good. I just baked my first cake."

"Really?"

"Yep, it's my dad's birthday, so I made him a cake. It was pretty easy."

"That's cool."

"What are you doing?"

"I'm just finishing up a new model of the Dreamliner."

"That's a Boeing plane, right?" I'm catching on to the whole learn-what-the-boyfriend-likes conversation techniques.

"Exactly. It's going to revolutionize the airline industry."

I make interested noises.

"So you want to do something tonight?"

"I can't." I find myself sorry to be busy.

"Oh."

"Yeah, see, we're having this family dinner for my dad's birthday." Then all of a sudden I feel a rush of guilt for not inviting him, so I lie. "And I totally asked my mom if you could come too, but she said she didn't think my dad would like that until we're um, married or something. Not that I think we're going to get—"

"It's cool. No worries. I've got stuff to do anyway. Just thought—"

"But I'd love to, if I didn't have to do the fam thing."

"Sure. Later."

"Definitely." I sigh as I hang up the phone. This just gets more complicated.

"They're here!" Mom screeches over the television commentator.

I'm putting the final touches on my cake. I had to improvise the shape because the layers stayed in the pan, so I scooped them into a pile and drizzled the icing over the top. I've seen more attractive piles of dog doo.

Mom stops by my side and stares at the cake. "It's a wonderful effort."

That's like saying "but she has such a pretty face" when the rest of her is Jabba the Hutt.

"I do have the bakery cake in the car if you're not happy with the results." She pats my shoulder.

I only wanted to make a cake, that's all; just a simple little cake for my dad's birthday dinner.

I'm about to tell Mom to get the other cake out of the car when Dad walks in, escorting Mike and Heather. "Wow," Mike says, stopping in his tracks.

There's still a little butter on the ceiling.

"That's the best cake I've ever seen," Dad says, ruffling my hair. The guy thinks noogies are synonymous with *wonderful you*. "Couldn't have done better myself."

Heather pokes Mike. "Doesn't that look like the dessert we got at Michel's last week?"

Mike looks at her. "Huh?"

"The chocolate soufflé cake you said was worth the fifteen dollars a slice."

"I said that?" Mike seriously blows the nice thing she's trying to do.

I smile. "Thanks."

"We brought takeout." Heather winks at me.

Thank God, we don't have to deal with Mom's massacring of the food pyramid. But then, who am I to talk? I look down at my cake again, feeling tears behind my eyes. Perhaps the apple doesn't fall far and all that. I must have inherited my mother's lack of culinary ability along with her ears.

"It's a great cake. I'm sure it'll be tasty." Mike smacks his lips and rubs his already expanding girth.

"Thanks." I take the plastic wrap off the paper birthday plates with rockets and spacemen on them. "Dad, you want to be an as-tronaut when you grow up?"

Dad grumbles as only he can.

"They were on sale, Gert." Mom shoots me an evil-eye thingy.

"Of course they were," I answer. At least Dad doesn't have to eat off the leftover Barbie plates from my birthday.

"I did always want to walk on the moon." Dad rubs my mom's hand.

"Oh," she says, rolling her eyes in that I-love-you-you-silly-man way.

I have a feeling I'm missing something.

We eat. I bide my time until I can get Heather alone. I must ask about the nipple quandary. I know of at least four people inter-ested in her answer.

"We'll do the dishes and get the cake," I say. "Come on, Heather, you can help me." I seize my head in the general direc-tion of the kitchen.

"Right," she says, jumping up.

I love girls. We speak the same language of herd animals. I wonder if sheep react the same way? Or cows? Am I just a heifer on two legs?

Tangent: sorry.

"What's up?" Heather lowers her voice and looks under her lashes at me.

It's a little disconcerting that I didn't have to ease into the question, but then I wasn't very subtle with the whole needing-to-talk-to-her thing.

"Were you serious that I can ask you anything?"

"Absolutely. I'm happy to help."

"Well, I don't know if this, you know, is a weird question or not." I turn on the water to drown out any still-audible mumblings. I really don't want my parents hearing.

Heather smiles at me. "My mother told me sperm came out of every orifice on a man just like a common cold, plus his fingers were infected so I could get pregnant if he touched my private parts at all—nose, mouth, hands and penis all off-limits."

I try not to laugh. "That's terrible."

She giggles. "Seriously, I was eighteen when I found out sperm weren't floating around on escalators or doorknobs."

Okay, that's seriously whacked. "Oh." What else can you say? I feel better.

"Look, I'm telling you that you're probably ahead of me and I promise not to laugh. My first date sneezed on me and I thought I was going to be pregnant for months."

I really can't help the giggle that escapes. "Sneezed?"

"No euphemism. An actual achoo with hanky. He had no idea why I freaked out so badly."

"What happened?" I giggle.

"When I demanded he marry me to give our child a proper name, he thought I'd lost my mind."

"I can imagine that."

"I never heard from him again. And I wasn't pregnant. So, what's the question?"

Maybe Heather isn't the right person to ask. She might not even know men have nipples. My dubiousness must show on my face, because she snaps to attention.

"Oh, wait." She holds up a hand. "I went a little wild in college, so you're not going to shock me. I was just illustrating a point."

"Okay. Are man nipples different than woman nipples?" I blurt out in a furious whisper.

"How so?" Heather doesn't even blink.

"Sensitivity. Liking the mouth-on-boob thing. Fingers, hands—fondling." I trip over my words.

"Oh. No. Why? Does Stephen have a nipple fixation?"

Oh my God, I don't know. "Could he?"

Heather bites back a smile. "You'd have to tell me. But like anything, there's no sure bet. Different people like different things. There's a vast range of sensation regardless of gender."

"Uh-huh."

"Give me the big picture."

"A guy dating another guy." I try to stay all anonymous. So confusing. And when does that ever really work anyway? "Guy thinks he likes it too much and therefore thinks he's a girl."

"No, it's a nerve thing, not a gender thing. My best girlfriend doesn't like her breasts touched at all—she has, like, no sensation and gets totally bored."

"Really?" I thought our boobs were our most pleasurable place. At least, that's what it looks like in movies.

"Men don't really get it. They think she's playing hard to get and she's not, but give her a foot rub and she's Jell-O. Everybody is different."

"Foot rub?"

"It's a continuum." She shrugs.

"Ah." This I understand. "It's a Rock and Barbie thing."

She gets all confused. "I have no idea what you're talking about."

"Don't worry about it. I get it, though." I nod and finish drying a cake pan.

"Just tell the guy not to make an issue of the nipple thing and when his partner is ready he'll tell him." Heather hands me a plate.

"That's what I was thinking, but I wasn't sure."

Her expression clouds. "I'm sure there are all sorts of worries being gay."

I hadn't really thought about it. "What do you mean?"

"Well, we're not really a culture that understands that sexuality and gender are two different things. We don't separate them—"

"Gals? Cake people?" Mike pokes his head in. "Our blood sugar is dropping in here."

"Sorry, I got caught up in my whole anthro thesis."

"Huh." Mike seems to know what she's talking about.

"Thesis?" I ask. Man nipples as a thesis topic. Sounds edgy.

My expression must show what I'm thinking. "Gender and sexuality," Heather clarifies.

"Oh, of course." Now don't I feel like an idiot?

"Call me anytime." Heather picks up the cake and hands it to me. She takes a match and starts lighting the candles.

"Thanks," I say.

We both begin singing "Happy Birthday" as we walk back into the dining room.

rave #8
butt swishing

I feel like a reporter for Animal Planet. The butt swish is usually reserved for females but I have seen Adam do it occasionally, so perhaps there are instances of gay men using it. I'm not sure. I couldn't scientifically say. It's a technique often seen at the mall, and often utilized during a rousing game of bob and weave.

It's a graceful, sophisticated ability to swivel the hips at a twenty- to thirty-degree slant. If done right, the butt swish is alluring, attractive and the evolution of man in motion. Done badly, it's seven kinds of wrong.

So beware, and practice with a rhythm of step, slide, swish, step, slide, reswish. I also suggest using a mirror before attempting a public display, which should only be done by advanced flirters or expert seducers. And if you are advanced or expert, then you probably don't need the explanation of mall flirting. It's just a thought, though; good to know.

 nine

Clarice is standing three people away at the entrance to the gym. We're waiting to make a grand entrance along with the rest of the soccer team. I really wanted to be sick today and not be here. "Gert," she whispers in a loud, un-whisper voice.

"What?" I can't really hear her over the band's "Wipe Out" rendition.

"Have you talked to Stephen today?" she asks, pantomiming her way through the question.

"What?" I still can't make out what she's asking. I push toward her.

"Stephen. Have you talked to him?"

"Why?" Why is she asking? I can't remember when I last talked to him. I mean, really talked to him.

She shrugs. "Spens asked me if you'd talked to Stephen today."

The pep band begins playing the fight song. "Why?" I shake my head. She must know more than this unhelpful tidbit.

She shoves her way closer. "Spenser and he were talking about GAGD and Spenser mentioned it to me."

"Is he taking you?" I lower my voice and raise my brows.

"Stephen?" she asks.

I roll my eyes. "Spenser."

"I don't know." She bites a hangnail. Very sexy habit.

I nod. "We haven't really talked about it. It's a couple of weeks away."

"Twenty-four days," Maggie says from behind us, moving forward. "Do we really have to run out there and jump around?"

We've been told to look peppy and school spirity.

"I guess." I peek around Karmel, our goalie, who pretty much blocks the goal with her hips, trying to see what the cheerleaders are doing. It sounds like they are passing out X.

"I'm so not into this." Clarice rolls her eyes. "I thought we were the kids who despised these rallies—how are we part of one?"

"Someone's bright idea to try out for the soccer team."

"How was I supposed to know we'd make it? My mom plays lotto all the time and never wins."

"The odds were much better we'd make the team," Maggie says. She's always right.

"I'd rather have won lotto," I say.

"Okay, people, look alive!" Mack yells down the line as the cheerleaders hold up a big butcher-paper sign for us to bust out of and run through.

We kinda jog through as the band plays "Wipe Out." Again. Could they have picked a better-suited song?

I can't breathe; the entire school is looking at me. I'm naked and no one told me. "Why are they staring at us?" I whisper to Clarice.

"They're supposed to. We're going into battle on their behalf."

There are times I can't stand Clarice's militant attitude about everything. "We play soccer."

"Exactly. It's not a blood sport, but it's no different than being a warrior in the Middle Ages."

I don't know about that. We have no weapons, a longer life span, good nutrition and . . . "No plague," I say.

"You haven't seen the Westside Cicadas, have you?" Maggie asks from my other side. "They're locusts. We're so dead."

"Comforting. Thanks," I say as Maggie's name is called over the microphone.

She steps forward and waves quick at Jesse and then at a random group of freshmen.

"You have a big crush on him," I say without moving my lips, so really it sounds more like "Woo 'avaigcrotch in 'im."

Maggie looks at me like I'm having a stroke.

I'm about ready to repeat myself when I hear Mack. "Another surprise talent this season is Gerrrr-trooood Garrrr-ri-ballldiii!" Seriously, the alphabet doesn't have that many syllables. He loves my name.

I wave at Stephen, who hollers and whoops. Wow. Over-enthused. I telepath that he needs to calm down, but he doesn't seem to understand my message and waves at me again. Boys.

"Be my partner?" Karmel turns to me and grabs my hand.

"Oh—for what?"

"Haven't you been listening? We're doing an egg toss."

Right. How could I forget the cheerleaders' insane need to humiliate and terrify us with fun games?

Karmel doesn't even wait for my answer.

All of a sudden there's a spoon in my hand and she's tossing an Eggland's Best scud missile at me. "Catch it!" she screams.

Right. As if this game is winnable when we have tiny salt spoons to catch the eggs. I manage to cradle the egg against my stomach.

Maggie and Clarice don't even try. They're such doody heads. A couple more exchanges and it's only me and Karmel left standing. I can feel all two thousand eyes boring into my solar plexus.

Sweat drips down my back. These nasty-ass nylon uniforms are too small and too itchy. The lights are strobed into my brain. Then someone starts the foot-stomping and then clapping. With every beat of my heart, another reverberation rocks the gym.

I see Karmel's mouth move but can't hear anything she's saying. One of the cheerleaders makes her back up a step before she can toss the egg to me again.

Karmel lets the egg fly.

Have you ever noticed how much like lightbulbs eggs can appear when sailing through the air? I'm sure there's a syndrome with acute egg-bulb displacia.

I was not looking at the egg sailing in a perfect arc across the basketball court to land without ceremony on the bridge of my nose; I was staring at the lightbulb.

Egg in the face. I'm that girl.

I hear a smack and blink furiously, trying to keep my focus on the "egg" I'm still watching hang air over center court.

The gym gasps. I look around, trying to figure out who we're all concerned about. Maggie and Clarice and Mack and the assistant athletic director, who is also a nurse, collapse around me. Or maybe I collapse and they just kinda follow my trajectory. Then I realize that there's blood on my shirt.

After that I pretty much black out. I come to in the nurse's office with paramedics shining a flashlight into my eyes.

Killer headache.

"Lie still, miss."

It feels like an alien crawled out my nostrils and took over the world.

The paramedics are a swarm of flies; they are everywhere and won't stay still. I blink, trying to keep up with the buzzing.

They all nod in unison. "You have a couple of butterfly bandages and swelling, but we don't have to do any stitches."

Mack leans down, a complete freaked-out expression on his face, covered by a film of fake-coachy optimism. "Gertrude, your parents are on the way."

"Huh?" What? No. Why? They've graduated high school, why are they coming back?

"They want to take you to the emergency room. To make sure."

I mumble and shut my eyes. The world is moving too fast. And here I thought February portended to be a great month. Holy-Mother-of-the-Shortest-Month, please don't get any worse.

"Fine, thanks!" I yell, waving at the freshmen staring at me. Two humongous black eyes and a glaring white bandage and I'm not allowed to stay home. Even the headache I have doesn't cut it with Dad.

"Nope, you're an athlete. You need to get back on the horse."

Huh, cuz I've always been such a jockey. What's with the stupid cliché? He all but shoves me out of our car. (I can't drive for a few days, either.)

"Are you okay?" Maggie and Clarice shove a couple of Oscar juniors who decide to reenact the whole scene in the courtyard.

"Wait." I finish watching the almost-actors in their dramatic roles. "Tell me there wasn't a stretcher involved."

Maggie and Clarice shoot each other looks. "They were afraid you'd broken your neck."

"Neck?"

"They put a brace on you and then put you on the stretcher. It was all very Discovery Health Channel," Maggie informs me.

"Lovely."

"You okay?"

"Yes, I will live. No practice today, though. I get to watch you run." At least there's an upside.

"See you after sixth period," says Clarice. They wave.

I nod and head down the art wing. If I'm lucky, today might be self-portrait day and then I can go all Picasso on my features and it'll be accurate.

Stephen doesn't even bother with hello. "How are you?"

I try to work up a flutter in my belly upon hearing his voice. I can't. I think the nausea has to do with the head injury and not Stephen. I think. I'm not totally sure. "Fine."

There's a silence. A very leaden silence. He's called for a reason; I can hear it in his voice. It's not like my nose is still a topic of discussion around school. There's no embarrassment being associated with Nose Girl anymore. April Collins ripped the seam of her mini and walked around with a rhinestone thong and her butt cheeks showing until one of the teachers noticed a commotion. Rumor has it she was walking around like that for hours, though how she didn't feel breezy, I'm not at all sure. So I'm not talked about now.

"The face?" he asks. The bandages are off and the bruises are going down, I tell him. Why did he call? Other than I'm his girlfriend and it's expected.

"Good," he says.

The silence is killing me. "So?" I can almost hear him trying to get the words out.

"So?" I prompt again.

"Yeah, so. I was wondering." He trails off like he's losing cell reception, but not really. More like he's losing nerve.

Is he breaking up with me? Can he do that? What else could he possibly want to ask me that requires this much lead-up? "What?" Oh, I sound bitchy. Must fix. I lighten my tone. "What's up?" Better.

"Um . . . well, when do you think you'll be ready?" He sounds all sweaty and nervous.

Not exactly what I braced for. "Ready?" For what? Space travel? A movie? Plucking the eyebrows, again?

He huffs out an exasperated, "You know."

Holy-Mother-of-Penis-People, do not make me play this game. "No. I don't really know."

He mumbles. Sounds like he's actually getting a little ticked off. "Yes, you do. When will you be ready for . . . ya know."

Am I a moron? What the hell is he talking about? "Spell it out." I don't like to decipher; if I liked it, I'd do those crossword puzzles my father seems newly in love with.

"Sex." He sounds like he's bowing down and submitting himself to my level. Like it's so far down.

"Sex?" Where did this come from?

"Yeah, when are you going to be ready?" He's gathering momentum like a television evangelist.

When am I going to be ready? I don't know. It's not like a switch pops on and then there's a blinking light that says "open" in red and blue neon. "I don't know. Sometime?"

"Sometime? That's kinda vague." Now he sounds even more discombobulated.

No crap it's vague. Perhaps if we talked about his kissing technique, I might feel more inclined to have him thrusting other appendages my way. I try reason and rationality. Logic, even. "It's not like we've been dating very long."

There's so much that happens between kissing and intercourse. I mean, isn't there years of stuff to do before you get to penetration? Petting and stroking, oral, dry-humping . . . I feel like Emily Dickinson counting the ways, or maybe that was Byron, or was it Shakespeare?

What's with the rush? We haven't mastered tongues with clothing on—why does he think we can be any good at sex?

"You don't know." Now he's pissed at me and I don't know what I did wrong. Okay, I have an idea the correct answer to the question is "now, right this second," but come on, he couldn't have honestly been expecting that . . . could he?

I try a different tack. "Are you ready?" This ranks as one of the stupidest questions that has ever come out of my mouth.

"Yep." He sounds like he's been a monk for decades and is tortured. Like the dude came out of the womb ready for whoopee.

What can I say to that? I need to get off the phone. Think. What will get me off the phone? I don't want to have this conversation. Give in. Give in. Live to be a virgin another day.

"Soon?" I'm lying. I don't know. Soon seems like a good answer. It's not like I'm telling him I want to be married or anything.

Relief floods the line. I can almost feel the blood rush to his ever-ready in anticipation. "Soon? How soon?"

Even I can feel the tension level decrease. Who knew one word holds so much power? "Soon." The word that rang around the world. "You want a date?"

"That'd be great. Like the fourteenth or twentieth. Or whatever."

You're kidding, right? I'm supposed to give a date I'm going to be ready for sex? Does he realize how ridiculous this is? Really, who asks this kind of question? I'm trapped in a reality TV how-stupid-can-you-be episode.

Be honest, or lie? I'm going to shoot for the middle and see what happens. "I don't think I can do that."

"Oh. Okay. That's cool. Just thought I'd ask." He chuckles like it was all a joke. It didn't feel like a joke. It felt serious and weird. "Talk to you later."

" 'Kay." Are we finished talking?

The click of the phone pops in my ear like a firecracker. That's why he called. All he called about. A date for sex.

I feel violated. I feel dirty. I feel pissed off.

rant # 17
define "ready"

When will I be ready for sex? For nipple action? For going down and playing Popsicle with a penis?

When will I know? I can say I'm not ready to be naked with Stephen. I'm not ready to remove my watch with him, let alone my socks. That boy ain't getting nowhere soon. So why am I dating him? Should it just be about the sex? If you'll have it, then date him, and if not—don't? What if you don't know? I don't know.

Lucas? Lucas I'd like to get completely naked and roll around in the sun with. Okay, only if I looked like Scarlett Johansson when naked. Not that I know what she looks like naked, but she fills out clothes better than I do, so she must look better naked.

So am I ready for sex, but it's completely dependent on the person I'm considering having it with? I thought if you were ready, it meant ready no matter who, what or when? Could readiness actually factor the who into the equation?

 ten

Mr. Slater's butt has a bit of a disco beat going on. Huh. Wonder if he ate too many bran flakes this morning.

"I've received several phone calls from concerned parents this week. Seems some of you don't understand our term project and need guidance on how to proceed. I am going to speak slowly and repetitively, so I don't have to talk to your parents again this year." He sighs like there's actual physical pain in having to repeat himself. "This semester's main paper will be a focus on the who in comparison to someone on the list I gave you."

"The Who?" Old-school rock boy in the back gets all excited.

"No." Slater stamps on him. "There are quintessential questions every writer must answer. You know these, kids. They've been hammered into you since third grade. Mr. Speltic, name one of the five essential elements."

Corey's face freezes in a comical if pitiful expression. "Who?"

I swear Slater rolls his eyes in response.

"Very good. We're talking about who, what, where, when and why."

Oh, those. I knew that.

"You will be writing a twenty-five-page paper answering the who question. Who are you? What will history remember about you? Are you taking full advantage of every opportunity or are you sleepwalking through life? A writer must know himself inside and out, his biases, his fears, his deepest desires—"

"Jessica Biel!" Drake yells from the back of the room.

"Mr. Duscoe, you will stay after class." Slater's feeling a little harsh today.

"A writer must understand what drives him. You will have to get into yourself. Dig deep. I am expecting great things, people. Great things. The due date will be no later than May twenty-fourth; however, you can always turn the work in as soon as you've completed the assignment."

Snickers throughout the class. I don't think anyone has actually ever turned this assignment in early.

"We will take the rest of the period to brainstorm possible topics for inclusion in your paper. I will be walking around and I will count your ideas—you will have thirty-five distinct topics about you before you leave this classroom. And don't BS me, people. I've seen it all and I will not be grading on a curve so you kids can get As on this paper. You know my standard—it's up to you to reach it."

He smacks a ruler against the wall. "That's your guidance. Get busy."

My GPA is screwed.

"No way," I say as Mom hands me the already-opened envelope.

"It's true, dear. I'm so sorry, I know you were hoping for more."

I got a 163? She's kidding, right? I so didn't score a 163 on the PSAT. I'd banked myself at least a 190. I'm stupid. That's the answer. All these years no one has loved me enough to sit me down and tell me that I'm really plain dumb. I'm not a Brain, I'm a Belch.

"Is that bad?" she asks, hesitating like I'm going to scream in her face. Tempting.

"It's not good."

"I'm not sure it's bad. I read this article about what parents should expect and anything over 165 is a good score."

"According to *Parenting* magazine?" And can we subtract, please? I'm pretty sure 163 is not above 165.

"It was *Woman's Day*, but still."

"It's not even borderline Merit scholar, Mom. I can get into State with this score."

"Doesn't everyone get into State, even the druggies?" Leave it to my mother to point out this glaring truth.

"Well, yeah." So much for spinning it like the White House.

"Okay, you take it again." She shrugs like landing on the moon was especially easy as well.

"Again?" Chills break out along my spine and goose bumps flap along my arms.

"You're unhappy with it. Can't you take it again?"

That's like making Lincoln free the slaves again. There are some things that should not be attempted more than once.

"Again?" I squeak. Must think. Must think.

"Gert, honey, are you sure you're going to be okay?"

"I'm not suicidal, Mom." I don't think I'm suicidal, but I haven't really had time to weigh the options.

She shoos the air with her hands. "I wasn't worried about that. But I have never seen you so upset."

Probably because you're rarely home.

"Thanks for opening the letter before me," I say, just to stop the flow of parental concern.

As predicted, she bristles. "I thought it was important."

"Whatever." I clomp up to my room.

How badly do I want a better score? Badly enough to retake the test? Badly enough to study for it? Badly enough to risk doing worse the second time around? What happens if you do worse? Do they keep track? Do they have a list of decreasing scores, like a blacklist? I bet there's a list.

I slam my locker door shut, hoping the dent in it will go away with the extra force. Stevie isn't here to walk me to Ms. Whoptommy's, which is weird.

"What'd you get?" Adam pauses long enough to backpedal. He's so going to run into someone doing that.

"On what?" I'm hoping the whole class didn't get their scores at the same time. It will so suck if this week is all about who scored what on the test.

"Gertie." He stops and stares at me.

"Don't ask. You?" I can't spend the energy discussing this right now.

"One hundred sixty-three."

"Great." I try to feign celebration. Adam isn't smarter than me.

"Can you believe the delay in us getting our scores?"

"What?"

"Didn't you read the letter? Some bullshit about natural disasters and a computer malfunction?"

"No." Hmm, did the parental take it or did I just miss it in the haze of seeing a lifetime of minimum wage flash before my eyes?

"Oh. Well. We should have gotten them a couple of months ago, but they screwed our school. Good thing we're sophs and it doesn't matter. I guess it screwed a bunch of Merit stuff too." Adam waves his hand around. "You must have hit two hundred easy, right?" He jogs backward several more feet until he smacks into a pillar.

"I don't want to talk about it," I say. It's written all over my face: I'm a total idiot. I should pick up a heroin needle now and go join the Cloud Riders. My membership in the Brains will be revoked at any minute. I should perfect my giggle in case I'm adrift in a world with no like people.

The warning bell rings.

"I'm so, so—" Adam's sympathy is lost in the chaos of scurrying to our next class.

Stephen never shows up to walk with me. Odd. Maybe he's sick or something? Or not here today? I don't think I've seen him around.

I slink into Ms. Whoptommy's, certain that if anyone is going to ask the class what their scores are, it'll be her.

Stephen's already here. Weird. I smile at him. He looks miraculously healthy. I mouth, "Hi!" His friend Charlie smirks at me.

Stephen gives me a weird half smile, half shrug. Maybe he *is* ill. I'm getting a strange vibe.

I make it through the period with my eyes glued to the clock, watching the second hand tick. What's that saying about boiling water in a pot? It goes slower if you watch it, right? Second hands are the same. I swear the thing goes backward a couple of times to make the torture last longer.

Tangent: sorry.

The bell rings and I jump up, ready to dart out of class. Boyfriend with plague is so on his own. Today is not a selfless day.

"Gert, wait up," Stephen calls to me.

I can't ignore him. It's in the code-of-conduct dating handbook. I stop and turn back. "Hi," I say.

"Hi." He pulls out a note from his pocket.

A love note? Today could get so much better. So much brighter. I can feel the sun on my face and hear birds twittering a Disney song.

"Here." He pretty much thrusts the lined notebook paper at me.

"Thanks."

"Yeah." He backs away like I'm the one with the weird contagious illness.

That's when I get a chilly feeling of evil. I'm not turning into a vampire killer or anything, but I really don't think reading this piece of paper is in my best interest. Really not.

Stephen is acting all weird. No kiss. No "save me a seat at lunch," no "tell me what's up with you."

I close my eyes for a minute, blinking away innocence. He's dumping me. I look at the crinkled paper, still warm with his body heat, and I know. I know. I move to the side of the hallway before slowly unfolding the paper. I'm going to vomit.

I read:

Dear Gert,

Our relationship is dying. I think it's because we have moved to a new level and we're not giving each other what we need. Relationships need growth and giving to be healthy and have longevity. Ours doesn't have staying power. So I liked dating you, but I have to move on for my own health and development.

Regards,
Stephen

Is he serious? This isn't a breakup note, it's a self-help book.

I stop the first girl who walks by. "Is he serious?" I say, handing her the note.

It happens she's a senior with all her crap together and we've never exchanged glances, let alone words.

"Cowardly little shit. You are so better off single, girl." She hands the note back and moves on.

"Thank you!" I call over my shoulder as I slump against the lockers.

I've been dumped. Dumped by Dr. Phil's evil twin.

"Hey, Gert, warm-ups are at three-thirty. Look alive!" Lucas waves at me as he ducks into a classroom.

Warm-ups. Soccer home game. Lucas seeing me with my I've-been-badly-dumped face on. That's a cherry for you.

Okay, here's the deal. I don't have delusions of athletic ability. Really, I'm not the girl who thinks she's a jock but is really a Brain on the inside. Nope, I really am a Brain. So how did I get roped into this?

Clarice is actually talented. Maggie is worse than I am, so she's an alternate and rotates in when other people need breathers. None of us are in such great shape that we can play an entire half without needing to pass out for a few seconds until the oxygen begins flowing again.

I take that back. The goalie, Karmel, doesn't need breaks because she never actually tries to stop the ball. She likes to play the odds. She's so wide that the opposing team needs a mathematician to calculate the best angle of assault. Otherwise it's just luck. She likes the luck form of soccer.

Candace and Becky are both seniors, have played soccer since they were in utero, kicked boy-butt on many a field and played weekends on club teams for fun. They must so want to kill themselves right now. It's pretty much them as our team, and us running, jogging or walking along the field until the other team steals the ball from them and tries to calculate a goal.

Is there really anything else to say? Oh, the uniforms are nasty-ass polyester from ages ago. The school district bought them on eBay from a Russian state hoping to fund terrorism. They got enough money for the clothes to make a tongue-depressor gumball launcher. Sad, really.

So we're stuck wearing nonschool colors and absorbing who knows what kind of nuclear waste. I swear these were the official soccer uniforms of the Chernobyl company team.

I take the field. The other team, Mount Henley, looks like they do weight training and all sorts of cosmetic preparations. They actually look cute in their outfits with matching ribbons in their hair. How come we don't have matching ribbons and pink lip gloss?

The ref blows the starting whistle and it startles me. I'm too busy waving back at Mom, Dad, Mike and Heather.

Whoosh! The ball speeds past me and I can feel the ground vibrate as a million elephants stampede in my general direction. I don't even have time to brace myself before I'm knocked to the ground by a Mount Henley assassin. Air. I need air.

The ref leans down and peers into my face. "Take deep, even breaths," he says, like I'm gasping on purpose for the fun of it. "She'll be okay." He points at Ms. Assassin and gives her a foul. "Pushing."

Pushing? You're kidding, right? How about murderous intent? Clarice helps me to my feet, but then leaves me as the ball goes sailing down the other end of the field. Clarice takes her position more seriously than my health. Good friend.

We don't have official positions yet. Mack wants us to get a feel for all the stations before we get assigned to permanent locations. Clarice is a forward today, and I'm a halfback. Maggie is a benchwarmer.

The crowd cheers and I blink, trying to bring the field into focus. We score. I think. No one stands still long enough for me to really get a good view of the scoreboard.

The ball flies past me again. I try to run after it, but it seems like every time I manage to get where the ball is, it's gone, replaced by nothing except empty air and me looking inept. I really try to keep up, but Holy-Mother-of-the-Sports-Bra, there's a lot of running in this game.

The ball comes toward me. I move to stop it and kick it back in the opposite direction. Some girl from the other team kicks me in the shin. "Ouch." I kick her back.

"Ouch." She swears, too.

"Stop that," I say, trying to kick the ball toward Clarice and Candace. Now shin girl and her teammates are all ganging up on me and kicking my legs as hard as they can. Isn't this bad sportsmanship?

Finally, I kick the ball free and pass it directly to an opponent who is lined up at the perfect angle to score.

Karmel yells at me. "Thanks, Gert."

Mack screams from the sideline and throws his ball cap on the ground. Lucas is shaking his head like I've let down the entire free world.

It's a lot to keep track of, thank you. I need steel-toed cleats so I can whack some serious shin next time. Although I could just not go after the ball and then I wouldn't get kicked.

My shins have to be broken. Everyone will feel really stupid when they find out I'm playing with two broken shins.

Mount Henley scores again. Perhaps I should have run in the general direction of the ball, but it really doesn't stay in one place long enough.

And again.

We score. Or more like Candace scores.

Clarice steals the ball, only to be tripped on her way to goal. Ouch. That had to hurt. She picks grass out of her hair as the ref gives another foul to Henley. How many do they get? This has to be number twelve.

The ball rolls toward me and I kick it as hard as I can. It moves down the field about ten feet. Pathetic. One of the other team grabs it with her toes and does a samba toward me. I make a few attempts to stop her that are the least likely to cause me physical injury. I'm not big on the pain thing. My shins are throbbing so much that at any moment I'm going to look down and see bone poking out of my kneesocks.

Halftime.

My parents are clapping. I think they're trying to be supportive. Mike is talking on his cell phone with his back to the field. He showed up, I guess.

I sink onto a bench in the locker room and look for open wounds.

"Good job out there, Garibaldi. You really showed effort." Mack hits me on the back hard enough to displace a rib or two.

"Thanks," I mutter.

"Don't worry about it." Candace walks by like she hasn't been running for forty-five minutes. She doesn't even seem out of breath. Her breasts are perky and her sweat glistens like in a bronzer commercial. It's not fair.

The rest of the game is a blur of ball, bodies, fouls and pain. I think I rupture my spleen.

The ref finally blows the whistle to signal the end of the game and I glance at the scoreboard. 12–2. Us losing a soccer game with a baseball score—not a good sign. The rest of the season sits in my future like the Grim Reaper.

Mack gives us a big pep talk after the game. I don't remember a word of it. I guess it's supposed to be all motivatey and unpatheticy.

Really not working.

"I forgot my history book!" I yell to my parents, motioning with my arm that I'm going to get it. They wave. Mike and Heather have already left.

I walk—stumble, really—toward my locker. My muscles don't want to do what my brain is asking of them. I have to slow way down or pass a group of cheering Pops coming out of the boys' basketball game in the gym. I hit the brakes.

"Did you see them?"

"They sucked so bad."

"It's not like they're playing because they like balls." They all cackle.

Why do I have that sick feeling they're talking about the soccer team?

"What do you mean?" one of the Pops finally asks.

"You don't know?"

"Know what?"

"Soccer chicks are always gay. Always."

"Turf munchers," says another Pops, shrugging.

I've been verbally punched in the stomach. *Gay?*

"What?" says Pops number one.

"You know. They like eating pussy."

I'm going to vomit. I duck behind a post. I don't need my soccer-team sweatshirt drawing their attention. I'm not ready to defend my sexuality, especially when I didn't know I had to.

They walk past me, moving on to other illustrious topics.

Gay? Eating pussy? I thought I was playing a sport. To get Lucas's attention. How does that make me gay? And how didn't I know I was gay? And how come my gay friends didn't think to warn me that this was the general feeling about soccer players? Dumped and gay all on the same day. Bloody brilliant.

rant #18
turf munching?
since when is
exercise sexual?

Is it true all female athletes are gay? Does that make me gay? Why aren't male athletes considered gay? Okay, so figure skaters are gay . . . and ballerina-boys . . . and oh there I go . . . I'm sure there's a male figure skater who's straight . . . isn't there?

Will people think _I'm_ gay now that I play soccer? Are male footballers really _ballers_? How to combat assumptions?

Do I care? Maybe. But I know I will never touch a manly-boy butt if I give off the butch vibe, even if only through association.

Clarice isn't gay. Maggie isn't gay. Or are they? No, that would have come up in conversation. I'm not. I guess maybe I shouldn't assume that the burly girl playing goalie means anything when she smiles at me. Do I have to be careful how nice I am? Will I be attacked in the locker room by fanatical lesbian players? Is Lucas our coach only because he thinks none of us are lusting after him?

 **eleven**

I tried just not getting out of bed this morning, but the parentals noticed my absence around the coffeepot in time to get me to school. Damn.

I so don't want to be here. I don't want to see Stephen. I don't want to see those bitchy cheerleaders. Basically I'd like a dark hole with a home theater system, Netflix and junk food to live in. I could stay there forever and not feel the need to see school again.

"I have Vaseline." Tim and Adam lean over me as I'm digging through my locker before classes start.

"For what?" I ask. Do I want to know what my favorite gay boys need Vaseline for?

"His locker," Adam says.

"Huh?"

"We're going to cover his locker with slime because he be a slimeball." Tim goes all ghetto gay.

"Uh-huh." Weird. Sweet, but weird. "Maybe I should be all mature and not make a big deal about it."

"That's Charlie over there with the Cloud Riders."

"So?"

"So he's pointing at you and they're all laughing."

"Smear away." I slam my locker door.

Adam and Tim high-five and all but run in the direction of poor Stevie's locker.

"Hi!" Clarice and Maggie show up.

Holy-Mother-of-Suicide-Watches, what's up with the friends putting in appearances?

"Hi."

Clarice pulls out a gift bag that says "Over the Hill." She points at it. "Sorry, had to make do with what they had in stock."

"What's this?" How do they all know already?

"Care package," Maggie says.

"For what?"

"For you. The school has already heard about the breakup."

"It has junk food, Kleenex, Sharpies for doodle cleanup on anything you might have drawn hearts or his name on, a scented 'single-and-loving-it' candle—"

GREAT! "From your older sister?" I ask Clarice.

"Both of ours," Maggie answers. "Mine said you need a copy of GI Jane, which is her favorite kick-butt girl movie." Maggie's sister is at NYU.

"Uh-huh." I'm touched.

"Plus I printed out a list of ways to get over a broken heart." Maggie points to the small ream of paper tucked into the bag.

"Thanks." How am I going to show my face knowing everyone is talking about me?

"You're welcome."

Bell rings. I stash the loot in my locker.

"See you at lunch." They wave.

Lunch. Huh. That's gonna hurt.

I can't do it. No matter how great my friends are, I can't walk through the cafeteria today. I can't pretend I'm superbusy looking for a superimportant group of superpeople to eat with.

I'd like to be the totally together girl who calls the dumping dude a wanker and moves on to the next penis person. I'd like to be. In fact, I'd sell my virginity to the devil to be that girl. I'm so not that girl.

I pull my feet up and push against the stall door as a group of Giggles arrives in the bathroom for after-lunch upchucking.

Is it always going to feel this bad?

He's a bad kisser.

He sucks at conversation.

He probably doesn't even remember my favorite color or my favorite group or the world's all-time best movie according to *moi*.

So why am I crying? I blow my nose in really cheap toilet paper when the herd leaves.

My mascara is turning into lip liner.

Why can't there be an expiration date on dating so you know when to abort the mission? Like those alarms in the space shuttle that scream, "Pull up! Pull up!"

I would have appreciated a little ejecting before the crash and burn.

He dumped me. And he sucks.

So why am I so sad?

I thought things were looking up, but they're not. It's a weird blip on the radar, me thinking that life was turning around and good.

Okay, he wasn't perfect.

Is he the only guy who will ever care when I'm going to be ready for sex? What if he's the only guy who will ever ask? And I said no.

I'm going to be wearing spandex, with wrinkles and white hair, talking to a ficus named Stephen and telling him, "I'm ready, I'm ready" while I water him every other day.

I'm an idiot. I should have named a date. I should have told him I wanted to have sex.

I should have just shown up at his locker naked and said, "Take me, lover."

At least he wanted me. What if no other boyly-man or manly-boy will ever want me again? I'll have to pay a street person to strip me of my virginity when I'm ancient and dried-up. No, I'll become a nun.

"Gert?" Maggie calls.

"Gert, are you in here?" Clarice obviously doesn't approve of Maggie's technique and yells louder.

"She has to be in this one. We've checked all the other ones."

"Come on. It's just us."

"Maggie and Clarice," Maggie says.

"She has to know our voices," Clarice says with exasperation.

"I'm here." I drop my feet back to the floor and stand up from my throne.

"Told you," Maggie says.

"Come out here," Clarice demands.

"I don't really think that's a good idea."

"Yes, it is." Maggie never sounds this demanding.

"Seriously, get out here," Clarice commands.

I open the stall door to my two friends leaning against the sinks with their arms crossed, glaring at me.

"What?" I ask. They look pissed.

"You're allowed to wallow, Gert, but you're not allowed to sit in the bathroom at lunch, over a guy who has a tiny dick."

"Clarice!" Maggie looks horrified.

They weren't supposed to know that. Only Adam could have spilled those beans.

"What? It's true." Clarice holds out a Sharpie.

I blot my eyes with recycled cardboard towels that could also be shoe boxes.

"Adam told us." Maggie shrugs with a lot of sheepishness.

"They're standing guard." Clarice nods toward the bathroom door.

"We've voted." Maggie takes the Sharpie from Clarice and pokes me with it.

"Voted?"

"He's a terrible kisser and has astonishingly bad breakup skills. You need revenge."

"Revenge?"

"On the wall." Clarice points to the white paint behind me.

"*What?*"

"We've decided you will be doing the student body a favor if you assert Stephen's rather numerous flaws in a locale that will be infectious."

"It'll make you feel better." Clarice gesticulates. "My older sister said so."

"Your older sister suggested we vandalize the school bathroom?"

"In so many words."

"Uh-huh."

"It's not like you're going to get caught. Adam and Tim are blocking the door. No one is going to come near here for another two minutes." Maggie glances down at her watch.

"Here, I'll start." Clarice writes, "Stephen Blasko is the world's worst kisser—bring your towels.

"See? Easy." She hands another pen to Maggie.

"You're not," I gasp as Maggie raises the pen.

"Oh, I so am. He's a jerk." Maggie writes, "Whose d is so small it takes only one letter to spell it? Mr. Dickhead Stephen Blasko."

I laugh. I can't help it. My sweet, straight-and-narrow friend actually wrote the word "dickhead" on the bathroom wall.

"Clever." Clarice high-fives her.

"Your turn." They look at me.

I consider.

"When are we ready to have sex with Stephen Blasko? Try never, nope, not gonna happen, *nein*, *nada*, zippo, zero, zilcho, *niet*. Keep the lotion handy, ol' Stevie, cuz you're never gonna—"

Clarice takes the pen out of my hand. "That's enough, ace."

I've never considered graffiti liberating, but I feel better. Much better. My stomach isn't quite so upchuckedness, nor are my eyeballs all swimmy.

"Guys?" Adam knocks on the bathroom door.

"Coming!" we yell, grabbing our bags and racing out the door.

"Okay?" Adam asks me.

"Better. Definitely better."

The feeling of taking back control lasts until I'm home and Adam calls with a question I'm not prepared to answer. "Who are you doing your paper on?"

What paper? "Paper?"

"Yeah, the paper due tomorrow?" He's speaking like I'm foreign or brain-challenged.

"What?" I don't remember hearing about any paper.

"The most influential artist of the twentieth century? Your opinion and all, but—"

This should ring a bell. It should, but it doesn't. "Crapping buttocks."

"You forgot?" he gasps, aghast.

I can be honest or I can play it off. "I did."

"You don't forget stuff like that." He doesn't sound like he believes me.

"Thank you." I never forget schoolwork. I'm always done with it days early. It's a curse, which apparently I've now broken without kissing any frogs. Or maybe Stevie counts as a frog.

"It's half our art grade for midterms." Again with the disbelief.

"Of course it is." The other half is whether or not we've given ourselves over to the art experience and mastered yoga's downward dying dog. I sigh.

"She talked about it the first week."

Okay, we've established my idiotness. Can we move on? I have a paper to figure out. "Right." I grope around for the clock and pick it up. 11:03 p.m. I'm so screwed.

Adam warms to his topic. "I'm doing Picasso. I'd let you copy me, but I think she'd be a little suspicious."

"Just a little." Though I could change a few words.

What am I thinking? I don't cheat. I'm not a cheater.

Panic. Panic. Think. Think.

"Want me to help you search online? I'm sure you can find stuff on all sorts of artists."

"No, go to bed." It's eleven, for goodness' sake. How am I going to write a paper in this amount of time? I'm exhausted. I'm heart-broken.

"You sure?" He wants to go to sleep. I can hear it in his voice.

"Yeah, I'll see you tomorrow." Crapping buttocks. What was that website Jenny used last term to buy a paper?

I fire up Google. I'm desperate.

I type "buy term papers." I can't fail midterms.

Theultimatetermpaper.com. I click.

I can't fail. Not acceptable.

It's written on my face, I know it is. I'm a cheater and it's written all over my face.

"Gert, we'd like to talk to you, please," Mom calls.

Oh, Holy-Mother-of-Felonies, they know. " 'Kay," I yell down the stairs. *Take a breath and stroll, Gert.* I try to stroll, but it's more like a limp without focused concentration.

The parentals look all expectant. "We've talked and we think you should retake the PSAT if it's really going to upset you this much."

"I take it again in the fall for real."

"What do you mean for real?"

"I take the actual SAT in the fall. This was just practice. It doesn't count for anything." I guess.

"Then why the hell are you moping around?" Dad shouts.

Uh. "I got dumped, too."

"Oh, dear, I'm sorry." Mom hugs me.

I mumble "thanks" into her bathrobe and pull away. Did they just call me down here for this? "That's it?" I can hear the shock and awe in my voice so I clear my throat.

"Was there something else, dear?" Mom cocks her head like she's a poodle and I'm a tasty morsel.

"Nope." I slam my mouth shut.

"Have a good day, dear." She shuffles back up the stairs in her robe and Dad turns on ESPN.

"What's going on?" I ask as I step over people sitting in the hallway. Is there a weird virus affecting people's ability to stand?

"Today's the weigh-in. We're protesting," a perky blonde with dimples in every cheek answers.

"Hoping to have all the kids sit in and not go to classes." Her utterly skeletal boyfriend says while holding her hand and gazing into her eyes.

As the feeling of cheaterness passes, I realize God does love me. Anything to not go to art and turn in someone else's paper on Georgia O'Keeffe!

"It's a total violation of our civil rights." A dreadlocked Rastafarian scoots over and pats the floor next to him. I think I can get high simply breathing in his vicinity, but he's kinda cute.

"Yeah." A perky freshman plants herself next to the dreadlocked Cloud Rider. He looks at me and shrugs in apology. I smile back.

"I can see that," I say. Like I'm getting on a scale. *You can just write "N/A" on my report card, thank you very much.*

I want a lithe, lean school board before I'm going to worry about my butt size.

"I'm game." I plop down, leaning up against a bank of lockers. All along the hallway, more people join in the protest until it takes on a feeling of utter party.

A guy from my bio class pulls out his iPod and minispeakers and starts jamming with drumsticks on his textbooks. This is a very eclectic protest.

I'm liking it.

"What are we doing?" Clarice leans down and tries not to step on me.

I scoot over. "Protesting the weigh-in."

"How long are we sitting here?" she asks as she tries to fold herself into the tiny space.

I shrug, jamming to someone's beat box. At least, their attempt at beat box. "I think we're going for all day." *At least through art class, please.*

"Really? Can that be done?" She looks impressed.

"What are they going to do? Pull out the dogs and rubber bullets?" I ask.

"It's been done." Maggie finds us.

"Yes, but over weight?" I ask.

"Hmm. Good point." Maggie plops down next to me. "You doing okay?"

"Yeah, I'm okay."

"Isn't this the coolest? Jesse, sit with us." Maggie pulls on the hand of a guy passing by. "You guys know Jesse?" She smiles at us like we should know something.

"Hi," he says, like he knows all about me. He has that look— like I've been the topic of conversation.

Pretty soon Adam and Tim are arguing over video games and stretching out their long legs across the hallway.

Princi-Pal Jenkins starts trying to walk through with a bull-horn. "People. You've made your point. First period starts in two minutes. Anyone late for class will be written up."

No one moves. I kinda think he made it sound like a dare. Not a good move if you're in the position of authority and we're sup-posed to be all listening.

Clarice leans over. "We should call Channel Six and see if they'll come film us."

I point to Jerry, one of the Oscar film nuts. "He's live-casting on the school website."

"Can he do that?"

I can't say I know how, but he is. I shrug.

Pal tries again, moving in the opposite direction. Once the sen-iors decided this was a worthy cause, the entire freshman class sat down as a unit. It's scary how packy they are. "Students, there are appropriate venues for voicing your opinions," Pal calls again on the bullhorn.

"You threw away our petition!" someone shouts.

"And laughed," another voice calls.

"I did not throw it away. I merely suggested that the adult com-munity of this school district might know more than the students who like to be overweight."

"Look who's talking!" a guy yells.

Jenkins whips around, trying to pinpoint the voice. "That's rude and against our school code. I demand you all return to classes now." He's sounding more and more like a petulant child.

No one moves.

I slide my gaze to Adam's. I am so sitting this one in.

Maggie snaps her phone shut. "Channel Six already has a crew on the way."

I point. "Isn't that the editor of the city paper?"

"I think someone must have tipped her off too." Maggie smiles.

"I don't think I'm going to be turning in my paper today," I say to no one in particular. Whew. Crisis averted.

Kinda. There's another soccer game tonight. More running.

 twelve

I pick up the phone and put down the book about Georgia O'Keeffe.

"Hello?"

"Gert."

"Mike?"

"I need a favor," he says, then silence.

Oh, this could be good. Since when has Mike ever asked me for anything? "Reee-aaa-lllyyy?" I draw the word out like it's its own language.

"But first you must swear complete and utter silence."

I try to be funny. "You've sworn allegiance to the Dark Side."

"Funny." He does not sound amused.

Notice the no denial. I knew it. Liberal on the outside, conservative and evil on the inside—that's the rotten stink of white man for you.

"What?" I ask, since he seems to be waiting for me to stop my mental tirade.

"You know that Heather and I have been dating almost a year."

I do the mental math. It doesn't add up. "Wait, you brought her home four months ago."

"Yeah. You should learn something from that."

Interesting. Either he's not as dumb as I thought or I am interminably doomed. "I've been dumped, so it's not like it really matters."

Mike sighs. "I heard. You're not going to ruin this with wallowing and moping, are you?"

I try not to be offended. "I don't even know what it is you think I could ruin." As if I'm wallowing or mopey. Puh-lease. "You've confused me with the Disney Channel."

"Ah, my mistake." He breathes heavily into the phone.

I take pity. "So, what's our secret mission?"

"I need to pick out a ring."

"You wear jewelry?" I now understand the vow of silence.

"No." Disgusted, he barely makes the word understandable.

"Oh. Oh!" I get it. Heather. Ring! "You're proposing?" I screech. Very maturely.

"Dammit, Gert, you think the parents got all that?"

"Sorry." No way did they hear me. The game is turned up so loud Dad couldn't hear God's voice giving him a directive. "You're asking her to marry you?" I whisper, to appease the brother.

"That's the idea."

"What do you need me for?"

"Obviously not relationship advice."

"That's low."

"Sorry. I'm nervous. Will you help me?"

"What exactly do you need me to do? I only have about a hundred bucks in savings."

"I don't need money. I need a girl's opinion. I want you to go shopping with me."

"Shopping?" Haven't they discussed getting married in a roundabout abstract-but-clear way so it's not really a surprise? And hasn't she pulled him over and gazed longingly at the perfect ring, which is always in the window of the jewelry shop? I need to stop taking my cue from movies. "I thought everyone had the marriage talk these days."

"Says who?" he asks.

"People."

"Well, we haven't."

"Do you know her size?" I ask, pulling out a notepad to make a list.

"I'm not buying her clothes." He sounds like a dying man.

"No, doofus, rings come in sizes."

"Shit," Mike mutters. "How do I not know this?"

Obviously didn't think that one through.

I pity him, yet again. "Leave it to me." I'll come up with something.

"If you give this away, I will kill you so slowly you'll be a grandmother before you're out of agony."

Huh. Who knew violent tendencies run in the family?

"I can be covert. Class rings. She wears one, right?" I think I've seen that bit of high school pride on her hand on occasion.

"I think so."

"So I'll call her and ask about it like I'm curious what my finger size might be in ten years."

"Gert." There's a warning in Mike's voice.

"I can do this. You came to me, remember?"

"I only wanted you to go with me to the store and pick out an engagement ring."

"I can do that too."

"Okay, then."

"I'll let you know when I know what size."

"Can you make it soon?"

"Why?"

"I'm aiming for Valentine's Day."

"Oh."

Crapping buttocks. Did he have to remind me? This was the one year I thought I was safe from the whole red-hearts-and-flowers thing as a single woman. "I'll let you know. Oh, and Mike?"

"What?"

"Thanks."

"Don't make me regret it."

"Hi, Heather? It's Gert. Mike's sister." Like she knows more than one Gert.

"What can I do for you?"

"Um, well, I'm curious about the ring I saw you wearing."

"My class ring?"

"Yeah. They're selling them and I just can't figure out what size to get. Mom isn't any help cuz she wants to know when they started giving out rings instead of pins."

"Huh."

I'm not sure she's buying this. She sounds skeptical. "Sooo, has your finger changed size since you bought your ring?"

"Oh, a little. But I'm still pretty much the same size as when I was in high school. I guess if you gained a lot of weight maybe the size would change. Usually you can try them on at the display table."

Crap, didn't know that. "That's what I was thinking. A four is a little tight and a five is a little loose. What size is yours?"

"It's a six, I think. I'd suggest you get the one that's a little loose."

"Thanks so much. I knew you would know."

"And Gert?" Heather asks.

"Yeah?"

"Don't let Mike spend a lot. I don't need something flashy."

"Uh. Uh." I have nothing to say.

"Night, Gert." She giggles and hangs up.

"Ni—" I put the phone down without finishing the word. What's the point?

I was so good. How did she know? What's with the covert conversation not being so covert?

I quickly dial Mike. "She's a six. Let's go Saturday."

"Did she—"

"Nope, doesn't have a clue." Sometimes lies are best for everyone's sanity and safety. I have a very low pain tolerance.

The away bus. This is what I ran for. I've missed my first three away bus opportunities due to blatant cowardice and bad hair. It's now or never. I must make a move—the season is waning and I'm still running after Lucas without direction. This is why I have put up with the huffing and cramps and the sweating. Lucas. And me. On an away bus. Oh, there are stories of dreams coming true on away buses. Fairy tales may have sparkly horse-drawn carriages, but reality has old yellow exhaust belchers. Road trips with only the light of the passing streetlights and cell phones. Ah, the allure.

It's really rather weird. We get let out of class two periods early. Of course, we have to do all the work, but we don't have to sit through class, which is great. We lug all our stuff onto a stinky school bus. But the adrenaline is running high and fast, so it feels cool. I know it's bizarre, but it's true.

Lucas walks by as I'm standing in line with my girls to get on the bus and I catch a sniff of his manly-boy smell. He's changed soap brands. Am I a stalker to know this?

Nah, that would mean anyone with a crush and a nose falls into that category.

I get stuck sitting at the back with Maggie and Clarice. Miles away from Lucas. But we're on the way to the game. It's daylight. This is not the important part of the trip, so I'm cool. I will bide my time.

Their locker room smells like ours. Weird.

We warm up. We run around a little. We practice kicking the ball. The game starts.

I barely have time to take a step before Candace is airborne and yelling, "Clear it!"

The other team looks like they're not sure how they happened to be here. I like the dazed and confuzzled look; it means we have a chance to win a game.

At least they don't try to run the whole time. I hate the opponents who dart around like a school of piranhas in cute shoes.

I study the sidelines. Do they have a coach? I really can't tell who it might be.

The ball comes at me. I hear yelling. I spin. I dive to get the ball. But I miscalculate and hit the dirt with my foot. It sticks. Have you ever noticed that dirt stops momentum? Especially frozen dirt.

Why does our goalie get to wear long pants and the rest of us are stuck in shorts in the middle of winter? My cleats are bright red. I like to pretend they are like Dorothy's shoes and they'll take me home if I click my heels three times.

The other team obviously just needed to warm up. Now they're all serious and speedy. Scary, too.

Clarice goes to throw in the ball. Why did she throw it right to the opponent? It's not like she couldn't tell the difference between our teams—they are lean, mean muscle machines that don't look human and we are the girls with curves, huffing and puffing. Look for the red faces and sweat and you can immediately tell who is who.

At halftime I hear they've won state like eight times in a row. Of course, three of those years there wasn't an opponent, so they were pretty much given the title just for showing up.

After second half starts, I think they're finally getting tired. The ball is flying toward me. Wrong direction. Must get it to go the other way. I swing my leg back and shoot.

"Foul!" the ref shouts like we're all hearing impaired. "High kick." He points at me.

Huh. Okay, so it looks more like a Rockettes line kick, but puh-lease, so not a foul. It's not like I actually kicked anyone in the head. She had really good reflexes and I missed making contact.

Candace takes the ball all the way down the field on her own. It's like everyone is too tired to stop her, and she just races down there at top speed. She can control the ball like she's attached to it with Silly Putty. I'm so unclear how she does it. She shoots, and the ball just misses the top of the goal frame. So close and yet so daringly far.

"Heads up!" Mack yells. The ball is in my section of the field and I am supposed to insert my body between the oncoming team and the goal. Yeah, right. Assuming way too much about my commitment to the little white and black ball.

Where'd the ball go? It was just here. I twirl around, trying to locate it. How does someone lose a ball that size?

Mack won't stop yelling. It's not like we can understand anything he says, but he doesn't quite get that. He yells a lot of stuff, hoping we'll pick out one or two percent of the whole; he believes in quantity coaching. Of course, I mostly hear "practice is over" and "nice job, Garibaldi."

We win the game, thanks to Candace, Becky and Krista. We sink-shower since it's late; we really don't have time to full-shower. Not that I really want to get naked in front of any of these girls. Clothes are armor. Armor is good.

I wait until the ride home to talk to Lucas. There's lots of cheering, but it's a two-hour trip and people are stinky and tired from the game. There's not much conversation and Clarice and Maggie know exactly what I'm up to. Hard to fool friends with good brains. They slide into the seat right behind Lucas and throw their bags on the seat next to him.

"Hey, Gert, we saved you a seat," they say in unison as I climb the stairs to the bus. They manage not to giggle. I'm near the back of the pack, having learned early that the back seats are taken up fairly quickly and the guys stay near the front of the bus. Pretty much it's a way to get closer to Lucas without being all transparent about it.

"Thanks." I shove their stuff to the side by the window and sit. This gives me a perfect excuse to sit nearer the boyly-man. Manly-boy. Such a fine line.

"Great game, Gert," Lucas says as we pull onto the freeway. "You know what plans Tim has this weekend?"

"No." Why ask me this?

"Just curious. You being tight with Adam, thought you might have heard." He shrugs.

"Nope, sorry." I grimace, frantically flipping through the Rolodex of my brain trying to think of something to say.

Miles zip past. iPods pop out. Lucas's included.

I have to tap him on the shoulder to get him to take out his earpiece.

"What?" He genuinely looks interested in anything I might say. Maybe that's his secret—looking like he cares. Not a lot of guys can pull that off.

"Can I ask you something?"

"Sure." He shrugs and pulls off his other earpiece.

"Have you ever been dumped?" I lower my voice, not wanting the entire bus to hear me.

He's surprised. Or I think that's surprise. It's kinda hard to tell with the streetlights whizzing past in the dark. He leans in. "Of course. Are you breaking up with me?" he says, smiling.

I roll my eyes but don't answer.

"This about that guy?" he asks.

My heart speeds up. He knows? He saw us together and wondered? This could be good.

"Cuz Tim mentioned it was pretty cruel."

Great. I deflate. Perfect. "Yeah, I guess I was curious if there's ever a good breakup. Or is it always like that?"

"First time, huh?" He nods. "That's the worst."

"Really?"

"Sure. It gets better, though. After you figure out that there'll be another girl, or guy, coming along. It's not like you're never going to date again."

I like his confidence in my dating future. Of course, he could just be speaking from personal experience and then it's not so confidence-building. Now, this sounds like good advice. Even mature. But think about it. This is blue-ribbon guy talking to me. Me. The odds of our oceans having the same number of fish are slim to none. Besides, scientists say there won't be any fish left in the next few decades, so there can't be that many now, right?

"Ya get me?" he asks.

"Yeah, I guess so. Thanks."

"Anytime." He puts his earpieces back in and goes to sleep. Either that or he just doesn't want to talk to me anymore so he's pretending. But there's drool, so I'm pretty sure he's not pretending.

I watch, trying not to be too creepy and obvious.

I put on a skirt. This is a momentous occasion. I must dress appropriately.

"You're sure she doesn't suspect anything?" Mike asks for the hundredth time as we climb into his tiny gnome car.

Hmm. Again I consider whether or not it's in my best interest to tell the truth. "No, not a hint."

Seriously, why do people ask questions they only want one answer to?

We walk into a huge jewelry store. One of those stores claiming to have cornered the diamond market that sells only hand-cut, magically mined perfect stones. The bling is blinding. "Wow."

Okay, either I underestimated the choices or I overestimated Mike's ability to make decisions. Or both.

"What's the budget?" I ask, glancing around at the display cases. Mike always has a budget. Dude had a financial plan when he was six, or so I've heard during the why-can't-you-be-more-like-your-brother-when-it-comes-to-money lectures from the parentals.

Mike's eyes are glassy and hugely dilated. "No budget."

"Huh?" I must have misheard.

"I don't have a set amount."

"Do you have a ceiling?"

"Reasonable." He shrugs. Sweat trickles down the side of his face.

What the hell is reasonable? That's like saying I'm going to have a rational tantrum. "Diamonds" and "reasonable" don't go together in the same sentence. "You do know that De Beers started the whole 'a diamond is forever' thing as an ad campaign after World War Two, don't you? This is the tradition that isn't even older than our parents."

That snaps him out of it. "Where do you get this stuff?"

"I'm just suggesting you not feel the need to get a diamond."

"I'm getting a diamond. Everybody gets diamonds for engagement rings."

We peer over a case with about a thousand solitaires in various sizes and shapes.

I continue. "Most diamonds have some blood on them, either

during the mining process or in the trade. Children are orphaned, maimed, killed."

"Charming." A saleslady with capped teeth and a sprayed updo smiles at me like I'm a leper at Miss America.

"Gert. Listen to me." Mike grabs my arm. "We are getting a diamond. We are saving the world another day."

I shrug him off and paste a smile on my face that replicates the one across the counter from us. "I'm trying to be supportive. I didn't want you to feel like you had to be a lemming if you wanted to be different and daring. I wanted you to know you have options."

He relents and pulls out a hanky to wipe at the sweat. "Thanks. I get that. I'm optioning my right to buy the ring that says Heather's name regardless of whether or not children have been orphaned."

"Okay. I'm cool with that." I lower my voice to a whisper. "But what's the budget really?"

"There's no budget."

"No, really?" Oh, buttocks, I must save Mike from himself.

"Can I help you?" Charming Lady asks.

I don't like her. She was a Pop-Giggle hybrid in high school, I can tell. She probably plans their class reunions because she genuinely thinks the world can't get better than high school. I wish we could go somewhere else, but Mike seems set on this store.

He nods. "I need an engagement ring."

"Who's the lucky lady?" Charming asks, looking at me like there's no way I could possibly be the lucky lady.

"His girlfriend," I answer.

"Heather," Mike says, like there's only one Heather in the world and Charming must know her.

"Splendid."

Who says "splendid"? Really, who says that?

She taps her perfectly manicured hands on the glass. "Sometimes it helps to know if the young lady works? What are her hobbies? What type of accessorizing does she prefer?"

I start talking to Charming to take the pressure off Mike. "She's a preschool teacher. Likes kids and wants kids." I glance at Mike to see if he's agreeing with my assessment of his future wife. "She doesn't wear a lot of jewelry, I'd say a few tasteful pieces. She prefers accessories that aren't flashy." I add this last knowing full well that Charming gets a commission on the size of the bill. Flashy takes out a few of the larger, more heavily secured tables of gems.

I'd also like to mention for the record that there are no price tags visible. Frankly, I think they should be color-coded so you know what you're falling in love with before you get socked in the stomach with the bottom line. It's sneaky, I say. Sneaky, sneaky, sneaky.

Charming Lady nods. "That gives us a starting place. If you'll allow me to suggest a few?"

Mike nods jerkily. It's even air-conditioned in here. It's February and they air-condition the place. I don't think it's because diamonds sweat. I think it must be the average condition of men walking through those doors.

She pulls out a couple more trays. "These are our most popular pieces. All are one to three carats total weight."

"That's nice." Mike points at one. "So's that one. That, too."

Okay, this is going to take forever.

"Are you focused on a solitaire?"

"Why do you ask?" I raise my eyebrows. I can tell she wants to say something but she's still sizing us up. "Well, if the young lady—Heather, is it?—works with children? Presumably she'll want to wear this every day? Perhaps she'd prefer a few small stones, even a band of small stones, rather than a single larger stone. Our professional clients tend to stay away from large single stones."

Yeah, some of these could permanently maim small children. I see blind preschoolers running around.

"I think she'd like those two." I point to a couple of heart-shaped diamonds. Smallish.

Mike gasps. "Heart-shaped. Yes, that's her."

"Good, we'll stick with rings that have a heart-shaped stone in them. Might I ask what your profession is?" Charming directs the question toward Mike. I guess she doesn't think I look old enough to have a profession.

Mike jumps like she's pointed a gun at him. Obviously, cogent thought is beyond him at the moment.

She sends me a small smile and quips a brow in question. "He's a professor at Simon Randalph," I say.

"Oh, that's a very well-respected private university." She beams. I guess it pays more than the local community college.

"Green!" Mike shouts this last word like he's got Tourette's.

"Green?" Charming and I ask in unison.

"Her eyes are green. Green's her favorite color."

"Uh-huh." I shrug. News to me.

"Okay, that's good. Let's look at diamond and emerald combinations."

"H-heart," Mike stammers.

"Yes, in heart shapes. Of course."

I wonder if she does this all day long. Trying to distinguish gibberish from the mouths of terrified buyers and finding a ring to match. I feel the need to apologize to her on Mike's behalf. "He's normally very articulate," I say.

She smiles at me, a twinkle finally warming her gaze. "They all are until they walk in here. Even the most sincere groom gets a little giddy at the prospect of buying an engagement ring."

Interesting. I wonder if brides all hesitate before saying yes, or if the hesitations come at night, in the dark.

A very painful four hours later, Mike selects a banded ring with three stones representing past, present and future. They're small enough that they won't injure Heather's kids and large enough that you can tell they're heart-shaped. They even have her size in stock.

I had to steer Mike away from the rings only worn in rap music videos or down the Red Carpet. Rings where he'd be dead before he'd had the chance to pay them off, even with the very nice finance package offered by the store.

Velvet box in pocket, we walk out into the brisk snowy air. Cupids dangle from the Plaza's streetlights.

"Thanks, little sis."

"You're welcome. Are you doing roses and candles and moonlight?"

"I can't really control the moonlight thing—forecast is cloudy. You think I should do roses and candles?"

I hesitate, as his color is just starting to return to normal. "What were you planning?"

"I don't know. One knee after dinner."

"Do you have reservations?"

"Yes, I do."

"Where?" *Please don't be Chuck E. Cheese.*

He names the "it" romantic restaurant.

How clichéd!

"What?" he asks.

Dude is a Mensa boy. You'd think he could be more creative than that.

I don't say anything.

"I'd rather do it at home, but she's not going to wait in the car for me to light all the candles and I'd never concentrate worrying about burning down the building while we were at dinner."

It's not like my Valentine's Day is going to be anything worth saving the date for. "Why don't I come over and light all the candles, turn on the music, et cetera, et cetera?"

"And then be there? Thanks, but this is scary enough without an audience."

"No, I'll watch out your window and sneak out. I can hide around the corner from your apartment door when you go in, then ride the elevator down and drive home."

"You'd do that?"

"Well, yeah. You're my brother."

He looks pleased. Touched, even. "You're sure?"

"Yes, have it all there. I can just set up. You do the shopping. It has more meaning if you've bought all the stuff."

"You're probably right. But it's tempting to give you permission to use my Visa."

"I can order you stuff, but she'll ask. You know she'll ask."

We are women, we're genetically programmed to find this type of tedium out.

He nods. "You're right."

"On one condition, though."

"Oh no, what?"

"Just call me and tell me what she says."

"That I can do." He smiles and hugs me to his side.

Clarice catches up with me in the hallway and tugs on my arm. "Are you going to the girl-ask-guy dance?"

The posters are everywhere. I see cute hearts and Photoshopped girls flirting with boys and I get the stomach pit of dread. I've been avoiding the heck out of this conversation. "That means I'm asking someone to go, right?"

She shakes her head. "Not necessarily."

News to me. How'd I miss the meaning of this one? "Oh?"

"Well, it's girls' choice, right?" Clarice's expression gets all hidden and blank.

"Right." I so do not follow.

"Can't we choose to go alone?" she hedges.

"You're not going with Spenser?" I ask. I can't believe what I'm hearing. They've been hooking up while studying for weeks.

Her eyes get all swimmy. She whispers, "No, he thinks that's too much of a relationship."

"Really?" Does dancing equate relating? I've never known the correlation, but then, guys hate to dance and most don't really like relationships, either.

She's studying the cement floor and poking at a black wad of last year's gum. "Hmm."

I take a deep breath and put on my best empowered-woman-go-get-'em persona. "You should ask someone else. Just to prove to him he's not the only roach in the kitchen."

"Huh?" She's confused.

I shrug. "I've just never liked the fish-in-the-sea thing,

especially now, since there aren't many fish in the sea anymore. So I'm trying on a few other sayings."

She giggles. "Roaches?"

I tamp down any defensiveness I feel. "They're fairly indestructible. It's not the insult it first appears."

"Whatever." She can't stop laughing. At least I've cheered her up.

"Are you going to ask someone else?"

She sighs. "Gert, I like Spenser."

"I know you do." I'm not blind, challenged or stoned.

She rolls her eyes. "No, I mean I *like* him. I don't want to go with anyone else."

"Oh. That's a problem."

"Is it? I mean, he could have thought that he just wanted to be benefriends and now that we've spent time together, maybe he's just waiting for me to tell him how I feel." She's all hopeful and puppylike.

How to explain that the bronze statue of the school mascot knows how she feels about Spenser? We're all pretending she'll get over it. Especially Spenser, who is going to take an Oscar for his portrayal of obliviousness. He's given it new life.

"I really hope he does like you as much as you like him," I answer.

The bell rings. Holy-Mother-of-Chiming, I'm saved.

cupid's seminal arrow

We do not celebrate Valentine's Day in this school. I wish I could say it's because all the girls have risen up and demanded we be left alone instead of judged on couples' day. But no. It's our school board.

The same school board that collectively weighs two hundred pounds more than it should but still thinks it's a good idea to make us stand on scales and get physique grades. This same group of rejects got together and decided that Valentine's Day promotes sexual behavior. They passed a board policy outlawing any mention, decoration or celebration of a holiday promoting sexual feelings or behavior. They even went so far as to suggest that the pressure to be in a couple on Valentine's Day leads to promiscuity among students and staff and therefore leads to an unhealthy workplace.

A bunch of Giggles and Pops are wearing black armbands in a show of solidarity and grief with the mighty Aphrodite.

Sex taints learning, basically. According to the school board, Cupid isn't shooting arrows, he's shooting his wad. And chocolates? They are aphrodisiacs. Flowers? The sex organs of plants.

Really. Maybe they have a point, but it's been lost in the absurdity of their politics and frankly, it doesn't curb the pressure I feel for not getting aphrodisiacs and floral genitalia. I'm not the biggest fan of the holiday. Mainly because I've always wanted the bubble bath with rose petals, candlelight, amazing kisses and lots of action.

I'm not really sure what my fantasy is beyond the kissing part. I know I want more, but I need to figure that out before I start the cameras rolling in my head. Seriously, nine-tenths of the being-ready-for-sex equation is actually having an idea of what to expect. I don't have a clue. I mean, I've seen movies, but I've also heard horror stories of girls who rip and bleed and pain and stuff. Which could very well be propaganda to keep my panties on, but I'd like to think the man I'm with would stop if I was bleeding and screaming, and I'm not terribly confident I've met him yet.

But that leaves me home alone without the parentals, knowing there are people all around me getting kissed tonight, and the best I can look forward to is a little CPR (Covert Privatalia Resuscitation) for Maya provided by yours truly.

Am I as pathetic as I feel? Huh. No good answer to that one.

 thirteen

So I did my part. Got the candles lit, rose petals strewn, champagne iced. Barry White playing in the background. Mike left a cheesy-ass saxophone CD out for me. Uh, no. Not Kenny G. Nothing says *no* like Kenny G. So that's the smallest adjustment I made and it's February fifteenth and I still haven't heard a word. He promised to call with details.

I dial.

"Jesus, Gert, it's five a.m."

"Good morning, sunshine. What'd she say?"

"Hang on." Mike mumbles something and I hear shifting and squeaking. He's still in bed.

"Gert, thank you." Heather's sleepy voice greets mine—apparently they're in bed together. This has to be a good sign. Unless it's pity breakup sex. But doesn't that usually happen before the no? At least, that's the order on TV.

"So?"

"So, little sister, you will have a new big sister-in-law."

"Cool!" I shout.

"I had no idea the whole class ring conversation was a setup." Heather's laughing, clearly enjoying the private joke with me.

"You had no idea, right," I say.

"Mike says you helped him pick out the ring and set up the apartment."

"Yep."

"Nicely done. Perfect. Here's Mike."

"Hey, no telling Mom and Dad until I call them later, okay?"

"Okay."

"And Gert?"

"What?"

"We really need to talk about when to play a Barry White CD." Mike chuckles.

I hang up with a smile on my face. Let's hope the rest of the month goes this smoothly.

I walk into the PSAT/SAT study class after school and sit down. I must study if I'm going to take the test again. I mean, I took it early as a sophomore: the real deal that counts I'll be taking in the fall with the rest of my class. I'd like help. Some support. Some pep-talkiness.

However, the conversation goes straight down the expected line.

"So, what'd you get?"

I turn the question back. "What did you get?"

"I got a 186." Crystal has the personality of a Pop Rock—fun for a while, but no substance. I got tired of her by the second week of kindergarten. Really. There were three days of friendship before *poof!* it all popped away.

"You should have already received your scores, Miss Garibaldi. Are you sure they haven't come?" Counselor interrupts to ask.

"If they'd come, I would be able to tell everyone what a great score I got, like Crystal, right?" I bluff.

I'm wondering if the school gets copies for our files, in which case Counselor knows exactly how badly I did on the test. She opens her mouth but closes it again. Perhaps she's smarter than I give her credit for.

"So what are you doing here?" Brian asks.

I don't try too hard to feign surprise at this suggestion, as it's a perfect excuse to get the heck out of there. "You know, you're right. I should go."

"Miss Garibaldi, don't let them run you off. Wanting to improve your scores isn't a bad thing and should be applauded, not ridiculed." Counselor rakes the room with a knock-it-off look.

"No, really. I mean, I told my friend I'd come to support her and she's not here—must have forgotten. I'll go find her." I gather up my backpack and coat.

"Stay. It'll be fun," Crystal says.

"Yeah, we can quiz each other on the hard words." Brian works his falsetto.

David gives him a high five.

I shut the door behind me. What was I thinking? Mom must have put moron pills in my oatmeal cement this morning. Huh, I didn't actually eat any of that glop. Maybe there's a hallucinogenic that can be inserted into toothpaste. I can see the headline now: "Terrorism Attacks Pearly Whites."

I am so doomed to go to State. Everyone gets into State. I lean against the wall. I should have gone out for cheerleading. At least there'd be an obvious reason to go to State.

I trail along behind Mom and Dad on the way to the awards night for the soccer season. It's finished. All eight weeks of the school's shortest sports season on record. I guess there weren't all that many teams for us to play. But at least I didn't have to run for half the school year just to get my letter jacket. I don't have to run again forever and ever. Unless I'm being chased by a pack of rabid dogs. Then maybe I'd think about running. Maybe.

The parentals are insisting on attending. They even wanted Mike and Heather to come, but thankfully they couldn't make it.

I try again. "We really could skip this."

"Gertrude, that's enough." Dad is totally looking forward to tonight's banquet. It's basically a potluck dessert thingy with lots of store-bought pastries. Coach gets to say a few words about what a great team we are and then we get our letters.

I think Dad is expecting me to get the MVP award. I can tell by the look on his face. He's full of hope. In an hour, that hope will turn to disappointment, but I don't have much to do with that. I sink lower in my seat and pick at a brownie.

"Welcome, welcome." Mack begins his big speech. I listen to most of it, but I'll spare you. "Blah blah great team, first season, lots to build on, can't wait for next year, blah blah."

I bite into a cream puff from Costco. Yum. Beats the dinner Mom made of Creole-style carbon and canned corn.

"Now for the awards," Mack says. "Can I get the team assistants up here, please?"

Dad sits taller at the mention of awards. I tried to prepare him for this part, but secretly I'm hoping. What can I say? I'm a competitive person. Of course I want to get the little trophy with my name engraved on it for being the best, or funniest, or most likely to go to the Olympics. Okay, most improved might be more my region of probability, but still. I can't help it.

The guys move to the front of the cafeteria and Mack introduces them. He calls Lucas's name and I swear Lucas smiles into my eyes in a moment of intimacy. We share one of those blurry magic moments. His hair is so perfect. The breadth of his shoulders is perfect. Just the right blend of muscles and bone. He's built, but not overbuilt. Like his neck is still a neck.

I sigh. I can't help it. He's the ice cream sundae my taste buds are waiting for.

Finally, Coach works his way through the JV team. Then it's our turn. "Varsity squad, please come up here." There are a few girls who played and suited up for both JV and Varsity, so they just stand there.

My parents clap and beam like I've been awarded a Rhodes Scholarship rather than just, you know, done a lot of running around.

We all get handed our letters with the school's initials on them and the little soccer ball patches. Mom was probing on the way here whether I want to get a sweater like in Dad's day or a jacket like in Mike's. I don't know. I'm leaning toward the leather jacket. The flashier the better. I wonder if you can get fake diamonds on letter jackets (I don't want real diamonds cuz that's just like strapping someone's hand to my chest and walking around all bloody and gory). Holy-Mother-of-Black-and-White-Orbs, I ran my ass off to earn the letter jacket. Leather. I want some dead cow to wear.

Why is dead cow more acceptable than maimed child? Hmm. I'll have to think about that.

Mack starts in on the awards. MVP: Candace. Spirit Award? "Every team needs a heart. Enthusiasm and grit to keep everyone going. The person who gives pep talks when the coaches are busy. The person who elevates not only the play of her teammates, but brings the quality of their interaction to a new level."

Holy-Mother-of-Political-Maneuvering, who is he talking about? We don't have a person like this on the team. There is no such person. They're all in New York at the UN trying to broker peace deals. They are not here, playing girls' soccer.

"This person surprised not only our coaching staff, but I think she surprised herself."

Why does he keep looking at me? He can't be talking about me? There's nothing elevated about me on this team except for the elevated medical insurance claims.

He's looking at me expecting something. *Can* he be talking about me? Did I really bring meaning and spirituality to this team? I'm good. I have no idea. I'm all smiley. Waiting to hear my name because you only look at the person you're giving an award to, right? You don't look at someone who is not getting the award.

"I didn't have a chance to ask before the awards started, but I'm hoping her teammate will come say a few words because she can't be here tonight to accept this herself."

I'm not listening to all the words coming out of his mouth. I'm trying to formulate my acceptance speech. Who should I thank? Who should I snub?

"Gert Garibaldi, will you come say a few words about our Spirit Award winner, Karmel Lennin?"

My stomach hits my knees and ricochets back up to my earlobes, all jiggly when it stops bouncing around. I start to stand, thinking the rousing applause is all for me, and then some part of my brain kicks on and points out the bit I missed the first time.

". . . baldi, will you come say a few words about our Spirit Award winner, Karmel Lennin?"

I blink. I didn't get the award. I have to say something nice about the girl who split my face open with an egg? An egg that is now on the FBI list of WMDs?

I stumble over my feet on my way to the stage. What can I say? I can't very well be honest and say Karmel's contribution to the team should be measured in calories because it was girth and not her skill that saved the goals. I'm not smacking her weight here, but geez, let's not pretend she's a rock star because she plugged the holes in the goal with her butt. More power to her, but I never heard an encouraging word come out of her mouth. And she always stopped working out when the coaches weren't around.

I find Maggie and Clarice's shocked faces in the crowd. Clarice gives me a thumbs-up, like "better you than me."

I clear my throat as Mack steps away from the microphone and leaves me staring at all the people.

I open my mouth, close it and lick my lips. "Uh, this is our first year and people had to learn a lot of stuff they didn't know."

Okay, I'm not sparkling with wit and eloquence. "Karmel was our goalie. She made it difficult for other teams to score. And—"

God, what else can I say? I can't even make anything up. My imagination is taking a sabbatical in Tahiti. "Her socks always matched and her uniform was spotless. Go, Karmel!"

I wave my hand in the air and kinda screech like a zoo animal. Clarice and Maggie join in the screeching and clapping, so I'm saved. I rush back to my seat. My parents look astoundingly proud of me.

"Gert, honey, can I talk to you?"

Mom pokes her head around my bedroom door without even waiting to hear if now is a good time. "Sure." *Now that you're here.*

She grips her hands and licks her lips. "I understand how the topic of sex could make you uncomfortable."

Let me save us from this horror. "Mom, we don't have to do the birds and bees thing."

Shock, then uncertainty, paints her face. "Oh, well, okay, but that's kinda what I was hoping you could help me with."

Huh? "You're the one with two kids," I say.

"You know so much more than I did at your age, and the ladies were talking at Bunko about this program one of them saw."

Oh, this could be good. "And?" I put down the textbook. I can feel a humiliating parental moment coming. I have hum-dar.

She takes a deep breath and blurts out, "What exactly is anal bleaching?"

I blink. I'm fairly certain I didn't stop breathing for long since I'm alive and not dead, but that's about all I can attest to. Of all the questions I thought might come out of Mom's mouth, that didn't make the list.

"Did you hear me?" She's peering into my face like there's nothing shocking about her asking me about anal bleaching.

"Um. Can I get back to you?" I have no idea what to say.

"You don't know?" She's crestfallen. Her *sigh* sounds old. "I asked your father, but he didn't seem to know about it either."

"Um, well, no, I think it's something people do who are interested in having anal sex. Or oral sex."

"Oral, there?" she asks, her eyebrows rising to her hairline.

I nod and pluck at lint on the comforter. "There. It's called a rim job." I push the mortification down into my stomach and try to act like we're discussing drapery patterns.

She nods as if she understands. "Oh. But bleach?"

"It's about the color of the skin, I think." Either that or there are some weirdly inclined germaphobes in the world.

"Thank you. I appreciate you telling me. I told the girls you'd know. You're so smart."

I choose not to dwell on the idea that a bunch of Bunko ladies are waiting to hear my thoughts on anal anything.

"Hey, Gert. Party at our house Saturday night. Bring a date if you want." Lucas pauses by my locker. Just a brief pause to get the words out.

I smile. "Sure. 'Kay."

"Hey, Adam? You and Tim are getting drinks, right?" Lucas turns to him and asks.

"Yep." After Lucas has walked on, Adam leans down to me and whispers, "He's inviting the whole soccer team, kind of an end-of-season thing."

My smile doesn't falter. "Whatever."

"Whatever?" Adam asks. "Word is he doesn't have a date to GAGD yet."

"So?"

"Just thought you might care. You bringing a date to the party?"

"You busy?" I ask with a grin.

"Taken. But you can be our favorite inny."

"Inny?" I'm not sure I really want to know.

"Girls inny, guys outy."

I giggle. "That's so juvenile."

Adam just laughs and walks away. He and Tim now have a secret language. I don't think I'm okay with that.

A date? Who? But bigger still, do I possibly have the balls to even ask someone?

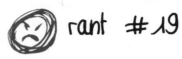 rant #19

term paper "who am i?" part one

Who am I? It's simpler to write a paper about who I'm not. I don't know who I am. I'm Gert. I'm a friend to Adam, Clarice, Maggie and a few others. I'm the daughter of Mr. and Mrs. Garibaldi. I'm the sister of Michael. I'm the future sister-in-law of Heather. The future girlfriend of someone. The ex-girlfriend of Stephen. I am a sophomore in high school.

I am a girly-woman, or am I a womanly girl? See, I don't even know what the truth is.

Life would be vastly easier if I knew who I am. If I had one part of me that I could hold on to and say, "Don't touch, that's me, that's mine." But I don't yet. I have days, sure, where I think I know what I need to know and what I want. But that feeling is fleeting.

I'm not a beautiful person. To compete I'd need about ten different plastics. I don't think so. I'm not a plastic surgery person. I mean, sure I'd love to have perky boobs and a nondescript nose, pouty lips and a tight tiny booty. But what if I change my mind after it's all over? See, here's the deal, I like to change my mind. I change it often. Occasionally, I've been known to change my mind simply because I've had the same opinion for too long. Maybe that's stupid, but it's true.

So I'm not beautiful and if a manly-boy were to tell me I am and really mean it, I think I'd probably cry. Because we all want one person who isn't our parental to think we're beautiful, don't we? Maybe it's just me, but I don't think so.

I'm not going to be a Merit Scholar with scores like I got on the PSAT. So perhaps I'm outgrowing the Brain definition too. Maybe I'm not as smart as some. I once had this friend who wrote an essay about how one girl she was friends with was her intellectual match, and I was her political and social match. We're not friends anymore. You're not very bright if you think you can easily sum up smarts like that.

I'm an American. I like being American. I don't like the rest of the world hating me, but there are very few other places I'd be happy having been born a woman. You know? There aren't a lot of choices for free, for me. So I'm not going to be emigrating anywhere or dissing the U.S. itself. She's been good to me, hasn't she?

I'm not big on God, but I'm not completely faithless, either. I just don't know how much of anything I believe in. How can you believe in something when you don't even know who is doing the believing? Don't I have to know myself before I can believe in anything remotely unseen?

I am the girl who plucks her eyebrows daily in the

hopes that this grooming makes me less likely to stick out and perhaps more likely to be considered attractive.

I am the girl who dates kinda-cute boys but not Lucas.

I am the girl who joins a sports team to be around a guy, though I secretly hate myself for feeling like I need to be around a guy in the first place. Aren't I supposed to be all feministy and complete without a penis in proximity? Does this make me a traitor to my gender? Or to women who can't vote? If I like to be around a manly-boy enough to run miles upon miles, does this make me the girl who cuts my hair the way he wants it to be cut? Who does my makeup according to his preferences? Who makes excuses if he hits me?

That's all I have so far. . . .

Fourteen

I arrive at the party with Adam, who picked us all up at Clarice's house. We're spending the night. Not Adam, just Maggie and me. But we're going to the party first so we can have something other than the upcoming dance to talk about. They've been trying to convince me that asking Lucas to the dance would be good for my development as a confident human being.

Clarice is so full of crap. They laid off when Adam laughed in the car and said that Lucas has been turning girls down since November. He has a date now, though. I guess he stopped turning girls down when Aubrey asked him. Or is it Amanda? Ashley? They all probably asked at one time or another.

The bass is thumping. I've been here before. It's still the normal-looking house with the amazingly terrible AstroTurf decorations with flowery bows. I'm working on my calm self-assured exterior, but I wish my insides matched my outs. It's still Lucas's house. There's only so much calm a girl can be.

"Hey." A guy I don't know opens the door.

"Hey." I can't think of anything else to say and he's waiting for a reply.

"Dude." He nods.

"Duu-dde." Adam makes it two syllables.

"Righteous."

I walk past, trying not to laugh. *"Righteous"? You're kidding, right?*

This is drunk-people conversation. Drunk people, or stoned people, for that matter, will want you to believe that being under the influence creates a higher form of consciousness. Like they're reaching a plane full of rainbow colors that makes them better or bigger human beings. But put any sober person in the middle of their conversation and it will be recorded accurately: it will be full of exclamations and pronouncements and a whole lotta crap. Really. There's not a nice way to put it.

I really don't get the attraction, but this party is full of people who want to surf the wild rainbow. I guess the end-of-season party means the end of spring, the end of hunting season, the end of wild-duck mating season instead of the tame and relatively benign interpretation I had, which was end of the soccer season. Huh. My bad.

There are tons of people. Lots I recognize from Jenny's New Year's party. A few who came to my birthday party back in the fall. And some I've never seen before in my life. I didn't think this town had this many people.

And really, if I need to be drunk to ask a guy out, maybe that's my sober self's way of trying to get me to pay attention to what I really want. If I really wanted to ask a guy out, I'd be compelled to act, rather than needing to drink Listerine in an effort to get the freshest breath and my stomach pumped. What's the point?

Tangent: sorry.

If I wanted it, I'd do it. So maybe I don't want it that much.

The party is okay. No real talking. Lots of making out. A few full-fledged coital hookups in bedrooms and a couple who decide the floor behind the couch is all the privacy they need. Holy-Mother-of-Hind-Ends, I don't need to see his full moon and its orbiting bits. If my parentals only knew.

I drink a Mountain Dew. A cold one. Munch on a freshly opened bag of chips. I saw them open the bag; I can't bring myself to eat any of the food that is sitting out. I've seen too many of those high school movies where the unenlightened eat or drink a very unappetizing ingredient.

Clarice disappeared with Spenser soon after we got here. She's intent on finding out exactly what he thinks about being in a relationship with her. She told us she wants to take her boyfriend to GAGD, but Adam and I shared this look that pretty much shouted, "But he *has* told you!" He wants to be benefriends, how much more obvious does he need to be?

But Clarice didn't pick up on it. Nothing. So Spenser is cornered in this house trying to explain for the three-hundredth time that what he wants he stated clearly the first time they had this conversation. Hmm. I can see why guys get exasperated with us.

Maggie finds me around eleven. "Help." She grabs my arm and all but attaches herself like a barnacle to my side.

"Whoa, personal space," I say, pulling away.

"Don't. Look like you like me." She hugs me tighter.

"Huh?"

"Gert, we're together. *Together*. Put your arm around me."

I am so not following this conversation, but I put my arm around her back while reaching for another can of soda. I will have to pee if I keep drinking this way, but what else can I do with my hands? Hmm.

Maggie whispers through clenched teeth, sounding all snakey and hard to understand, "Jesse is following me around hinting that he wants to go with me."

"So?" I ask.

"So, I like him. Kiss me." She tilts her head up toward mine.

I snort Doritos and Mountain Dew up my nose.

"Thanks. You're so supportive." She glares at me but doesn't even give my snort secretions room to maneuver.

I pull away, wiping my nose on a used paper towel. Beggars and all that. I try to point out, "You like him."

"Of course I like him. He makes me insane." Maggie turns around and starts rearranging the stuff on the table.

"So, what's the problem?" I can't begin to unravel this one.

"I'm not ready to like him. I certainly am not ready to ask him to go to a public function with me."

Again with the rational thought. "So, don't ask him."

"But he's getting pretty close to asking me to ask him and I can't say no because then he'll think I don't like him, but I really am not ready to talk to him every day and kiss him and have sex with him and meet his family and—"

"Breathe," I say.

She inhales.

"Exhale," I demand. She does. "Better?" I ask.

She tenses up again. "He's coming over here."

"Don't freak. He'll think he smells bad." I pinch her cheeks.

"What?" She looks at me like I've lost my mind.

I don't expand and tell her that my worst fear is a group of people recoiling from me because I smell and haven't figured it out.

"Hi, Gert. I got you a soda, Maggie. I didn't know what kind to get." Jesse holds out four different ice-cold, sweating cans.

"Hi, Jesse," I say, but he's not even looking at me. Maggie is speechless. She's back to looking like a puppy that's been kicked for peeing in the wrong place.

"Thanks." She takes the top can.

"So, you like Sprite," he says, nodding.

"Huh?" Maggie says.

"Yes, actually Maggie here loves all types of beverages." I jump in to rescue her.

"Good to know," Jesse says, all sagey.

Maggie is still speechless, pinned to my side like a Halloween costume.

"So," he says. His head swivels to take in the room, but I'm not sure his eyes ever really leave Maggie's face.

I rack my brain trying to come up with a topic of conversation because I'm starting to lose blood flow to my left side and Maggie isn't loosening her grip. I can't flee from the scene. Painful as it is.

"Do you like comic books, Jesse?" I ask.

"What?" He swings his gaze back to me.

No wonder she's creeped out. He has the I'm-going-to-nibble-on-you, very manly expression on his face. I feel my own fear beast and step back. He's all manly and intimidating.

I repeat myself.

"I used to," Jesse replies.

I happen to know he still collects a bunch of different kinds. It came up in a guy conversation I overheard one day. I think Adam also told me. He's reliable.

"Really?" I raise my eyebrows and my falsetto. I'm quite the actress. "Maggie here loves Spider-Man."

She nods quick, like a rodent scenting cheese.

"Huh. Well, I have a couple of first editions," he says, trying not to sound too excited. But he has that little-boy-trying-not-to-let-on-that-it's-Christmas-morning expression.

"Oh. Um, um," Maggie stutters.

"Maggie, you were just saying the other day that you didn't think anyone we knew could possibly have first editions, weren't you?" I may lay it on a little thick, considering the looks they both give me. What can I say? I'm not an actress.

I push Maggie off me and toward Jesse, only half listening to him expand on his very favorite topic of graphic novels. They move away and I'm left alone again. Until I spot a familiar face.

"Ricardo," I say, smiling.

"Jesus, chica." He smiles broadly at me and moves in my direction. He's really quite cute.

"Hi," I say.

"Whassup?" he says. I guess in the two months since he's been here he's become fluent in teen-speak.

We look at each other for a few seconds. I don't know how long. But then it comes over me. I want to kiss him. He's supercute and waiting for me to say something inspired. And more importantly, I've had eight Mountain Dews, so I'm as high on caffeine and corn syrup as it's possible to be. I'm inspired. Feeling reckless.

"What's Spanish for 'kiss'?" I ask with what I hope is a twinkle in my eye and not a total turn-off expression.

He blushes, but takes a step closer to me. "Uh—" He's obviously trying to find the right words.

Okay, so his English hasn't improved that much. I must be drunk—it's the only explanation for what I do next. Only I haven't been drinking, so I have no explanation. I scrunch up my lips and smack them. "You know, 'kiss.' " I pause to assess his reaction.

He's smiling broadly. *"En español?"*

"Sí," I say.

"I show you." He takes my hand and pulls me toward the more darkened recesses of the living room.

I don't have much time to process this swift change in climate before his face is literally a heartbeat away from mine and he stops. *"En español."* He lowers his lips to mine.

I don't close my eyes because I'm (a) startled I had the *cojones* to flirt to this extent and (b) waiting to see if it's me or are there really good kissers in the world?

I try to focus all my attention on my lips and my senses so I know exactly how different this kiss is from the first few ridiculous excuses. He smells good.

His lips move against mine with enough pressure that I know they're there (as if I could remotely forget) but not so much that I feel like I'm being eaten alive. It feels good. Really good.

He pulls me closer and angles his head so his lips slant more or less across mine. His tongue touches my bottom lip, just a quick little lick asking permission. That's what it feels like. I don't feel impaled. I feel gooey.

I open my mouth and our tongues introduce themselves. We don't get the same rhythm right away, but it's *fun* kissing a boy.

I was under the impression that kissing could only be good if you like the person you're kissing. Like there's an emotional attachment that must take place before anything can be gooey. I can't even try to say that Ricardo and I have any kind of emotional attachment. It's not like we bonded over soccer trivia. He's not my soul mate, but he sure as hell is good for my self-esteem. I'm kissable. Definitely kissable. And good at it. It's *fun*.

I don't really pay too much attention to anything else going on around us. We kiss. We stop. We start talking to other people. At some point, I lose track of Ricardo. Maybe that's best. What would I say, really? Thanks for helping me to know I'm not the problem? Keep in touch? Nice technique?

Maggie and Clarice and I head out, meeting Adam by the car. I don't even say goodbye to Kiss Boy.

"Wow, Gert, I didn't know you were that kind of girl," Adam whispers to me outside.

"*I* didn't know I was." I shrug. If that kind of girl means knowing that making out should be good for me, then I'll embrace that title. I'm that-kind-of-girl. I giggle. Who knew?

We're all jammied up at Clarice's with blankets and sleeping bags heaped on the floor of her family's media room.

I can't believe I heard correctly, so I ask Clarice to repeat. "He what?"

She shrugs. "He asked me to go down on him."

Maggie puts down the bag of Twizzlers and swallows. "And?"

"Yeah, what'd you do?" I scramble out of my sleeping bag. This is too exciting to be weighted down by down.

She chews on her lip a little. "I did."

Oh, to have a friend who's been that up close and personal with a penis. I have questions. Lots and lots of questions. Most importantly, "How was it?"

She smiles. "Odd."

I want details. "How so?"

"Did he pressure you?" Maggie demands, breaking my flow of question energy.

Clarice is startled. "No . . . I mean . . . I don't know."

I demand clarification. It's so not cool if she didn't actually want to. "Wait, this is vastly different. You didn't want to?"

"No, I did, but he never really gave me a chance to say no. It was so fast. It was—"

"He forced you?" Maggie's face is turning red.

"No, I could have stopped, I guess. I just wasn't really thinking. And it was cool. Fun. Fine." Clarice grabs a Dr Pepper and gulps it.

This requires the entire story. Maggie and I put on our invisible detective hats to figure out if Clarice was duped into kissing the snake or if she bit that apple on her own. "It was what? Start at the beginning and leave nothing out."

Now she's all scared and shy. "I don't know if I really want to talk about it."

"I would really like to respect your privacy and not force you to go into graphic detail, but I'm not that nice," I say.

Maggie shakes her head. "Me either. Spill it."

"Oh, Maggie, you're starting to sound like me." I'm impressed and give her a golf clap.

She half smiles, half grimaces. I'm not sure how to read her expression.

"Okay, but aren't you not supposed to talk about this kind of thing?" Clarice looks uncertain for a minute.

I chomp on a handful of gummy creatures. "Why?"

"Because I don't want you thinking I'm a slut or anything."

"We don't. Scout's honor." Why is a girl a slut when she's

enjoying doing the things boys want her to do, but he's not a slut for his part? I hate double standards. The hypocrisy is beyond unreasonable.

She sighs. "Promise?"

I cross my heart like I'm in second grade, which is weird considering we're talking about open mouth/insert penis.

"His parents don't get home till late. They work a lot. And so he asked me over like he always does."

An editorial aside here: Clarice secretly hopes Spenser will be her boyfriend if she puts up with the booty calls long enough. I don't have enough life experience to really try to convince her otherwise. She wouldn't believe me if I tried. Maggie agrees with me. So we're just biding our time until Clarice catches on—or her older sister kicks her butt.

Clarice continues. "Anyway, we hooked up like usual."

I interrupt. "Define." "Hooked up" is so freakin' ambiguous I refuse to settle for it.

"Kissing with tongue. Topless."

"Braless?" Maggie asks, grabbing a corn chip.

"Yeah, he took off his Wonderbra and I was totally disappointed. Boy is flat." Clarice giggles.

We crack up. The visual of Spenser in a Wonderbra is quite delightful.

"Anyway, he kinda took my hand and put it on his pants. This isn't the first time, but I've only ever just sorta laid my hand there. He was sticking up against the denim and all hard and he rubbed against me. I don't know what came over me, but I undid the zipper and all of a sudden there he was."

"No underwear?" I'm gaining a picture of commando Spenser that I'm not sure I want in my virgin brain.

"He had boxers on but he was poking out the top of them or something. I don't know." She shrugs, exasperated. "I wasn't really studying for a pop quiz."

To me, it's really quite simple. "Then let's be clear from now on that you are studying for our exams—as the only girl in the proximity of any dick, you really have to be willing to cart back details and share."

"I second that." Maggie nods like it's a UN accord.

"Whatever." Clarice glares at me. "He was just there."

"What did it feel like?" Maggie asks.

"Soft like an old T-shirt, but superhard under that, like a—"

"Bone?" I ask, trying to keep a straight face.

"Thank you." She giggles.

"So he was all rocking his hips and kissing me. He had his hands on my boobs, which was making me totally bored, but he's a really good kisser."

"Did he ask you to in words? A complete sentence?"

"No. He didn't. I guess. He did this thing with his eyes and sort of guided my head. I just leaned down." Thoughtful, she continues, "I was curious what he tasted like. And besides, it's this total rush of power. He couldn't think at all and seriously he would have given me anything to not stop. It's weird how completely in my control he was."

Even for me that seems— "That's a little diabolical."

"What? I didn't say I was going to start charging him or demanding he be my sugar daddy. It's just an observation."

"Interesting." I must consider this.

Maggie asks, "So did you like it?"

"Yeah, I did." Surprise colors her tone.

We've all heard horror stories, and it's pretty much assumed that if you're a good girl you don't like giving head. I mean, no one I know would ever admit to liking it. It's supposed to be dirty. It's supposed to be that thing guys like that girls do only if they really like the guy.

"Really?" I insist.

"Yeah, it's fun." She smiles.

Hmm, must think. I'm utterly relieved. "Thank God."

"What do you mean?"

"I mean, it's like this huge thing that guys like to have us do, right?"

"Aside from sex, it's like the only thing," Maggie offers.

I shrug. "Right, and I thought it was a given that it'd be gross and totally unfun."

Clarice giggles. "It's not. I mean, I guess it could be with another guy, but I had fun."

"Thank God," Maggie echoes me before we dissolve into laughter.

"Oh my God, I am so sorry." Tim and Adam bound up to my locker.

That what? It's a school day? The Mideast is still fighting? The planet is getting too hot to support life? "For what?"

"Stephen, aka Teeny-Weeny."

"Stop." I hold up a hand and plead for them to stop. I don't want to hear anything about him. I don't. Okay, I want to hear he's miserable without me and desperately wants me back. I can't resist. "Okay, what?"

"He's dating someone," Adam says.

Tim elbows him. Hard.

I'm stuck on the idea that he could find another girl to date so quickly. It's only March. My body isn't even rigor mortised yet.

"And?" Tim prompts Adam.

"What and?" I ask. Trying to keep track of the looks they're shooting each other is like watching TV and talking on the phone. I'm exhausted in about ten seconds.

"What? Spill," I say.

"Jenny." Adam drops his tone.

"Jenny what?" I ask as the reality dawns on me. "No," I gasp.

"They're dating." Tim nods.

"No." The pain. The humiliation. Where is that damn Sharpie when a girl needs to poke some eyes out?

"I saw them groping in the science wing," Tim says.

"I'm really sorry." Adam gives me his sincere look. "Want Tim to beat him up?"

"I will," Tim jumps in.

"No. We broke up. He can date anyone," I say, seething. *Anyone but my archnemesis.* Doesn't he care? Did he ever?

Adam hugs me. "We didn't want you to be shocked or hear it from Jenny first."

"Joy. I have history next." *Way to ruin weeks of a perfectly awful semester.*

"We know." Tim squeezes my shoulder.

The bell rings. When do I start to think Stephen's my friend and we laugh about the time we dated? When does that happen?

Ms. Whoptommy looks even more hassled than usual. I don't think she's counting points correctly for her notorious post-holiday diet. She usually drops a few small children by now, then puts them back on her hips by June. I really don't think she's sticking with the program this year. Perhaps she has an inner rebel and feels the need to buck the system.

"Your project this month is an in-depth look at the Bill of Rights. We will read, discuss and dissect each of our rights as Americans. Then you will pick the right that is most important to you. The right that speaks to your soul."

God, not another paper. Persuasive writing? A clear journalistic rehash? A pro-con debate fit for a Congressional committee? I can't wait.

She continues as if I hadn't been having a personal internal conversation. "However, we will not be writing our feelings."

I love the "we." Such a royal definition.

"We will be making a visual statement, an artistic impact."

Like the great meteor that killed the dinosaurs?

She passes out papers with specifics on them. It's always a bad sign when the criteria are stapled together in a packet.

"You can use any material that speaks to you, excluding bodily fluids, or excrement from any animal, including yourselves."

Holy-Mother-of-the-TP, it says something when using poop to visually describe the Bill of Rights has to be explicitly ruled out. She's probably referring to Bobby's brick-and-mortar art project from last semester. Let's just say the bricks were collected in a dog park.

"Also, if you choose the right to bear arms as your personal right, you may not actually use guns, pictures or photographs of anything remotely resembling a gun. We are a gun-free zone, people." She clears her throat.

Ashley raises her hand. "Ms. Whoptommy, is that why the Civil War photos were all blacked out in the textbooks?" That unit was four months ago. She's only now realizing this?

"Exactly, Miss Gray. As I was saying, no weaponry of any kind may be referred to, but you may use arms as your substitute."

Mannequins all over the county are crying out in fear.

"Like human arms?"

"This is not gross anatomy, Mr. Wilson. You may use pictures, photographs, models or replicas, doll parts or molds of your own arms. They just have to clearly be arms and we'll count them as a substitute for guns. However, there are many rights I'm sure will speak to all of you—"

In other words, only the really brave or really stupid will actually try to make the right to bear arms into an art project with actual arms. I think I might feel a spark of inspiration.

"You will have four weeks to complete this project and you will not be working in groups."

There is a God; I don't have to endure grouping. I sneak a glance at Jenny and Stephen; they're holding hands across the aisle. I swallow and pray for the period to end or for a brain hemorrhage. Either one would be fine.

rant #20

to ask or not to ask
(that is the question)

Okay, here's the deal. The idea of asking a guy out is utterly and completely terrorizing. It's like one of those chocolate Easter eggs filled with Ebola instead of tasty cream. Eat at your own risk.

I mean, what if he says no? I know it's not the end of the world, but it would ruin my life. Depending on the guy, I'd have to change my schedule so I didn't have any classes with him, and come up with routes around school taking me completely out of his path so I wouldn't have to so much as glance at him.

It might mean a whole new group of friends, or even moving to a new school. I don't think my parents would be happy about that one. I'd have to come up with a good reason.

I don't know how guys do it. They ask out multitudes of girls and have to get told no at least once in a while. Except for Lucas. I don't think Lucas has ever heard no in his life.

Then I think about Adam and Tim. They're as close to in love as two people can be without admitting that they're in love and they're fighting about

194

being seen in public. Which is just cruel. I hate it that they're worried about the wrong person getting all vigilante, and here I am quaking at the thought of being told no. "No." It's a little word.

So how do I grow a pair of balls (temporarily, you understand. I don't really want testicles) and ask? And who?

You know that saying "go big or go home"?

Well, do I go big and ask Lucas or do I go home? Bad example, but you know what I mean. How do you know who to ask? Is there a signal? An encrypted code? A flashing light?

I need the handicapped dating sensors—like the crosswalks for blind and deaf people, loud beeps and flashing lights. That'd be perfect.

 fifteen

The question that's been plaguing me for weeks pops out.
"What is GAGD?"

"I don't know." Clarice shrugs. "A bunch of seniors voted on
names. Girl Ask Guy Dance won. Personally, I like GAGD. We
could make it into a verb—say, are you going gagging this
evening?" She laughs at her own joke.

"Can I just point out one itsy-bitsy thing?" I can't resist asking
this question and perhaps I'm the only one who actually got the
memo, but here goes: "Can't girls ask guys to *any* dance? Are we
really limited to one event a year to be forward?"

"Point for Gert." Maggie licks her finger and writes in the air.

I take a sip of water. "Do guys like it when we ask?"

"I don't know." Clarice is surreptitiously watching Spenser eat
a handful of French fries.

Maggie is folding her napkin into an origami thingy.

I continue, albeit in a lower voice since Victor appears to be
eavesdropping on our conversation. "It doesn't seem fair."

"What do you mean?" Maggie asks.

"Well, they have to ask first for everything and suffer the nerves and humiliation when we say no. So it's not fair."

Clarice shrugs. "Putting it that way, how could they possibly object to being the one getting asked instead?"

"Unless their manliness is somehow hinged on it." Maggie sails the birdy toward the garbage can.

"Oh." Clarice looks at me.

"I hadn't thought of that," I say.

"That could be possible." Clarice nods.

I'm not sure I follow. "How would that work, exactly?"

"Well, what if the pain and humiliation are like the manly equivalents of menstrual cramps?" Maggie says.

"Huh?"

"It means you're a man when girls giggle at you when you walk by," Clarice translates.

"I guess. But back to my point. Isn't this the twenty-first century? Since when do we have to wait for a guy to think we should go out before we go out?"

"I don't know. It feels like there's something wrong with asking a guy first."

"Does that ever work out?" Here's the part I'm more interested in.

"I don't know. I keep reading in all the major mags that guys like aggressive women who let them go along for the ride. But really, isn't it supermodels who aren't thought overly aggressive? Like seriously hot chicks who the guy wouldn't have the balls to ask out? It's okay for them to ask the guy because it would never occur to him to ask them first?" Maggie is so smart, she's mind-boggling.

I think there must be fine print in those articles *Cosmo* writes about assertiveness being "the new sexy." The fine print states you must be Gisele before asking a guy out. That makes sense.

"So are you?" Clarice gets to the point.

"Huh?" I say, still trying to figure out how to transform myself into Gisele by the end of the week.

"Asking Lucas?"

"I don't think so." I glance around to see if anyone is eavesdropping. Even Victor has gotten bored with us. I forget I'm not the most interesting thing in everyone else's lives.

"You should. I mean, what have you got to lose?"

Dignity? Self-esteem? Face? Pad Thai with a side salad?

"Are you?" Maggie asks Clarice.

"No, Lucas really isn't my type." Clarice smiles.

"I meant, are you taking Spenser?"

"I don't know yet." She shrugs.

"What are you waiting for?" I ask.

"Some indication that he wants me to ask him, I guess."

Maggie nods. "I couldn't do it."

"What? My Brainiest friend gets cold feet when the invitations are hers to toss?"

"Yeah. I don't have the nerve." Maggie looks sheepish.

"But then you won't be going," I point out.

"Yeah, so?"

True. Does it really matter if we go? "She's right. The world won't end if we're not there."

"But we have to wait around for the guys to think about asking us the whole rest of the year. We should at least exercise our right to be turned down." Clarice nods like she's come to a big decision.

"Hmm. Maybe that's the lesson? We're not big on dances when we really have a choice? We're not much on boys, either."

They both look at me, horrified.

"I don't mean that. I mean we prefer *men*." Men who understand the importance of being asked because they've been turned down more than once in their lives. They should know a good thing when she invites them.

"Men scare me." Clarice shudders.

"Me too." Maggie shudders. "They're so big and silent and intimidating."

"No, they're not." I feel the need to disagree for the sake of disagreeing. Men scare me, too. Who are the girls who are eighteen and dating thirty-year-olds? Obviously, they're not petrified by shaving prowess and five-o'clock shadow. I wouldn't know what to do with a man if I was given the opportunity. They're a little like truffles, all earthy and mysterious and take digging to find. I'm talking about the fungal truffles, not the chocolate kind.

"Yeah."

"Right."

We all drift to our next classes thinking man thoughts.

"He's such an ass." Adam throws his history book against the wall.

"Whoa." I duck yet another projectile.

"I'm sorry." Adam looks contrite when he focuses on my face. But his eyes have the glassy glaze of rage and pain. Like a wild animal.

"What happened?" I ask.

Adam roars. "That's perfect. Just great. You're taking his side."

A Sharpie almost blinds me as it javelins into the pile of dirty clothes.

"I'm not taking anyone's side. You called me, remember?" I walk a little farther into the room.

"I know." Adam punches a pillow.

"What—you know, why am I here?" I'm tentative about my word choice. So far I've escaped bloodletting, but just barely.

"He's an ass."

What "he" are we talking about? Must be the only he with the power to make Adam this upset—Tim. "Tim?"

"Who else?"

"Uh-huh." I wait for the coming avalanche.

"He thinks we should go to GAGD as a couple." Adam slouches down on his bed, laying his head in his hands.

"Aren't you?" I step around the mess and slide down next to him.

"Not at school. Not like that."

I put my hand on his knee. I don't need to say anything.

He continues. "He wants to get tuxes with, like, the same colors and matching flowers or something."

I can see the problem. The matching outfits would undo anyone's fashion sense. "I thought gays were supposed to be aware of fashion faux pas? Matching outfits?"

Adam rolls his eyes. "Dude, it's not the outfit."

Oh. How to proceed? Hmmm. I think it's too late to leave and pretend I never got his message. "You don't want to be a couple anymore?"

"It's not that. I think I'm falling for him."

"That's big." *And the rest of us knew this months ago. Why are you only now getting the news?*

"Yeah." He doesn't sound pleased.

There has to be more. "And?"

"I'm scared."

"About falling for him?"

"Yes and no."

I roll my eyes. He's being all girly. It's annoying. "Help me out here."

He wipes his eyes. "A pack of hyenas cornered me in the locker room the other day."

"Jocks cornered you and did what?" My heart speeds up.

"They didn't touch me, but they got in my face."

I swallow back the urge to go kick jock ass. "They threatened you? Why?"

"The obvious. They'd seen Tim lean in and kiss my neck—it was a quick, thoughtless bit of affection between classes."

"Oh." That's all?

"We're so careful. I'm so careful and I let my guard down for a second and those goons, they said things." Tears roll down his cheeks. "I shouldn't have to be careful, Gertie, I shouldn't have to watch where I kiss."

I hug him toward me and hold him.

"It's not fair." He cries into my shoulder.

"No. No, it's not." My own tears streak my face. "You deserve to go anywhere you want with anyone you love."

"That's a joke." He stumbles over the words, trying to speak, breathe and cry all at the same time.

"Did you tell Tim?"

"Tell him what? His boyfriend is scared of some jocks?" He chokes out a snorty laugh.

I shrug. "For starters. Personally, I think it proves your intelligence that you're scared."

"Right." He's not convinced.

"Adam, those goons are dangerous in large groups. Their already minuscule"—I pause for effect—"brains shrink in proximity to each other."

We sit on his bed with our arms around each other until the tears slow. "You have to tell him the truth."

"I know."

"And you have to decide if you want to take on the idiots."

"It's not fair. I don't want to be a hero. I just want to go to a dance with my boyfriend."

"I know. I'm sorry." And I am. So very sorry. What's my excuse, huh? Hearing a boy say no? That's not much of an argument, is it?

I work and work and work up the nerve to ask Lucas. If Adam has to decide whether or not going to the Saint Patrick's Day GAGD is worth getting the crap kicked out of him, then I really have no excuse not to ask a guy, right? I mean, it's not like anyone is going to beat me; Lucas will just say no and how bad can that be?

I know he'll say he can't go because he already has a date. Which is exactly like asking your long-term boyfriend to go because you know he'll say yes. Hear me? So asking a guy who you know will say no is almost like asking a guy who will say yes. (That sounded much better in my head. Sounds kinda pathetic now.) So I'm going to ask Lucas knowing he's taking Aubrey, Amanda, Wellesey or Laura. It's all good.

Clarice and Maggie think I'm insane. They don't follow my splendiferous logic. But when I see him, my mouth goes from wet and wild to dry and desolate in a tenth of a second. My palms itch and my feet freeze up, so walking forward is like walking on two clubs. Weird and highly unattractive.

Twenty feet and closer. Look at that hair. Those lips.

A leggy brunette walks up to him and wraps herself around him. My steps falter. She plants a kiss and walks away doing that highly Giggle wave of several fingers. I can read her lips: "Ta-ta for now."

I push the toxic carbon dioxide from my lungs in a huff. I can hear the clock ticking down. I have only about a minute or so before the class bell rings. I force my legs forward.

Ten feet and closer.

Five feet.

"Hi," I say, from about four feet away, because I don't want to sneak up on him. He's the lion in the grasslands and I'm the antelope. He would eat me using that analogy and I really don't think we're going to be getting oral at this point in our relationship. He's either ignoring me, or he didn't hear me.

Could be because the hello came out in a croak. Very unattractive.

"Hi," I say a little louder and right behind him.

He jumps. I think my voice was more in the decibel range of "Fire!" than in the close-promixity-conversation place.

"Oh. Gert. Hey." Lucas slams his locker door and turns around.

"Hi," I say, but I can't quite get the words out of my mouth. They're stuck there like Mom's meat loaf. All scratchy and looming and breath-stopping.

"Hi," he repeats. He's expecting me to say something else and I'm trying. Really trying, but I just can't.

The bell rings.

"See you round?" He takes off without a backward glance.

"Right," I say to his back. Maybe I'm not supposed to ask Lucas to GAGD. I think the Goddess wants me to start smaller than a definite no. The mystery is good, right?

Clarice and Maggie grab me after our next class.

"I'm telling you, you have to start with guys who are sure to say yes and work your way up." Clarice is in instructor mode.

"Really." I'm dubious.

"I'm serious. You have to start on the training wheels before you get to off-road in the Hummer."

Bad, bad word picture. "So I shouldn't ask Lucas. Is that what you're saying?"

"Well, yeah. What's the point?"

Maggie jumps in. "It's not like you don't know he has a date. And he's so not dumping her for you. No offense, but she's so, so . . ."

"I know I'm not *sooo*." I try to not be offended by my friends' assessment of my lack of sooo-ness. But I get it. "Who should I start with? If you were me." I put that caveat in there because I'm not after the same type of guy as Clarice.

"Ryan," Maggie says with a nod.

"Sean," Clarice says. "Or David. Or even Bob."

"You're kidding, right? Bob?" Maggie asks.

I'm not sure if Maggie thinks I'm out of Bob's league or he's out of mine. "Should I be insulted?"

"The kid wears Star Wars pajama bottoms to school." Maggie shrugs. "And he's not a challenged kid, either."

As if it would be much more believable for me to ask out a guy who is special ed and wears Star Wars pajamas. Not that I wouldn't ask out a special ed guy if he was— Oh, forget it.

"Okay, so not Bob."

They can't come to a consensus. My mind wanders and I try to make my own decision.

I decide to ask Lance. Lance is a total geek, but he's about my height and very nice.

"No way does he already have a date," Clarice confirms.

"Good choice." Maggie approves.

"Who are you asking?" I'm sure that my friends are going to be inspired by my example.

"You're kidding, right?" Maggie turns red at the thought.

"Oh." I turn to Clarice. "Spenser coming?"

"I think so." Clarice doesn't look very enthusiastic. I'm going to have to plumb those depths later and see what she's not telling.

"Here goes." I spot Lance across the cafeteria and all but run up to him. I must really look scary because the expression on his face is utter terror; he kinda scuttles like a rodent. I'm not sure if that's a trait I could come to like. It's a little creepy. But I must go through with my plan. To stop now would be silly and, well, wussy.

"Hi," I say.

He gulps.

I have to wonder if I have food on my mouth or a stray boob hanging out.

"Want to go to GAGD with me?" I ask.

"What?" His face turns a purple shade I didn't think possible in nature.

"Do you want to go to the dance?" I have a really bad feeling in my stomach. I think I'll have to puke if he doesn't answer soon. This is terrible. This is awful. How do guys do this on a regular basis? I really think our species should have died out ages ago if it all comes down to asking the other sex out.

"No," he blurts.

I blanch. "No?"

"No." He scrambles away without even saying thank you or coming up with a lame excuse to make me feel better.

I close my mouth and swallow.

Clarice and Maggie can clearly understand the outcome of the exchange because even from across the room they're all sympatheticy and suitably upset.

I really need to crawl into a hole.

"Hey, Gert, did you want something earlier?" Lucas taps me on the shoulder. "Sorry I had to run on you, but I had a big test. Did Lance turn you down?"

"Oh. No." I try to smile through the tears threatening to humiliate me further. I can't bring myself to say anything else. Obviously, Lucas witnessed that debacle.

"Okay." He shrugs and moves by me. "Later."

I lift my hand and limp-wristedly wave at him.

I can die now.

Really. Anytime.

A lightning bolt would be lovely.

Right. Now.

rant #21
neon lights aren't concealers

I have a zit the general size and shape of Ohio on my chin. That's right, there's very little of my chin showing around the pimple. I'm trying not to pick it. I really am trying. But it's throbbing like Ms. Whop-tommy's mole and frankly, I don't want to have skin anomalies in common with that horrid woman. I'd rather not even use the same type of toilet paper she does. Of course, I don't know what brand she uses, but you get the idea.

Why does concealer always match in the store and never at home? I now have a patch the shape of Ohio a shade or two darker than my cheeks. I don't know what the point is of concealer. So people can guess at the enormity of disgustingness lurking below the surface? I could sell tickets to how much pus we could get out. Put myself through college selling tickets to the grand-prize pimple exhibition.

I try really hard not to pick it. I try.
I can't. The temptation is overwhelming.
I'm only human.

 sixteen

Saint Patrick's Day starts in a big way with a very informative announcement from Princi-Pal Jenkins.

"The following statement is from our school board and this school's administrative team. It has come to our attention that Saint Patrick's Day brings with it several traditions that are illegal and immoral. The tradition of pinching anyone not wearing green will not be tolerated. This constitutes sexual harassment and will not be allowed in the school environs.

"If a student is caught pinching another student or faculty member"—lots of groaning and comments about the idea of touching a teacher like that. Yuck—"the offending student will be disciplined accordingly and the police will be notified of said behavior.

"Signs for the dance that have a leprechaun and say 'Get Lucky for GAGD' must be removed from all school walls. They are inappropriate, and any student caught hanging the posters will be disciplined.

"No green Silly String. No confetti. And this year we will not have the annual special green lunch from our cafeteria's food team. Thank you. Please have a good learning day."

Absurd, anyone? I mean, sure, no one likes to have their butt manhandled. That's why I'm wearing a kelly green shirt today. It hasn't stopped the pinching, though.

Seriously, I think the only part of that whole announcement that made any sense to us is students who get caught getting punished. The moral—don't get caught. Lots of pinching fingers will be hidden behind backpacks and books.

A stupid person is so going to report a pinch, though. There's a pool going to see who will report and if they'll file charges at the local police station. Can you say "scapegoat"? A freshman geek is so going to be expelled trying to impress the upperclassmen. It's inevitable.

Other than the fingers, it's a scurry-and-hide kind of day. Only girls with the best dates, or people totally hooked on each other, are making conversation today. The rest of us are living in fear that someone is going to ask if we're going to the dance. And then we have to mutter and mumble, or act all singular and proud or, even worse, pull the fire alarm or call in a bomb scare, just so there's a new topic of conversation.

Here I am in history class with a whole period of library for our rights assignment and I'm spending the whole time avoiding Stevie and Jenny because that's so vomilicious. I swear Jenny can astrally project herself right into my line of vision.

They can't keep their hands off each other. They seem to think the tables have an invisibility force field allowing hands to wander and rub ad nauseam without anyone watching. Of course, I'm down on the floor behind the nine-one-something decimals, peering over the tops of books. But still. The nerve.

I'm almost jealous. Almost. And then I rein myself in and remind myself in a loud whisper that he was a terrible kisser.

"Really?" The librarian's substitute reshelves a book above my head and walks away.

I should have checked my personal space before speaking. Must remember that.

Please make the rest of the day zoom. Please. I don't ask too much, do I?

Everyone in the world is at the dance but me. I look at the clock and three minutes have ticked by since the last time I stared at it.

To be honest, none of us from the group are there. Tim and Adam have made up a little but are taking a break this weekend. I don't think it's a good thing when couples need a break. Doesn't that just mean they're trying on being single again? And if you think you want to be single again, even for just a moment, isn't that a bad sign?

Tangent: sorry.

Maggie has the stomach flu, though I think maybe the idea of going with Jesse was just too much for her. But she says it's a virus so I'm letting her believe that.

Clarice decided not to ask Spenser since he doesn't want to be her boyfriend. She's hoping he'll have regrets about not going to the dance and want something more with her on Monday. I didn't point out that I'm fairly certain no straight man has ever felt regret about not going to a high school dance. They're not exactly boy-friendly functions, are they? Need I repeat the erection slow dance of last semester?

And I'm here. Alone. Lonely and pathetic. Boring. I hear a parakeet calling my name. On my navy-puke comforter. I decide to sort and throw away the Mount Catalog of college brochures that is the corner of my room. It was the size of a hill; then it became a mountain with a bunny run for skiers; now it's close to making the Seven Wonders list of natural amazingness. I'm almost overwhelmed by the size of the pile, but hell, I have nothing better to do while the rest of the world is dressed up and dancing and making out.

I have three piles on the floor. The throw-away-because-I'd-rather-waitress-than-attend pile, the maybe-backup tier of places and the consider-applying-here pile. Pretty much, I'm screwed with my current PSAT score. Really screwed.

The statistics are staggering. Every single applicant to the Ivy League was valedictorian last year. Not just the two percent they admitted, but all the applicants.

You know the bottom-of-the-pile person, the person that is worse than everyone else? The person no one wants to be, but someone has to? That person was valedictorian, scored a perfect on the SAT and donated a kidney to an orphan in Zimbabwe. At least, that's what I've heard.

If that's the bottom person, I need to reality-check myself. I think my reality check bounced.

I toss Bryn Mawr, Scripps, University of Texas. Good schools, maybe, but not me. I close my eyes and randomly pick ten to put in the maybe pile, just to make sure I'm not limiting myself because of natural or taught biases.

I pick up an extra-thick booklet. It's the one Princi-Pal Jenkins gave me after the Brangate controversy. I guess I tossed it out of my bag when I got home and never looked at it again. It feels like the Toys "R" Us wish book. Not that I know how that feels since I haven't read one since I was . . . oh, it's been so long I can't remember that the Barbie stuff starts on page 42.

Anyway, this wish book has pictures from all over the world, not the toy catalog, this catalog. It's called the Passport Program for High School Students. It's a semester long. You visit six to eight countries. The list of cities is impressive. Rome, Oslo, Tokyo, Paris, Hong Kong, Amsterdam, London, Cairo, Lima—and those are just the ones I can pronounce without spitting on myself. I'm intrigued. It's salvation. I can hear angels singing. I must fill out the application. I bet they don't have school dances. I bet they don't have Things, Giggles and Oscars in France. Europe is too sophisticated for that stuff.

Because let's face it: unless I join the cheerleading squad, I'm so going to have another terrible year.

I dump another blue Pixy Stix into my mouth and make that inevitable sour face before flipping the page and reading on. Students are assigned to families or schools for three weeks in each place. You do schoolwork with the help of an online tutor and spend most of your time seeing the sights and meeting the peoples. You do day trips in each country with other Passport students who are there from different schools, so you get to meet people from here, too.

Look at their shiny, happy faces. They're zitless, their teeth sparkle, even their outfits have the international flair of sophistication.

The catalog headline reads: "Do you seek adventure? Tired of

the same old high school experience? Feel like there must be more to life than school dances and football games? Apply today to broaden your horizons and change your world view."

You know that movie preview announcer? I feel like he's in the room reading this to me. All boomy and authoritative. My heart races.

I've never really thought about leaving the country. I mean, I've joked about it, but could I? Meet people I haven't known since before I had my adult teeth? People who don't think the world revolves around our school campus? People who don't care if our football team has a losing season, or if the track team makes it to state finals? Do such people exist?

I flip through, more than intrigued. Visit Aztec ruins or take a Roman bath. Bungee jump or spelunk. (I'm guessing spelunking is a cave thing since they're in a cave and smiling—I don't think it's a German word for torture or anything). Eat baguettes in Paris, or sip European chocolate in Barcelona.

I pull out the application. I glance at the clock. It's only 7:46. I have hours to fill and visions of Stephen and Jenny having sex to beat into submission.

I glance around my room. The mountain has been split into two large garbage bags and a small stack of pamphlets to keep. I have too much time to kill. I look at my bookshelves. Nothing jumps up and shouts "Read me!"

My toenails are polished.

I shuffle through the Passport application again. Why not? It's not like I'll get the scholarship portion, which is the only way my parents would consider letting me go. You probably have to be a valedictorian to get into this too.

I fill out the first two pages of mostly boring stuff. A couple of essay questions about why I want to participate. I do my best impression of a Miss America. World peace, feed the children, make a difference, blah blah, woo-hoo. I reread and smile. I sound all Gandhi and Mother Teresa's love child.

Uh-oh. Must write five pages about myself. You've got to be kidding. What is it with everyone wanting to know all about me? It's weird. And stalkerlike. Creepy, in fact. I wonder if Mr. Slater is a weird pervert who drinks beer in his tighty-whities while reading our essays. No. Bad mental picture. Really bad mental picture.

I debate spending more time on this. I decide to print out five pages from the draft of my Slater assignment. I cut and paste and edit a little and put on the correct title info. Print it out. Sign the application. Forge my mother's signature. Slide it into the envelope. I don't have snail mail stamps in my room.

"Mom! You have stamps?" I yell as I go down the stairs.

"Yes, Gertrude. They're in the desk in the stamp drawer next to the bill box." She says this like they've been there my whole life. Which now that I think about it, they pretty much have.

"What is that?" she asks.

"Oh, just this thing for school. Pen pal thing."

"That's nice." Mom beams at me like I've delivered the Messiah and won the lottery. "Just put it in the mail-out basket and I'll take it first thing."

"Thanks." I drop the envelope with its three stamps in the basket and head back up to my room.

"Your father and I are just getting ready to watch a film. Would you like to join us?"

"Does it have subtitles?" I ask.

"No. I don't think so."

"Won any major awards?" I press.

"I don't think so."

The clock reads 9:05. "Okay, why not."

It's a homework weekend. Delightful. I'm making a collage of mouths for my history project. I figure the right I appreciate most is freedom of speech, so they're all mouths in midword or sentence, not just smiles. Smiles are boring when you think about it.

"Gert, what are you doing?" Mom knocks and pokes her head around my door at the same time.

"Knocking usually requires waiting for a response," I can't help but point out. See? Freedom of speech.

She only looks at me.

I roll my eyes at her. "I'm working on my Bill of Rights project for history."

She steps into my room, gingerly avoiding piles of clothes and papers. It just appears messy. I know exactly where everything is. "On what?" she asks.

I shove a pile of old magazines over as she tries to sit next to me on the bed. The good part about having really old parents who don't throw anything away is the fact that I have, like, fifty years' worth of *National Geographic* and *Time* to find mouths in.

Mom points to the poster board. "Explain this?" I can tell she's wondering if it's one of those signs they talk about on *Dateline* for mental illness issues. She totally thinks I'm goofing off and not really doing an assignment.

"We have to do a visual representation of the right we'd miss most."

"And yours is?" She leaves this dangling like it's not completely obvious.

"Freedom of speech."

"Why the lips?" She still doesn't get it.

"They're talking, you know, speeching."

"And you can't put the whole face?"

"No, that would cross over into body language, and frankly, freedom of body language is not covered in the Bill of Rights."

"Oh, Gert. I think it's inherent in the law." She shakes her head.

"Nope, not there. Doesn't mention it." I won't hear her opposition. I'm exercising my freedom of hearing, too.

"Okay. You have a nice variety of mouths in various degrees of, umm, open." She pats my head.

"I was going to do the right to bear arms just because we have to use actual arms—well, not actual arms, but we can't use guns and so it just seemed cool to mangle a bunch of dolls."

"Uh-huh." The should-I-call-a-shrink expression comes back.

"But see, I haven't ever held a gun, so it's not like I'm going to miss something I've never done, right?"

"I see."

I don't think she does. "Anyway, working here." I look pointedly at the door.

"I'll leave you to it, then." She exits like an international spy, all quiet and tiptoey.

The phone rings. I have paste all over my hands. How does it always get everywhere?

"Hello?" Caller ID indicates Tim's house. Also Lucas's house, but that would be asking way too much.

"Gert?"

My heart ripples, then jumps into a rumba. I think it might be Lucas. "Yes?"

"Hey, it's Lucas."

I bite back the unattractive screech that threatens to fly out of my throat. "Hi," I say. "What's up?"

"Tim's miserable. We should do something." He gets right to the point.

Not the declaration of undying love I'm hoping for. "What?" I wipe my hands on Kleenex, trying to get the paste off.

"You know, Tim and Adam. You and I need to make it better."

This sounds suspiciously like a plan I'd hatch. Damn, I wish I'd thought of it. Who knew Lucas had girly-interfering tendencies? "What do you have in mind?" I ask, intrigued.

"Here's what I'm thinking."

I pull out a pad of paper and start taking notes. I do like a good scheme.

Must remove father from living space. How? The truth? Or a big lie? I'll try truth first. At least a version of it. "Dad, I need a favor."

"Now?" He doesn't take his eyes off the screen. It's the 1992 Duke win against Kentucky.

"Yes, now," I insist.

He is not taking me seriously. "I'm watching the game."

"Dad, Duke wins when Laettner hits a half-court shot." I click the remote off. It's a calculated measure.

"Gert." *Now* he wants to pay attention and get all ticked.

I shrug. "Well, it's not like it's gonna change; it happened a lifetime ago."

"It's still one of the—"

I finish his sentence. "—best all-time endings to a college game. Yes, I know, but I need you to finish watching it in the garage."

"I don't have ESPN Classic in the garage."

"Dad, please," I cry out in desperation. Lucas and I can't interfere with Tim and Adam if we have to make small talk in front of my father. It's not like he'd be a good relationship counselor for gay men, as it requires being completely comfortable with the idea. Besides, there's no way in hell he'd let three guys go up to my bedroom. He'd think they'd gang-rape me, then kill him and Mom.

In my dad's world, pretty much anyone who isn't on the television playing a sport is a criminal. And when those same people *aren't* on television, they're most likely criminals too. He's fairly paranoid across all time and space continuums.

"Gert, I should be able to watch television in my own house." Dad pushes himself to his feet and continues mumbling. But he's moving, which is a good sign.

"Faster. Faster," I say, wishing for a cattle prod. Or a Taser.

"Going. Going," he says.

I stop following him once he gets to the kitchen and go look out the window in time to see Adam pull up and get out. "Hey, do you mind parking next door?" I yell out at him.

Lucas thinks that if we manage to get them in the same room, with no escape routes, Adam and Tim will get over their issues. I'm dubious, but the first part is getting them in the same room. Adam's arrival and partial car hide should help.

"Where?" he asks.

"Behind the hedge there. They're out of town and Mom is being weird," I say, pointing. Mom being weird is such a frequent occurrence that Adam doesn't even question her fake request. Sad world.

"Better?" He shuffles up the sidewalk and steps past me.

"Thanks so much for helping me." I've made up this huge story about needing his manly shape for my art project.

"What are you doing?" he asks as I point to a chair and pull out a roll of duct tape.

"It's a photo collage of a kidnap victim."

"Uh-huh."

"Don't worry, I won't show your face, just parts of it in each of the photos. I want the audience to feel the despair and hopelessness of a hostage." As I say this, I begin taping his wrists to the wooden arms and his ankles to the legs. I also tape across his chest just in case.

He keeps going on and on about Tim and how he isn't giving in. It's the same heartbreak sludge that comes out of every broken mouth. I stop listening when I can karaoke the conversation.

I glance up at the clock. They're late. I pull out my camera. It's a film kind my dad picked up around the time he still had hair. It's also empty. So I pretend I know what I'm doing and I play with the lens screw thing and do stuff, snapping the shutter every couple of seconds like it's a photoshoot. Where's my wind machine?

"Gert, the tape is kinda tight. I think it's cutting off circulation," Adam mutters behind the tube sock I've tied around his mouth.

I didn't know exactly how to do this as I've only ever seen it done in movies. I pause. "Do you still have feeling in your toes and fingers?"

"A little, maybe."

"Then stop whining. This is art." I totally get into my imagined role of pissy French cartographer; after all, I'm making a map of the human condition.

A car pulls up. I hear doors slam.

"Who's that?" Adam asks.

"Probably Mormons." I swallow.

"Huh?"

"I should go tell them I've found God hiding in the dryer with all the socks. You should be quiet or they may call the police. And that'd be bad." I back out of the living room and go open the front door.

I'm speechless. Lucas is carrying his brother over his shoulder, so it's Lucas's face, next to Tim's butt, that I see first.

"All clear?" Lucas asks, pushing past me. "He's heavy."

Tim's sweaty red outraged face shoots me a look of utter and complete contempt. He has duct tape on his hands and mouth.

"Hey, Adam." Lucas greets Adam like this is something that happens all the time.

"Ah, shit." Adam's tone tells me he's figured out he's been Punk'd.

"Yeah, sorry about that." I close the living room door behind us, hoping Dad's hearing is as bad as I need it to be.

Lucas rips the tape off Tim's mouth as I finish taping his ankles to the chair.

"You asshole. I am so going to kick your ass." Tim's a little angry.

"It was her idea." Lucas points at me.

"You called me!" I shriek. "He did; he called me." I turn to Adam, knowing this is an important detail.

We sit them facing each other in the living room. Aside from rigging a face-holding device, we can't really force eye contact.

I clear my throat and begin. "We're going to work this out."

"Yeah, you two are goners. Why don't you just admit it?" Lucas is strangely verbal about his brother's heart.

"Look, don't hate me," I say to Adam. "But you're miserable, and the only way that's going to get better is if you work things out."

Both guys remain stubborn and silent.

Lucas and I share a look. This may take longer than I'd expected. Lucas shrugs. Obviously, the actual talking part of the plan is my domain. So I put all the hours of watching reffing on ESPN to use.

"Fine. Here's what we're going to do. Adam, you're going to tell me one thing that bothers you about Tim. Then we'll switch." I wait.

To say the next three hours are painful and utterly devoid of progress is an understatement. But in the last few minutes, when I'm ready to give up and kick Lucas for having such a brilliant idea, Adam sighs. "I wanted to go, you know. But I'm scared. I don't particularly want my ass kicked by a bunch of redneck homophobes."

"Like I do?" Tim squirms. "I stopped feeling my hands about an hour ago. I won't move, just untape them. Please?"

I get the littlest scissors I can find and start snipping.

"But you're so fearless. You don't give a damn," Adam goes on.

"Yes, I do. I'm terrified," Tim insists.

Lucas chomps on an ice cube.

Adam persists. "Then why force it?"

"Because they'll still be there, even if we don't make a show of being a couple. Even if we pretend we're two straight guys hanging out, the hate and fear are still there."

"I don't get it," I can't help saying.

Tim turns to me, rubbing his hands together. "It's not going to matter when we step out. Those jerks who want to make an issue, they're still going to be there. Only they'll be older, or be our bosses, or landlords."

"He has a point," I say to Adam as I begin snipping at his tape.

"I don't want to be a flag bearer for gay rights." Adam bites the words. "I just want to have my life."

"Your life includes having a boyfriend, right?" Lucas says.

"So?"

"So you're not living your life if you make decisions based on not upsetting the goons or not being a role model."

Adam sighs. "Can you guys wait in the hall for a minute?" he asks Lucas and me.

I stand up. I'd like to say no, but that wouldn't be very nice of me. "Fine." I grab Lucas's sleeve and pull him into the hallway, shutting the door behind us.

"You think it worked?" he asks.

"I hope so." I rub my face with my hands. I'm hungry and cranky and frankly, Lucas is more human than he was before we started this. That's good. He's not quite so godlike. Though, of course, he's still the most deliciousness boy in the world.

 # seventeen

"Gert, you looking for a job? There are listings in today's paper." Dad really knows how to ruin a perfectly decent day.

"Yes, Dad, I'm looking for a job that works with my specific skill set." I like the way that sounds. As opposed to not really looking.

"Which is what?" Dad has the audacity to sound like I'm bullshitting him. Which I am, but he's not supposed to notice that.

"Stuff."

He waits, with his patented drill-sergeant expression.

My brain whirls. "Like specific matching criteria."

He shakes his head like an oracle. "You're being too picky. Gotta start at the bottom."

"I know." But how far down the bottom do I have to start? There's bottom like scooping dog crap and there's bottom like running the personnel department of a small Fortune 500 company. I'm not looking for CEO, mind you, simply a job where it matters if I show up.

He clears his throat, preparing a full-scale lecture—in between plays, of course. "That means doing something you're—"

"Dad, I know." I inhale and inch toward the door. "I want fulfillment, that's not asking too much."

He barks a laugh at me. And keeps laughing. I've never heard him laugh so long or so hard. "Fulfillment?"

I slam the living room door as I retreat to my bedroom. He's laughing at me. Laughing. Holy-Mother-of-Booger-Appearing-Snorts, my father finds me amusing. That can't be good.

I have to get a job. I realize there are people my age who have been working for years. But they'll die young and decrepit. I have years ahead of me to work—why start early? I had a reprieve during soccer, but the season has ended and the parentals are making all sorts of job-finding grunts, and barking laughter at my answers.

Why do I have to work? I don't want to work. I want to play. I'm not very good at it, but that's just it—I need to get better at playing before I am forced to work for the rest of my life. I need memories to draw strength from when I'm too old to know what the latest chart-topping hit is. Which is what—like, thirty?

Jobs. Jobs. Jobs. What do I want to do? Mom stuck the classifieds under my door this morning. I think that's another grunt.

I haven't showered. I haven't changed out of my pajamas. Really, what's the point?

I pull out a highlighter. Food service is out; I don't like touching other people's spit. I can't handle having to clean up after anyone—busing tables is out. Waitressing is out, since you have to start as a buser.

I'm so not interested in delivering papers or mowing lawns. I flip the page.

Dog walker. I'm an animal person. I'm not a crazy animals-have-feelings person, but I think dogs are cute. I could walk them. I read further. Six a.m.? Five bucks an *hour*? I don't think so. I wouldn't walk small children at six a.m.; why in hell would I get up early for *five bucks* to walk a herd of poodles? Someone needs to call and tell them they need to offer more in the way of *dinero*, or those dogs are going to be walking themselves.

I keep reading. I draw a smiley face over the office tech positions. "Donut shop looking for hard worker for after school and some weekends." My interest is piqued.

Hmm. I sit up and turn down the latest CD Clarice burned for me. Femme rock with minor screaming. No big surprise.

" 'No experience necessary. Free donuts. Competitive wages,' " I read out loud.

Oh, I bet they pay twelve bucks an hour. At least.

I like. I circle the ad with my Sharpie. Not the same small-penis Sharpie we used in the girls' bathroom at school, but a different one. This one is purple.

This has potential. I go to the computer and type in the donut shop's URL for a copy of the application. I like donuts. I can sell donuts. It's food, pre-spit, with no cleanup.

We're having Heather's family over for an engagement party dinner. Mom has been insistent that she meet the whole new clan of in-laws. That's what she's calling them: a clan. I think the argyle/plaid outfit Heather wore the first time she met Mom must have seared itself to Mom's brain. It's like she thinks it was an ethnicity thing rather than a fashion faux pas.

We've never met Heather's parents. After hearing her mother's take on sperm as an infectious disease, I'm almost positive this will be an evening I won't, or perhaps can't, forget. I'm trying to figure out how to work sex into the conversation, if only to see Mrs. Dean's reaction. Maybe I can ask about Mike and Heather having babies. That might work.

Mom has worked herself into the tizzy of all tizzies. She's having this delightful event catered, not because she has arrived at the conclusion that no one she loves should be forced to swallow her food, but because she's obsessed with having French cuisine. Somehow frogs' legs and snails spell romance. Can you spell "whacked"?

Personally, I'd like a steak and kidney pie. Termites? Chocolate-covered crickets?

Kidding.

Hmm, what do I think is the most romantic food? I'd say a double grande caramel coffee concoction because that's what I ordered on my first date with Stephen. But I can't really smell Starbucks right now without getting nauseated. I hope it's a phase and I'm not off coffee forever. That would be rough. I'll have to order stuff I don't like on all my other dates in case I become allergic when things don't work out.

The caterer has been here for hours setting up. There are smells wafting around that I'm not sure I've ever come across before. My stomach is lurching.

"They're here!" I close the curtains and yell toward the dining room where Mom has coerced Dad into helping her move the furniture around. She even cleaned out the room of all her crafty stuff so we could eat at the table tonight. I'm sure it'll be back tomorrow, but it's a nice change of venue.

"Don't yell, Gert!" Mom shouts back at me.

"Whatever," I mutter, and roll my eyes.

I peek out the window. Mike and Heather picked up her parents so they wouldn't get lost on the way here. Heather's mom looks just like her. Only very blond, five inches shorter and about a hundred pounds heavier. She's a bustling hurricane of activity, stomping and fluttering out on the front walk, wearing a sweater with appliquéd hearts and butterflies.

Heather's dad is also extremely short, but with salt-and-pepper hair that melds into a beard. I think he has a mouth and a chin, but I wouldn't bet anything irreplaceable on it. It could be a shadow, but short of a total lunar eclipse, I'm not thinking so.

Mike has never looked happier. He isn't even sweating. Then again, it's a balmy forty degrees, so maybe his sweat's evaporated.

I open the door before they even make it up the stairs.

"You must be Gert." Heather's mom envelops me in a cloud of floral perfume and a hug that invades my personal space.

"Come in," I squeak, squirming to break her hold.

Heather's dad prods me loose. "I'm Art." There was no trick of shadow: His beard takes up most of his face. However, he does have a place where a voice comes out. That's a good sign for a mouth.

My mother rushes forward and it's a battle of perfume and effusiveness. Rather *Wild Kingdom*–y. "Phyllis, it's so nice to finally meet you."

"And you, Betsy. Heather's told me how welcoming you've been."

"Ah, she's a sweet one. Our Michael is lucky to have found her. Come in, we're going to have wine and canapés before dinner."

Mom has hearts and wedding bells, the tissue-paper kind you get at the Hallmark store, hanging from the ceiling. There's crepe paper and confetti. It's like wedding decorations suicide-bombed themselves in protest. Just a little over-the-top.

I stuff a cracker with cheese into my mouth and sip a goblet of sparkling cider. No wine for me.

The evening divides itself into the women discussing wedding plans and the latest in event trends. The men sit together as if the women are contagious, talking about fishing, golf and the stock market. Art isn't terribly into sports and Dad doesn't know anything about stocks, so it's a grunt-and-pause type of interaction. Mike pretty much tries to keep things going. I sit by myself eating things I recognize, like grapes and cheese. The rest of the food all appears alien and brown. "Romance" isn't the word that comes to mind.

We move into the dining room for dinner. The caterer is wearing a white apron, has a terrible fake French accent and is serving us. It's a freakin' good thing I filled up on cheese when I see the main course. I'll spare you the gagging and the breathing through the nose.

The engagement cake is finally brought out, with little cups of espresso and cookies. I have a big slice of cake because it's four hours after the canapés and I'm falling asleep from boredom.

Finally they leave. Mom looks pleased. "Did you have a good time, honey?" she asks me. She appears momentarily fragile.

"It was great, Mom." I kiss her cheek.

"You think so?" She brushes my hair from my face. She hasn't done that for years.

"Yeah. Night." I slump up the stairs.

"I love you, Gertie."

I pause. She doesn't say this often. "Love you, too."

Dad's asleep on the couch.

My phone rings before the sun is even up. " 'ello?"

"This is Darcy at the Donut King. We got your application. Am I speaking with Gertrude?"

"Yes."

"Come in Monday. You'll be taken through orientation. Plan on being here for four hours. See you then."

"Wait." I rub my eyes.

"What?"

"I got the job?" I ask.

"Yep. That's what this says." She hangs up.

Whoa. I'm a working girl now.

THE FOOD CONTINUUM

Raves: Romantic Food
Ice cream: one bowl, two spoons
Tiramisu (just sounds romantic)
Chocolate truffles
Champagne
Grapes and strawberries
Toasted cheese sandwiches

Rants: Very Unromantic Food
Spaghetti
Swapped gum
Internal organ meat
Fish eggs, aka caviar
Stinky cheeses, like Brie
Soup

Hmm, what else? There must be something
I'm missing. . . .

 eighteen

I have a *terribly* bad feeling in my stomach. I think there's something very, very wrong with Clarice. She hasn't returned my phone calls and I'm certain she's ducking around corners to avoid me at school. I can't think of anything I've done, so I'm clueless. I track down Maggie outside her third-period class. "Is Clarice avoiding you?"

Maggie pauses. "I haven't seen her today."

I nod. "I'm pretty sure she saw me and then ducked into the main office so she wouldn't have to walk by me."

"Do you think something's wrong? Is she mad at us?"

I feel much better hearing Maggie say "us" rather than "you." "I don't think so. I can't think of anything she'd be mad about."

Maggie shifts her books and looks at the big clock on the wall. "I have her in the next class. I'll let you know."

Here's what's bothering me. "Have you talked to her since her date with Spenser Saturday night?"

"No, I've left a couple of messages." Maggie grimaces. "You think it went badly?"

"I can't think of anything else."

"Hmm. Me either." Maggie walks off while I scoot into my next class.

Lunch is just Maggie and me.

"She said she was throwing up sick." Maggie drinks her water and opens a travel pack of Goldfish crackers.

"Did you see her puke?"

"Nope. And she wouldn't look at me."

I lean in and whisper, "Does Spenser seem tense to you?"

"Yeah. More pissed than usual."

"Yeah. You think it's connected?"

"Definitely probable." Maggie munches on her crackers.

"We have to figure it out."

"Your first day at work?"

"Yep. I didn't even have to officially interview or anything."

"Is that good?"

"We'll find out."

I'm surprisingly nervous as I follow a fellow worker around getting the grand tour of the Donut King innards.

"This is the back room." Dreadlock girl has a tattoo of some type of spider on her neck. Either that, or it's a pine tree. I'm not sure. Seriously, though, trying to figure out each of her visible tattoos is vastly more interesting than this orientation. Am I destined to be a donut serf? I'm not thinking so.

"We make the donuts from the mix." She points at bags that say Drisco King's Famous Donut Mix. "Don't ask what's in the mix. I can't tell you. Not even the managers know what makes the mix. It's a secret."

Ah, good to see the Cold War is still sizzling on the fried-dough front. "Uh-huh," I say.

"That's the mixer. Where we mix the dough."

Holy-Mother-of-Trans-Fats, this is painful.

"You don't need to worry about making dough, though, since you're new. It's a seniority thing. I was just trained and promoted."

"How long have you worked here?" I'm wondering what type of company loyalty it takes to be able to turn on the car-sized KitchenAid.

"About five years." She shrugs like the time has flown by.

Lord, I never want to be here long enough to get the coveted training.

She points. "Be careful around the oil. They keep it really hot. We change it, but you won't be changing it because you're new here."

"Right." There's a theme.

"This is where we throw away the day-old donuts that don't sell overnight. But you won't be doing that because—"

"I'm new here?"

"No, because you aren't working the early-morning shift."

"Oh." And to think I thought I'd cracked the code. I scratch my head. The paper cap thingy is hot and itchy. So chic.

"Basically you're going to take orders at the counter. Make sure you listen carefully and put the right donuts in the boxes. Nothing ticks a customer off like getting a cream-filled instead of a pudding-filled."

"Really?"

"Yep, and they're impossible to tell apart, so don't worry if you mess up a couple of times."

Okay, so maybe I'm really bright, but it looks like the whipped-cream ones have blue sprinkles and the pudding ones have red sprinkles. "Do the sprinkles change?"

"What?"

"The sprinkles—one's blue and one's red." I point.

Her eyes get all big and buggy. "Wow. Never noticed that."

"Oh." I give her my best I'm-an-idiot-too-just-got-lucky look.

"So anyway. That's it." She turns in a complete circle as if she's making sure nothing else has changed.

"How do I work the cash register?" Color me silly, but taking money does seem to be the primary reason for running a business.

"You don't. You'll be scheduled with someone who has been trained on it."

I don't get to touch money? Is this close enough to the bottom, Dad? I'm not trusted with the secret recipe, the oil or the cash. And I'm on probation until they figure out whether or not I can keep cream and pudding straight. Challenging.

"You get paid every two weeks."

"That's cool." Do I ask about my starting salary? Is this my place?

"And when you work the late shift, not the early-morning shift but the late shift, you can take up to four dozen day-olds with you. It's a perk."

"That's almost as good as getting a company car."

"Huh?"

"Nothing."

"Personally, I took donuts home for the first few weeks. Gained weight and got really sick of the smell. You'll smell like them in a few weeks. Then you probably won't want to touch a donut for the rest of your life."

"Oh." That's a piece of divine wisdom for you. Smell like donuts? How bad can that be? People like donuts, right?

"I have to go make some dough. Kelly has the register. Holla if you have any questions."

"Sure . . . holla!"

"What?" She turns.

"You said to holla if I had a question. I— Never mind. What's my starting salary?"

"You make five twenty-five an hour."

"What?" That's it? No. "Really?"

"Yeah, I know it's a good start. And they give you a quarter raise every six months. I have to go make dough now." She disappears.

At least one of us will be making dough.

A raggedy office lady rushes in. "Miss? Miss? I need three dozen, please."

"How may I help you?" I put on my best please-the-customer smile and pull on gloves. With my hairnet and little paper booties, I feel like asking for a scalpel, but I'm sure that's higher up the career ladder.

When I get home I crawl into bed and hit the messages on my phone.

"It's Maggie. Clarice won't talk to me. Her grandmother says it's because she's too sick to come to the phone. But then she whispered that Clarice has been crying all day."

"Should we go over there?"

"If she wanted us to know, wouldn't she tell us?"

Maybe not. Maybe it's bad. "Do you think Spenser and she got into trouble?"

"Like pregnant?"

"Maybe."

"They haven't had sex yet, have they?"

"I don't think so, but it's not like we're there or anything. And she could be pregnant without actually going all the way, if the stuff . . . you know."

"True, but I don't think they've progressed to no bottoms."

"Would she tell us?"

"We demanded details the last time."

"Maybe she doesn't want to tell us."

"She has to. We're her friends."

"I say we give her till tomorrow, then force her." I'm not feeling like dealing with crap with kid gloves.

"Deal. How was donut land?"

"Fascinating."

"Tell me tomorrow, 'kay?"

"How's Jesse?"

"Don't ask me that." Maggie hangs up.

Well, okay then. What's that mean?

We don't even make it to first period the next day at school before Clarice and Spenser blow.

Spenser slams his locker door. "I told you I didn't want to have a relationship."

I pause, grabbing Adam's arm so he'll stop moving. If Clarice won't come clean, I am sure as hell going to watch this so I know what's going on.

Clarice sniffles. Her eyes are puffy, her cheeks are blotchy and her nose is red like Rudolph's. "But—" She can't get any other words out before breaking down.

Spenser stands there and says, "I'm way too young to limit my possibilities."

I've seen enough. I move toward Clarice. I think we'd all have placed bets this wasn't going to end in the fairy tale she had hoped for, but it still sucks. Clarice sobs against my shoulder.

Spenser spins out of Adam's reach. "Jesus, I was honest about it. What do you want from me?" He storms off, slamming the outside door behind him.

I lead Clarice to the closest bathroom while Adam flags down Maggie and fills her in. I glare at Pops and Giggles whispering behind their hands. Great, Clarice has made the gossip train. Lovely.

Spenser has a point. We girls beg and beg for honesty, but when we get it, we don't want to believe it and hope it'll change.

"He wanted sex." Clarice says this like one equals the other. "It was nice."

I stay quiet.

"I thought we were together-together. I thought it meant something. Didn't it mean something? He hates me." Clarice sobs.

"No, he doesn't hate you," I say, without adding that he probably regrets the sex as much as she regrets it, but for vastly different reasons.

Mr. Slater starts the class, facing us for a change. "Mr. Alexander, how are you going to spend your beautiful week of April's spring break?"

"I'm going to Corpus Christi with my brother."

Everyone has plans but me.

Slater narrows his eyes at Tommy. "You're finished with your paper, then?"

"Uh, sure," he says, squirming.

"That's what I thought. I'll look forward to seeing it turned in early on Monday after break. Ms. Millman, how about you?" Slater turns his attention to the Spanish Club's human mascot.

"The Spanish Club trip to Colombia." She even speaks English with a put-on accent, like Spanish was her first language. In her dreams.

"And your paper?"

"Coming along nicely." She smiles.

"Of course. Mr. Chapman?"

"Working on my paper, sir."

"Very good. You are all obviously the most self-motivated group of students I've ever taught. So you'll have no problem reading Conrad's *Heart of Darkness* in addition to your plans."

There's a collective groan. At least I'll have plenty of time to read.

"We'll have a quiz on Monday. I suggest you use the rest of the period to begin reading." He passes out the books and goes back to sit behind his desk and shuffle papers. I try to start the book, but I keep thinking about Clarice. I can't help it, because that could have easily been me crying.

rant #22
and
rave #9

sex versus the state of relationship

Here is the age-old battle of the sexes. Man means sex. Woman means relationship. Maybe not always. I think if I knew from the start that it was only sex, I'd be okay with that. I can't see me wanting to settle down with every guy who makes me gooey. I mean, talk about limiting possibilities. But I'm not ready for sex as someone's girlfriend, let alone sex as sex.

But are we, as the gentler sex, genetically programmed to be that way, or is it something society tells us we want? Are guys that much more unemotional and we're that much more driven by emotions? Or is that how we're supposed to act and mostly we flail around somewhere in the middle?

Do men ever want the relationship without the sex? And could I have both? Great sex for the sake of feeling good, and a great relationship for other reasons? Would I date a guy who didn't want to have sex with me? Or would Maya get frustrated and put an end to that?

I pull out a pad of paper and work on my "Who Am I?" assignment.

WHO AM I?

I am a sexual being. What does that mean?
I like the idea of sex, but do you have to
have it before you know if you like it? Or
is it like coffee or wine—an acquired
taste? Does doing it more make it better or
just . . . more-er? Is there a chance I
won't like it? What if I like it too much?

 nineteen

Spring break has begun. I hate my family. We don't go to Disney World or on a cruise. All of my friends are going places for spring break and I am stuck here, expected to work at the Donut King's bidding. Expected to feed myself and clothe myself and clean the house for Mom's dinner party.

Adam is with Tim. Clarice is with her older sister in Vegas. The older sister assured Clarice that she'd survive but that shows and sunbathing would quicken the pace.

Even Maggie has a date this week, with Jesse. Okay, so they're studying for their bio exam together. Not really a date, but hey, it's being in the same room with a penis person. That's a date in some cultures.

And I'm stuck here listening to British rock—everything sounds better with an accent. Not that I'm stuck listening to it, but that I'm stuck, period. I want to go someplace new. Have an experience that's unexpected and surprising. Encounter new people to broaden my horizons.

I can feel the spring break clock counting down. I'm wasting precious seconds wallowing. I should paint my ceiling. With nail polish. I wonder how many little jars of enamel it would take to get the whole ceiling. Like pony skin on crack. Could be good.

I may not be allowed to paint my walls, but there's no rule implicitly stating no painting the ceiling. I grab a jar of shimmery teal and climb up on the old navy-puke spread.

Hmm. I'm not quite tall enough just standing on my bed. I pull a couple of pillows over to stand on and begin painting, but it's not the most stable of stances.

I jab at the ceiling with the little teal brush. I cover a rectangle of about three by two inches before my neck starts to hurt. I should be able to cover a full square by the time summer rolls around. Maybe if I work hard at it. I jump on my bed while I'm here. I've missed jumping on my bed.

"Gert! Gert!" Mom's screaming. I drop the nail polish and it rolls under my bed, leaving a trail of teal goo.

I've never heard Mom's voice sound so big. I run to the stairs, hoping she's mad at me for something, but she sounds different. Scared. In pain. My heart races and my mouth goes dry.

I stumble down the stairs in an animal sprint.

Dad is half in his chair and half slumped against Mom and the floor. Like a rag doll. He's sweaty and pale. He doesn't look right.

I grab the phone. Dial 911.

Mom's crying and screaming. I help move Dad to the floor since he's already mainly there.

I don't know what to do. Mom is going to hyperventilate. "Mom, you have to breathe."

The calm voice on the other end of the line asks my dad's symptoms. "What do you feel?" I ask him.

He gasps. "Pain." His face is all gray and sweaty.

"Where?" I ask.

"Pressure." He touches his chest.

"His chest. Left side with pain," I repeat into the phone.

She tells me the ambulance is on its way.

I stay on the phone with her while Mom loosens Dad's button-down chamois shirt. She's frantic. Dad isn't saying much. His face is all scrunched and his hands grab on to Mom.

"They should be outside your house now. Do you see the ambulance?" the calm voice asks me.

I throw the phone down and dash to the door. I fling it open. "In here! In here!" I yell as the medics race past me.

They do their stuff. I can't really see, but Mom holds on to me like I'm the only thing standing between her and hell. Not a pleasant place to be. I'm sure I'll have bruises. I can barely breathe. The room smells funny. I hear the television in the background like static.

I've never seen my dad like this. Correction, I've never seen anyone like this. I've never happened on a traffic accident or been at the scene of a crime. I know to call 911, but that's where my expertise ends.

I can't even do that right, as I realize I've left the calm voice hanging on the phone. I grab the phone as the paramedics get Dad on a gurney and wheel him out the door. "Sorry. Sorry," I say into the dead air. I hang up.

"Gertrude, I'm riding with your father in the ambulance. You'll have to call Michael. He's teaching today, maybe we should wait to call him."

"What hospital?" I'm already moving to grab the car keys. I need to be there. I can't be left home.

"Memorial. Don't you dare drive." Her face takes on an

inhuman expression of panic. "Ask Mrs. Nelson next door to bring you."

I can barely stand up. I put down the keys and watch as they put Dad and Mom in the back of the ambulance and close the doors. I must have an expression of terror on my face because one of the medics pauses to look at me. "You did the right thing calling. Giving him the best shot. It'll be okay."

As if. How does he know it'll be okay? He doesn't know that.

I speed dial Mike's cell. Wait for his voice. Tears stream down my face. I feel so helpless. So alone. It goes right to voice mail. Crapping buttocks, he's in class. I tell him to call me.

I look around the room. I need someone to tell me what to do. What do I do? I don't know.

I grab Mom's phone book and dial Heather's cell. Praying she has it on in the middle of preschool.

She answers and I start sobbing. Really crying hard. The kind of crying that makes snot run freely and makes it impossible to talk. "What's wrong?"

I try to tell her in gasping bits and parts. She must understand enough because she says, "It's going to take me a few minutes to get coverage. I will call your brother's TA and have him meet us at the hospital. I will come pick you up. Okay? Why don't you pack a bag of your dad's pajamas and his toothbrush and stuff, okay? That would be helpful." She speaks slowly and enunciates each word.

I mumble. Thank God Heather is able to think.

I scurry up the stairs to my parents' bedroom. Rooting around in Dad's underwear drawer has never felt this—well, I've never actually done it, so that tells you something.

Soon I have a large duffel bag packed with everything Dad

likes. Including the *Sports Illustrated* that came in the mail yesterday that still has the clear plastic wrapping on it. I can't make decisions; I grab everything I think he wants.

I'm standing at the front door with my coat on, clutching my backpack (I might need something later—what, I don't know, but I want it). I walk the length of the living room.

Looking at the clock.

Looking out the window.

I wonder if Dad is dead.

Or in surgery.

Or Holy-Mother-of-the-Ratings, being attended by attractive but stupid residents like on TV.

Heather pulls up and I'm out the door before she even has her foot on the brake.

"What exactly happened? Have you heard details yet?" she asks as I stuff the duffel and my backpack in her backseat.

"I don't know. Mom kept saying heart attack. The medics wouldn't comment on what they thought was wrong with him." I'm shaking. She has to help me put the seat belt on.

"Okay. We'll go see. I talked to your brother. He's on his way. He's going to meet us at the hospital." She holds my hands. Hers feel hot.

"Okay." I nod. Fear claws at my guts.

Heather glances at the duffel bag Dad could use to travel around the world on foot, but bless her, she doesn't comment on how ridiculous I am. "Got everything?"

"Maybe." I'm sure I forgot something seriously important.

"We'll be okay." She starts the car and we drive to the hospital in silence.

The hospital is chaotic. We go in the emergency room entrance and look around for my mom or Michael. We don't see anyone we know, but there are lots of sick people, and bleeding people with towels wrapped around their heads or hands. It's really kinda creepy. I feel faint.

Heather takes my hand and we go to the front counter. "We're looking for our father. He was brought in by ambulance."

"Name?"

I look around, trying to identify the stagnant odor assaulting my nose. I don't pay too much attention to Heather and the gal in really old faded scrubs. Isn't that what they call those professional pajamas?

The waiting room is huge. White-gray, with weird abstract paintings and more uncomfortable chairs than I have ever seen in my life. It's the world's largest graveyard for dead, decomposing furniture. The tables are scuffed and the laminate is coming loose like that gum you can get in rolls. I don't know what's worse—the waiting room or the fact that I've been sitting here long enough to recognize that laminate can start coming off the particleboard underneath it. Definitely the amount of time.

My mom is arguing with Heather. "But they don't get enough sleep."

"Betsy, please calm down, you're going to make yourself sick. The doctors are doing the best they can."

"But they don't get enough sleep. The average doctor in a hospital gets three hours of sleep in a twenty-four-hour period. Can you imagine? Three hours, when the human body needs at least eight to ten to function fully and completely."

"Mom—" I try to save Heather from having this conversation for the fifth time.

"They said it. On *Dateline,* or *Primetime,* or one of those other shows. They reported it. Doctors in Denmark average eight point seven hours each night. I wish we were in Denmark. He'd have better care in Denmark."

I think Denmark probably has better waiting room furniture, too. What is that painting? Watercolor exploration of vomit?

"I'm sure the care here is excellent." Heather pats Mom's hand.

"A doctor." Mom leaps up and rushes at a guy I'm sad to say is neither attractive nor competent-looking. And yes, he looks like he saw his pillow about a week ago. Joy.

"Mrs. Garibaldi?" he says.

Mom nods like a bobble head on meth.

"We've taken your husband to the cardiac floor. The nurses are prepping him for surgery. He needs an immediate bypass. Perhaps as many as four."

"You're operating?" Heather does a terrible job of masking her disbelief that this man could perform an oil change, let alone a quadruple bypass.

He at least doesn't have the nerve to look shocked by the comment. He must get it a lot since he isn't an A-list Hollywood actor. "No. I will be assisting Dr. Matthews. He is the top cardiothoracic surgeon in the region."

"Really?" I ask. I guess I'm not predisposed to believing that the top anything would choose to live here.

He doesn't even blink in my direction, just ignores my comment. Makes me want to do a drunken naked dance on top of the crappy tables and the magazines from 1997 just to see if I can get his attention. I choose the better part of valor and refrain from dancing, or getting naked.

"A nurse will be out shortly to take you up to the waiting room on floor seven."

Gee, another waiting room. Wonder if this one has a watercolor depiction of poop hanging on the wall.

"Can I see him?" Mom asks.

"I'm sorry, but he was moved straight into prep for surgery. Time is critical." He doesn't look sorry.

Mike wraps an arm around Mom almost as if he is literally holding her up.

"I'll check back with you as we have news." He turns and walks back down the hallway as if the hounds of hell are biting at his heels. I'd like to do a little nipping. Guy's a robot.

We go back to our row to wait for the nurse to move us. Only I can't sit because another family has stolen our seats and there aren't four seats together anywhere in the enormous room. There are a thousand terrible chairs in here and most of them are full.

Heather hands me her cell phone. "Do you want to let any of your friends know? Adam, maybe?"

I shrug but take the phone. Not exactly the best news to share over the phone. Not that Adam cares about my dad, but my throat is so tight I have to swallow three times to clear it. I'm scared. I don't know how to be brave about this. Bravery isn't my strong suit. Coward. Woo-hoo, that's me. There's something to add to my list of shameful characteristics when this is over.

I dial Adam's cell number. He answers without a full ring. "Where are you? I'm stuck waiting for Tim's practice to be over. It would be so much quicker if you were here."

That's not even an appealing offer when all I'm thinking about is painting my bedroom with nail polish. "I can't. I'm busy." Good, I sound normal. Pretty normal.

"Where are you?" he repeats.

"The hospital."

"What?" Adam yells into the phone.

I can hear voices in the background asking Adam what is going on.

Adam says, "Gert's in the hospital." He says something I don't catch. "Hang on. Tim wants me to put it on speaker so we can all hear."

Holy-Mother-of-Technological-Advances, this isn't a conversation that needs to be broadcast. "No, Adam, don't you dare."

"Hey, Gert. How are you? Your face find more airborne eggs to get in front of?" Tim croons. I can hear a crowd of guys laughing. Perfect.

I slump down against the wall and lean my head on my knees. "My dad had a heart attack. He's in surgery."

"Oh, shit," Tim says. Adam takes me off speaker.

"Are you okay?" he asks.

"Fine." As if I'm more important than my father.

"Sorry. I didn't know. I thought maybe you'd been beaned with a soccer ball again." He's all apology.

"No." I start crying. I can't help it.

"I'll round up the gang as soon as I can and we'll come."

I snivel. There's just us breathing on the phone together.

"Where are you? What hospital?"

I mumble the name of the hospital and the info about the new waiting room. I can't talk much. I'm not worth anything at the moment.

"Okay, hang on." Adam's already yelling for people to meet him at the car.

I flip the phone closed as a nurse walks to the gaping mouth of the waiting room and yells out, "Garibaldi? Mrs. Garibaldi?"

We all stand like someone's stuck a needle in a butt cheek. "Here." Mom jumps up and down like we've won a game show.

We follow the nurse to a smaller, crowded, overly warm room with glass walls on three sides. There's an old television set broadcasting daytime soaps. I have no idea which ones.

"There's a run on heart problems today," I say to no one, but my mother shoots me the shut-up look I'm so fond of.

It's hours. I won't lie and say time somehow flew by. It's hours and it's excruciating and we're stuck in a tiny room with a whole UN contingent playing musical chairs. Leave your seat at your own risk. Don't pee. Don't go get coffee. Don't move or you'll be stuck on the floor, and who the hell knows what's crawling on that floor.

Aren't hospitals the dirtiest places in the world? Don't more people get sick in hospitals than anywhere else? Cheerful. I'm utterly hearts and flowers at the moment.

Tangent: sorry.

Mike's snoring. Heather's reading a book she bought at the gift shop with a half-naked Viking on the cover. I wonder if it would keep my attention. I'm thinking it's possible. Mom is doing her third Sudoku, also purchased by Heather in the gift shop. I should have let her buy me one each of the latest magazines.

Finally, when I think I can't keep my Kegel Kegeling any

longer, I look up and see Adam and Maggie sneaking into the waiting room. They're wearing scrubs, face masks and those bootie things. They look like extras from a *Grey's Anatomy* set.

"Sorry. Sorry. Hi, Mrs. Garibaldi." Adam hugs Mom quick, then embraces me.

Maggie sits on the coffee table between our chairs. "It took us forever to sneak in here. How's your dad?"

"We haven't heard." I look at the clock for the umpteenth time when I compute her words. "What do you mean, sneak?"

Adam rolls his eyes. "They wouldn't let us up. This room is for family only."

Huh. That's why it took so long for them to get here. "So what'd you do?"

"We had to sit down there for a while under the watchful gaze of a volunteer gatesperson, who I swear I've seen in history books about Nazi Germany."

Maggie shakes her head. "Startling resemblance, but not old enough. We had to listen and figure out which rooms they had visiting hours in. It took a while. Then Adam faked a phone call from you. He's a very good actor." She nods approvingly.

"So you gave me the room number and said come on up."

"Right, but we're not in a room."

"I know. We followed a janitor to the laundry supply. Grabbed the correct attire, then we've just been getting off and on elevators until we found the right floor."

"You're good friends." Mom pats Adam's hand and goes back to her puzzle. She's got the glazed-donut look.

Mike's still snoring. Heather's smiling. She doesn't appear quite as tense.

"Do you need anything? We can get pretty much anywhere. It's pretty amazing what the uniform will get you. Victor and Greg are both on trips, but they texted sad faces. Clarice is willing to hop the next plane back from Vegas if you want her to," Maggie says.

"Can you get me an update on my dad?"

"I don't think they'll let us in the OR. But we can try." Maggie's game to do whatever I need.

I shake my head. I can see my friends going to prison trying to help me.

"Garibaldi? Garibaldi?" A little man is wiping his face with a blue towel. He doesn't have a face thingy and his scrubs have sweaty armpits. It looks like he's just finished a triathlon.

We all jump to attention. Adam and Maggie squeeze to the back of the group, but I really don't think the guy even notices they're wearing identical doctorly outfits. Minus the sweat.

"It went well. I'm pleased. He's in recovery and then he'll be moved to a room. He probably won't wake up tonight, so I suggest you get food, get some sleep and come back in the morning."

"I don't think so. I want to be with him as soon as possible."

"Ma'am—"

"Thank you." Mom's chin thrusts up. I've never seen her so full of steel.

"I'll let the nurse know." Dr. Sweaty nods and heads back toward the nurses' station.

"Adam, will you be a dear and take Gertrude home, please?" Mom grips Adam's arm.

"Of course."

I don't like this plan. "But—"

"Gertrude, honey, this isn't the hard part. He's going to be in the hospital and then he's coming home and I'll need your help. You remember Jerry had this same thing happen last year?"

I nod.

She cups my cheeks. "It's a long road and we're just getting started. I need you to go home and eat a good dinner and get some sleep. Are you working this week?"

"Yeah."

"That's good. Mike and Heather will help me here."

"We're gonna stay, Gert." Mike touches my shoulder.

"We'll stop and get ice cream, okay?" Maggie pipes up.

Adam nods. "Absolutely."

I'm too tired to argue. I'm torn. I really just want to go home and crawl into bed and wait for the world to make sense again, but I also think I should be here, stiff-upper-necked like Mom.

I hug Mom. I feel tears building behind my eyes.

She kisses my cheek. "He's going to be fine."

Here's the deal about growing up: you begin to recognize the times when parentals can't necessarily keep the promises they make. "I hope so."

rant #23

the einstein factor

Okay, here's the deal: I'd like to kick Einstein's phenomenally annoying butt. Time should not be relative. Time should not, depending on whether I'm having a good or a bad time, change the speed at which it ticks by. Time should be the one freakin' constant in an otherwise inconsistent and inconstant world. I'm not talking about getting old. I'm not all fountain-of-youthy or anything, maybe because my neck looks fine and my boobs are growing out not down. I get it. I understand, but that's not the kind of time I'm talking about.

I'm talking about the tick, tick, tick of the second hand. The second hand stutters, it pauses, it's the Eeyore of the scientific world. It loves misery. It pauses slightly each time it notices a horrible moment and keeps pausing until it's sucked the life out of the people experiencing said torment.

Okay, maybe not literally, because we'd all be dead, but six hours of surgery should not feel like sixty. And good ol' Al brought it to our attention and he's a hero. What's with that? Why didn't he do something great and figure out how to get the second hand to take happy pills and get over it? That's what I'm saying. . . .

WHO AM I? (CONT.)

I am mortal. I have an invisible expiration date. I am human. I am an animal. I will die. Maybe not today, but maybe tomorrow. When I'm not ready. When I still have a to-do list. When I'm looking forward to reading that book or seeing that movie. When I'm supposed to show up for a special occasion like a wedding, or a birth, or a party I won't be able to attend because I'll be dead. Weirdness.

I'd really rather be like milk and have the date of my demise stamped on my forehead. Cuz then I could apologize for not being at the special thing, or I could eat Chinese takeout as my last meal instead of a grapefruit because I'm feeling fat.

Why does it have to be unknowable? Why isn't science working toward knowing the date instead of knowing the sex of unborn kids or putting off death by a decade or two? I don't want a delay. Okay, maybe if I was ninety I'd want a delay, but what good is a delay if you don't know that you would live that long anyway? Like why put people through nasty-ass cancer treatments if we could decode the date of their death? Then they could have a party and not feel guilty about choosing not to spend their last weeks in the hospital feeling worse than death. Or they'd know they're supposed to live another fifty years so the chemo is worth it. See? Much more useful than face cream to fight wrinkles. Do wrinkles matter? Who ever died and the one thing they regretted was the extra wrinkle on their forehead? I think face creams are covering up the bigger issue. We don't know when we're dying. Big issue. The biggest.

I don't know if I believe in God and heaven and hell. I don't know if I believe in reincarnation or in ghosts or spirits. I don't know if I believe there's something better out there. I'd like to. I mean, it would make missing the new flavor of Ben & Jerry's a little more acceptable if I knew heaven had it too. And in heaven there aren't calories, right? That'd be nice. I wonder if I could pick my body? Like one day be Angelina's prototype and the next try out Tyra's. That'd be cool. Sort of like when we used to dress up Barbies, except I could be the Barbie. I am above all uncertain of the post-death future.

I am my parents' genetic history. I am the conduit that will pass on what our ancestors have passed down. I am male-pattern baldness. I am heart disease and high cholesterol. I am so far immune to most kinds of cancer. I am good with words, but awful at math. I am someone's grandmother or someone's crazy nunnish aunt.

I am a girl no more, but a woman not yet.

I am at the start, but my parents are at the end.

 twenty

We pull up outside my house, but I can't make myself get out of the car. The dark house is staring back at me.

I don't know why today feels different. But it does. It's weird. It's scary.

Maggie and Adam settle back like they've got all the time in the world and don't think I'm losing my sanity by sitting in the car gawking at my house. Finally, it gets a little uncomfortable on Adam's vinyl upholstery. I can tell they're getting antsy, but I feel leaden.

"Ice cream?" Maggie asks Adam.

"Check," he says.

"Pizza delivery number?"

"Check," he replies.

"Carbonated beverages?"

"Check," Adam answers, and they both turn to look at me.

"Gert?" Maggie is tentative, ready to sit back and wait another fifteen minutes if that's what I need.

"Uh, check," I say, and grasp the door handle. I have to take a deep breath and open the door on the exhale.

Maggie and Adam flank me as we march up to the front door. "Keys?" Maggie asks.

I didn't bring them. "Uh, I don't—"

"Spare still under the frog statue?" Adam asks, already moving to retrieve it.

I nod.

He finds the key and opens the door. Maggie flips on every light switch she can find, including several that don't actually turn anything on, but I'm suddenly too tired to care. I wander over to the couch and curl up. I'm shaking.

Adam directs Maggie and they find every pillow in the house and most of the blankets. They make a nest around me, tucking me in tightly, and settle on the floor near me.

At some point, Adam calls for pizza and I think I eat a couple of slices, but it doesn't taste. Not bad, just doesn't taste.

I fall asleep, listening to the television and my friends chatter. "Stay?" I ask.

"Of course," they answer.

The house doesn't feel so menacing. I sleep.

Days run together. Dad's going to recover. It will be slow going, given the whole cracked-chest part. Mom and Mike take turns with Dad and let me make cameo appearances. I wish Mom would let me do more, but she doesn't want the burden to fall on me. I feel useless and insist that I'm not a child. I want to be helpful.

I can see the exhaustion in dark pools under their eyes. Mike's facial hair is spawning and Mom's got a helmet head from not getting her weekly set at the hairdresser's.

Now that I'm here, on day four, to take my turn sitting with Dad during the night, I wish I hadn't insisted. I've never really been in a hospital for this length of time. I mean, I've been in the emergency room a couple of times with stupid kid stuff, like the egg/nose incident, but I've never known anyone who spent time in one as an admitted patient.

My grandparents died before I was born, or shortly after, so this is all new. Mike and Mom left me in the lobby because I insisted I could find Dad's room on my own.

I pause outside his door.

There's a smell. I can't put my finger on it, but it's there. Like antiseptic and pus. Does pus smell? If it does, it's part of this odor.

I volunteered to take a turn spending the night with our favorite patient since it's my spring break and I don't have to work until later tomorrow. Plus, Mom's all loopy exhausted and Mike has a real career he's been absent from.

Now that I stand outside Dad's hospital room, I want to go home. This wasn't one of my more intelligent highly altruistic ideas.

I've seen him since his surgery. I've even seen them change his bandage. He has the world's most horrific-looking wound. Bad B movie horror-film horrific. So bad it looks fake. So bad I almost vomited right there. I think it must have shown on my face because the nurse made me lie down and she rubbed my face with alcohol to cool me off. How's that for humiliating? Dad thought it was cute, though; he smiled and asked me if I was okay. I was the entertainment. Yippee.

I don't want to go in. He's small in that bed. Somehow smaller than I can fully comprehend. He's shrunken and frail. He's not commanding or intimidating. He's old.

The nurses are wondering what I'm doing. I'll either have to go in or come up with a brilliant explanation for why the door won't open.

I push open the door and trudge in. How does anyone sleep in this place? It's a constant barrage of beeps and footsteps, and the sound of phones ringing, and the low murmur of conversations that are none of my business.

Dad turns his head and gives me a half smile of welcome. It's his most effusive expression. He's trying, I can tell. I don't think he likes me seeing him this way; he'd prefer I wasn't here. "You're staying tonight?" he asks me. He's creeping me out, looking at me all serious face. I can't remember the last time he looked at me like this. Studying me like there's a test later.

"Yeah. Are you okay?" I put my backpack down and sit in the plastic-covered recliner next to his bed.

"Fine. Fine." He never once looks away from me to stare at ESPN's latest episode of *Get 'Er Done*. He loves this show. I'm even more creeped out.

"You sure?" I ask. "Want some water?" I point at the pitcher and the bendy straws.

He shakes his head. "I asked the nurse to bring us hot fudge sundaes at seven. She should be here any minute."

I nod. "Right." Need I mention the heart attack? I'm fairly certain hot fudge isn't on anyone's heart-healthy food plan.

He pats the bed like he'd pat my head if I was closer. "I did ask. I hear there are pretty good vending machines. The cafeteria sells donuts twenty-four hours a day." He's feeling pretty good to be giving me such grief, so I relax a little.

I groan. "Don't remind me of donuts, please."

Dad chuckles like it hurts, which it probably does. "Sorry. Not the kind of career fulfillment you were looking for?" He hands me the remote. "What do you want to watch?"

Surprise ricochets around in my brain. "Huh?"

"What's on?" He dips his head toward the screen.

Never in my life has my father given me the remote, nor has he willingly volunteered to watch anything of my choosing. "Do you need me to get the nurse?" I lean forward in the chair, ready to spring into action.

I'm desperately afraid he'll die while I'm the only one here, and I'll never know if there's something I could have done to save his life. If only I'd paid attention at Girl Scouts when I was seven.

"No, I'm fine. Just thought you'd like to pick, that's all. Staying with me can't be the best offer you had on spring break." That's the closest Dad's ever going to get to apologizing for something that's so not his fault. Even I'm not self-centered enough to blame him for ruining what—let's face it—was going to be a sucky break anyway. I wave my hands. "Don't worry about it." I pick up the remote and he pats my hand. I try to smile. I do the best I can, but I'm sure it misses the mark.

Thinking I should ease us into this quality time together and not shock him into another MI, I rule out the obvious choices: reality TV, MTV, Court TV. "How about CNN?"

Surprise blooms on Dad's face. "You're into current events?"

"You're not?" This is a safe question. Dad watches the news only when he's not watching sports or home-improvement shows.

"I just never knew you were."

"Occasionally." Okay, so I don't pay too much attention to current events, just the ones that interest me. Sue me.

At one point, I go get us SweeTarts from the vending machine because Dad is allowed hard candies. It's the closest thing they've got to hard candy in the machine. I think he has one before he falls asleep. Mom said to expect him to mostly sleep. He's still recovering, so his body is tired.

I know from home that changing the channel or turning off the television can startle him awake, so I just leave the headlines rolling. I read the week's book assignment, *Heart of Darkness,* which, who knew, is an apt title for this week. Of course, Dad's heart isn't dark, just broken. His snoring is comforting. I've missed the sound of it while he's been here. The nights seem emptier at home without his rhythm.

I'm beyond tired when I report to work the next day. Recliners are not the most comfortable places to pass fourteen hours. Don't let anyone fool you into thinking they're better than beds. They're not.

Here's the deal with the donut shop. After about an hour at work, I reek. Really, really reek. Like dead donuts left in the trunk of a car on a ninety-degree day to decompose. Stink. It's not me. It's the air in here. Thousands of screaming carbohydrates leave a putrid essence behind when they are dunked in hot oil or consumed by customers who should be next door at Jenny Craig.

No, I'm not kidding. Next door is a Jenny Craig. The other side of us is a gym for women, and across the street is the huge twenty-four-seven gym for serious athletes. And then there's us. Which personally I think is rude beyond all get-out. It's like karmic sabotage. But the odds are good that people who shouldn't be eating donuts (not that any of us should eat donuts—Homo sapiens didn't evolve eating fried dough, did we? No, bark and berries, that's us) might go into one of the other establishments rather than here. I think the opposite happens. They work out, they've lost a pound in the last month, whatever it is, so they deserve a treat.

I know we all have free will and the right to eat whatever we want, but really, if you have to buy two seats on an airplane to get enough butt room, then you shouldn't waddle into the donut shop.

I'm not skinny. I'm not saying I'm perfect, and there are lots of people out there who might be crying that I'm being mean and "ist" and don't know what it's like to live with the disease of obesity, but if you're built to sustain your life through a famine that never comes, should you really consume a week's worth of calories in a bite of fried dough? I don't think so.

I know I'm not supposed to impose my own judgments and I've been all brainwashed by the media, but if you need help tying your shoes, perhaps a dozen filled, iced, fried-chocolate-sprinkled, high-calorie hot pockets aren't for you.

The UN shouldn't parachute rice and beans to starving people—they just need to open a donut shop in the world's most desolate places. Donut boxes could fall from the sky and no one would be too thin again. Really, it could revolutionize the charity movement. Think about it. Think of the trucks and trucks of fifty-pound sacks of rice and flour they show on the evening news. The same calorie equivalent could be easily distributed in neatly lined pastry boxes, and for a tenth of the work. There's never enough rice. But there are enough donuts.

Tangent: sorry.

Mr. Four-Chin, Toga-Wearing Not-So-Roman is still contemplating his choices. And he's hostile. He has that I'm-going-to-

eat-five-dozen-all-by-myself-and-I-know-what-you're-thinking
look on his face. He's filled two boxes carefully before his wife or
girlfriend walks into the shop to ask, "What's taking so long?" I
don't make eye contact with her because I'm sure she'll blame me
for the delay.

"I'm coming," he snarls.

She taps superlong nails on the counter. "You said you were
getting one."

"I am." He doesn't look at her.

One times sixty, perhaps, but that's just me.

"Honey, you know what the doctor said about your heart." She
tries the pleading tone one uses with an errant toddler.

I perk up. Heart trouble? Mr. Toga has a bad heart? Doesn't he
know how insidious that is? He shouldn't even be breathing in
here.

"Don't nag. I can't deprive myself, you know what happens
when I do that." Again with the snarling.

She takes out a piece of stop-smoking gum. "One is modera-
tion," she says, and pops the gum in her mouth.

"Don't. Don't. Don't!" he yells at her, and stomps his foot like
he's three.

Huh, guy doesn't like to hear "no." Shocking.

"I don't want you to have another heart attack. You heard what
the doctor said." She snaps the gum.

"The hospital wanted me to feed my cravings with low-carb
crackers. Crackers. Like crackers will do it," he says, like they put
him on the rack and pulled off his fingernails.

"Crackers probably won't kill you." Crap, I said that out loud.

They both swivel their heads and gape at me.

"Excuse me?" demands Mr. Toga.

What's that saying? In for a pound, in for a ton? "My father just had quadruple bypass surgery and he's the size of your thigh."

"You little bitch." Mr. Toga doesn't appreciate my candor.

I can't blame him, but I can't stop either. "He carefully measured out a half cup of oatmeal in the mornings. Never smoked. Never drank. He's maybe eaten a donut once or twice in his life, but he sure as hell didn't stand here contemplating the moist goodness of the blueberry versus the tang of the lemon-filled with the expertise you seem to have. So if you got off with a mere heart attack that didn't scare you enough to at least make an attempt to eat better, then you don't deserve it. You don't." I pant my breath out.

"Gert." The manager on duty carefully takes my arm and pulls me into the back room as I hear the woman wail, "See, she gets it, why don't you get it?"

The manager's face is green and purple, mottled like an Easter egg. "You will not work here anymore."

I could see that coming. I float up above my body.

"Our customers are our livelihood. We do not judge. We do not condemn. And we do not talk to them like that." He hands me my paycheck that I was supposed to get at the end of my shift today. "After we give that man any donut in the store he wants and take it out of your pay for today, if there's so much as a cent left over, which I highly doubt, I will mail it to you." He grabs the apron from my waist and the King Crown cap we all have to wear.

I nod. I know I messed up, but I don't care enough to grovel.

And you know what? That damn check smells like grease and that awful secret mix.

Mike's car is in the driveway and so is Mom's. I let myself in the front door quietly, in case they're sleeping.

I hear voices and then I hear my name. I stop in my tracks and listen. Obviously they didn't hear me arrive.

I don't make a practice of eavesdropping; I only do it when it's absolutely necessary, which is whenever I get the feeling I'm not getting the whole story. When I'm getting the censored, you're-not-old-enough version.

"Mike, I don't know how we're going to do it."

"Mom, we'll figure it out."

"But it's Gert's college fund. All of it. All of our savings. Do you know what that woman said to me? She asked what I thought my husband's life was worth and said obviously I didn't value it very highly or I wouldn't be in her office asking how I'm supposed to pay the bills. Can you believe that?"

Anger vibrates in Mike's voice. "No. I wish I'd been there. I have money saved up. I'll take out a loan. We just need to get Dad home and better and then we'll take the next step. What about insurance?"

"Ten-thousand-dollar deductible and then they pay fifty percent. The premiums were so high. Oh, Mike, we should have paid them. We should have paid whatever they wanted."

"Mom, you did the best you could."

"It's not good enough. Don't you see, it's not good enough. What do I tell Gert?"

"Right now, nothing. She can get a break on tuition at Simon Randalph. She can take student loans. There's scholarships. She's capable of working. She's got a job now."

Great, now my being fired has capital "L" loser implications. I'm going to make my mother cry. I know it.

She sniffles. "But she's just a kid."

"She's more mature than you give her credit for. And she'll have help."

"Mike, what if we die before she's ready? We never thought about it, but it's possible now. We're getting old and—" I hear Mom crying, but it's muffled, like she's holding on to Mike.

"Stop. Please, Mom, stop crying," Mike pleads with her. He's not big on tears.

I can't catch all of what Mom says, but I hear, "I can't lose him. I'm not ready."

"Dad is going to be fine. He is. And Gert's sixteen. She'll be officially an adult before you blink."

"I'd feel better if she knew what the world was like. If she'd been exposed to more—"

"You've done the best you can. And Heather and I will always be there for her. Always. She'll be fine."

Tears cloud my vision as I listen. I had no idea Mom worries like that about me. I tiptoe past the living room door but stop and meet Mike's eyes over the top of Mom's head. She doesn't know I'm here, so I just keep tiptoeing up to my room.

A few minutes later, Mike knocks and pokes his head in. "Hey, kid."

"Hey."

"She's tired. She's worried. Don't think about it." He sits on the edge of my bed.

"Mike." I sit up. "I'm going to think about it. I didn't know they worried about money. I've never thought about it."

"Gertie, they're fine. The hospital is expensive and not all of it is covered by insurance. It adds up quick. But you don't need to worry. Look, you're working, which is great, and Dad's proud of you for taking that on with such authority."

My face falls and I tear at a Kleenex. I mumble, "I got fired."

Mike goes still. "Are you going to tell me it wasn't your fault?"

I think about it. "No, it was completely my fault."

"Criminal?" he asks.

I snort. "No."

"Then you'll get another job and you won't make that mistake again, right?" he asks.

"Right."

"You're taking responsibility for it, that's big. That's good."

I nod. Still feeling like I should have kept my mouth shut. I didn't do the guy any favors and I certainly shouldn't care enough about his health to get fired over it. Especially if Mom is so worried about my place in the world.

"You holding your own in school?" Mike asks.

"Yeah, break's almost over."

"Don't worry. You don't need to take this on, okay?" Mike stands up and ruffles my hair.

" 'Kay," I say, not really believing him.

Days blend into weeks and before I blink we're well into May. I slide into my seat for art just as the bell rings. I seem to be ten steps behind everyone else.

"You look like hell." Adam sniffs me.

"Thank you." I pull away, wondering if I forgot deodorant this morning. I can't remember.

"You smell funny."

"Cut it out." I grit my teeth. That's not helpful.

"I'm not trying to be rude, but have you washed those clothes recently?"

To tell the truth, I grabbed clothes off my chair. I don't have the energy to fold the laundry, so it all gets piled in my room. "Of course."

"Cuz they smell like the hospital."

It's been weeks since Dad's attack and it's taking me that long to catch up to my life. "Okay, maybe I haven't worn this since then."

"Do you want me to come do your laundry?"

"No, things are getting better. I'll get to it." Soon. Sometime. Maybe. All these words are applicable. Frankly, if I'm not so disgusting that people run screaming from me, I have other things to worry about.

Ms. DaVoe starts class. "I'd like everyone to take a flower crown from your table group."

I glance at the pile of daisies, pansies and green stuff. "That?" I whisper to Adam.

"I guess."

We each gently touch a circle of flora like it's infectious.

"Place one on the person next to you." Ms. DaVoe crowns a kid in the front row, who looks like he'd like to slide down to Mother Earth's level and hide. "It's come to my attention that someone in the family of a student in our class has suffered a heart attack."

I pause midbreath. Who?

"Ms. Garibaldi's father was stricken recently, and he has inspired this assignment."

I turn to Adam. "How does she know?" I try to talk without moving my lips.

He shrugs. Baffled too.

"The crowns are to help you find your inner self. And we will be making self-portraits of our hearts. You're welcome to use any of the materials you find in the room. I don't want Valentine hearts, people, I want beating hearts."

I raise my eyebrows. First, how did she know about my dad? And second, how in the world did he inspire this activity? It's like saying Jimmy Carter inspires consumption of dumplings. One does not rationally beget the other.

"We will be working on this all week. Feel free to take your time and personalize your masterpiece. For those of you who need time to center yourselves, please come to the front of the class and we'll begin with a session of yoga." She whips off her scarf skirt to reveal shiny Lycra pants topped by a tank top desperately trying to keep her parts hidden. It's a tired tank top.

Adam leans in. "I swear I didn't tell her."

I shrug. I can't work up the energy to care. But I do know what my self-portrait looks like. I walk over to the materials cupboards and rummage around.

"What are you searching for?" Adam appears beside me, shuffling through cardstock and a jar of buttons.

"Remember those macaroni necklaces?"

"From kindergarten?"

"Yeah."

"What about them?"

I'd like to go back. I'm not ready for adulthood. I'm just not. "That's part of my heart." I pick up a bottle of red food coloring and a bag of pasta.

"What's the other part?" Bless Adam for not questioning my idea.

"Money."

"Uh-huh. You're going to put money on this heart?"

"Color copies." Lord knows I can't afford to glue money to posterboard, at least not until I find another job.

" 'Kay."

"You?"

"Froot Loops." He smiles.

I giggle. "That's good." I hand him a big bottle of paste. "I think you'll need this."

WHO AM I?
PART THREE

I am not graceful. I've always wanted to be a lithe ballerina type who glides instead of walks and who only bumps into boys on purpose to twitter, instead of accidentally, like me. Pick the most attractive guy in the room and I can guarantee I will somehow manage to dump liquid on him, trip on an invisible boulder in front of him or give him a concussion by passing too closely.

I have a sixth sense. I don't see dead ghosts. My sixth sense comes from instinctively knowing where the sharpest corners on furniture are, where the carpet is peeling just a wee bit, where the doorjambs zig into walkways so I can run into them.

It's not that I'm terribly clumsy. I would even go so far as to admit to being rather coordinated, if you define "rather" as "occasionally." It's more than a pure clumsy. It's a hybrid form of self-flagellation: monks use that whip thingy; I use whatever is most handy. It's a trait I was born with. Really wish I'd gotten a different recessive gene. Like red hair or deep green eyes.

I am not a people person. It's clear to

me that I would not be the one to build the ark or throw myself on the grenade for just anyone who might become collateral damage. Nope.

I don't like people in general. In mobs the collective IQ drops to a negative number; common sense, if there is any, runs in the opposite direction. I'm fairly certain I don't care about people for the sake of their peopleness.

Take polite conversation. I suck at it. I hate it. I don't want an answer to the "how are you?" question. I certainly don't want you to answer me. I don't care about your dog's gallbladder, your aunt's bad back, the cost of a postage stamp or Oprah's latest hot topic. Just say "fine." Really. That's all I want.

If we lived in another culture, I'd ask "are you well?" and you'd probably give me a list in minute detail. Don't. Resist the urge to honestly answer. Say "fine." Or "well." "Well" is okay, too. I don't want to hear about your hemorrhoids, the boss who hates you, the trash that you think is filling the airwaves and corrupting young minds. I don't care. I like my corrupted mind.

I really should have known this about myself before I applied to the donut shop. Because I've learned something. I think I could go days without speaking. Really. I'd like to try it, but Mom would probably ship me off to a boot camp in Arizona for ornery teens. Retail is obviously not for me. It requires the ability to act like you give a crapping buttock about the person holding the debit card.

And I don't compare to anyone else. It's not as if I think I'm better than Cleopatra, Princess Diana or Mother Teresa. I'm not. In fact, I'd bet money that I'm more flawed, more screwed-up, less deserving than all of them. But I'm me. I will not spend my life comparing myself to other people, who live other lives, walk in other shoes, shuffle their butts into other jeans. Cuz, see, what's the point in comparing us? At best I'd feel inferior and at worst I'd feel superior. What's the point? Besides, we all know you don't give As on this project, Mr. Slater. There are lines. This is mine. I don't want to be anyone else. I can't be.

So I guess we know I'm not a terribly good actress, either. Not a people person and not an actress. There are things I won't do even for an A. And my heart is made of uncooked red macaroni and photocopied dollar bills. What enlightening revelations will tomorrow bring? Can't wait. Goody.

twenty-one

I throw myself down next to my friends at lunch and put my head on the table. Ten minutes of sleep. Sleep would be good. What day is it? Crapping buttocks, I don't know.

"What day is it?" I ask without raising my head.

Clarice pokes her head under and looks at me. She squints like I'm a roach. Kafka, here I come. "What?"

"Day?"

"Friday." She draws this out like I'm a freak. I *feel* freakish. Since Dad's come home from the hospital and school's back in session, I'm a zombie. I can't even work up the "p" in "perky."

"Friday?" I close my eyes. Good, another week. I think I'm caught up on homework. I'm holding my own. "Wake me up when the bell rings?"

"Sure." Clarice taps my head like I'm an orangutan dressed up like a teenage girl. She might not be far off.

I throw my book bag on the kitchen table and grab a glass, fill it with four ice cubes, ginger ale and a little cranberry juice, grab a bendy straw and a yogurt and glide toward the living room, where Dad's propped up on a hospital bed they moved in so he won't have to do stairs for a while. "Hi, Dad. How's it going?"

This is our routine. I don't ask how he is, because it's clear he's been better and he's bored out of his mind.

He nods and takes the glass from me. "How was school?"

"Okay." I peel back the lid of the yogurt and hand it to him.

He wants to argue about eating it. Nothing tastes good to him, but we're supposed to get lots of little snacks into him until he feels like full meals again. I wait until he's finished sipping the pop, then hand him the spoon. "Cherry," I say. "Mom?"

"Napping. She went upstairs about ten minutes ago." This too has become our routine.

I kick off my shoes and pull up a chair. "Who's playing?"

"Marlins. You have homework?"

"I'll get to it."

He nods. "Why aren't you working right now?"

I haven't exactly told Dad I got fired. "Uh, I got fired."

"Why?" He doesn't react with the explosion I'm expecting. People in our family don't get fired.

"I told a customer that he shouldn't be eating donuts if he'd had a heart attack. He was on his way home from the hospital."

"That's all?"

Isn't that enough? I nod.

"I got fired from my first job."

"What happened?"

"I was working in a grocery store. I left early with friends and a delivery of ice cream didn't get put away."

"Really?" I've never heard this side of my dad.

He nods. "It melted. I had to clean it up and work another two months to pay for it, then I got fired."

"Seriously?"

"You looking for another job?"

"Yeah, I'm hoping there'll be something in today's paper." I can't take time off. Mom's counting on me. I know this. But she doesn't know I know she needs me to. Secrets are so complicated.

"That's good. Don't worry about it."

"You need anything?"

"I think I'll just close my eyes for a while. You go get to your homework."

"Want the TV on?"

"Yeah."

I nod, but he's not watching me. "Thanks. For, you know, telling me about the ice cream."

"Stuff happens." His eyes are already closed.

"Hi, hi. I've got dinner." Heather lets herself in, carrying bags of deli food from the place my dad likes. This too is the new routine; every other day Heather brings dinner. On the off nights, I'm learning to warm things up and throw them together. The sad part is that my efforts are actually tastier than anything Mom's ever made. "How're you?" Heather asks me as I walk into the kitchen.

"Okay, I guess."

"Sounds dire." She pauses. "Anything you need help with?"

"Need to hire a teenager?"

"Hmm, no. But I think the pediatrician who works in our building is looking for someone to file."

I close my eyes. "Really?"

"I can ask if you want?"

"Thank you. No one is hiring. I can't find a single person who'll talk to me." Part of me is secretly terrified that word of my firing has made the gossip circuit and I will be thoroughly unemployable for the rest of my existence.

"I'll ask. How's Dad?"

"He's better. He took two walks down the street today," Mom answers as she comes in, rumpled from her nap. She squeezes me and Heather gets a kiss. "Thank you, this is such a big help. Gertrude, is your homework finished?"

I am doomed to repeat this conversation for weeks. Mom shuffles in, asks a couple of bland questions, shuffles out. This is my life.

I fill a plate. "Thanks, Heather. I have to finish a paper for English."

"Your term one?"

"That's the one." I roll my eyes. I know more about myself than I ever wanted to know.

I'm almost asleep when Mom knocks on my door. She waits. This has to be a first. She knocks again.

"Come in," I call.

"Honey, can we talk?"

I turn on my bedside lamp, fuzzy pink shade and all. "You have more questions about anal bleaching?" I crack a smile.

She laughs. "No, I'm clear on that. I'm worried you're doing too much."

"I'm fine."

"I know you're managing because you're strong and capable. I've never been more proud of you. You've really stepped up to help this family." She has tears in her eyes. "The thing is, I'm grateful for your help, but I think maybe you're taking on too much."

"I'm doing—"

"Fine, I know. But is your schoolwork caught up? Do you want to go out this weekend? Have some fun?"

She's the most sincere I've ever seen her. I can't say I really thought she'd noticed—not that I blame her with Dad sick and all, but I didn't expect her to care. "I have editing to do on the big paper for Slater, and homework, the basics. It's caught up."

"Yes, but do you want to have fun? Have your friends over?"

I shrug. "Thanks, but not right now. I have to study for finals."

"Will you tell me if you need anything? I don't want you to get lost in all this."

"Thanks."

She kisses my forehead. "Dad's going to be better than ever. He's getting stronger every day and pretty soon things will be back to normal."

Normal. Really? I don't think so. I nod as she's leaving the room.

"I love you, Gertie."

"Love you, too." I turn out my lamp and stare at the ceiling until sleep claims me.

Heather brings by an application on Monday. "I told him you were very responsible and dedicated. I might have implied you're interested in pediatrics because there was this other kid they were considering who's all premed and, like, fourteen. I suggested you were willing to work a lot this summer if they needed you."

I throw my arms around her and hang on perhaps longer than is strictly polite. "Thank you. Thank you. Thank you." I pull away, gripping the application.

"You don't have the job yet."

"I will get this filled out and sent in right away." I stop. "Do you think they'll call the Donut King?"

Heather gets a sheepish grin on her face. "I might have said this would be your first official job."

"You're a brilliant liar."

"Don't tell anyone, they may kick me out of preschool!"

I grin.

She's thoughtful. "You're looking good."

"I'm getting my game back." I nod. "School is winding down and I'm going to get good grades, if I don't screw up finals. And Dad's moved back to their bedroom, and he doesn't need as much help."

"You still cooking dinner?"

"Yeah, I like it. Not as much, though, because Mom is back to her charities and stuff." Dad still isn't eating full meals, so most nights I'm snacking or nuking a precooked dinner.

Mr. Slater's butt must be plugged into a new playlist, because he's got a new tempo going on with the butt clenching. It's all rave jam.

Our paper is due today. May twenty-fourth. The one I've spent months working on? The one about *moi, yo,* me? I've finished it and I even had to edit out pages so I wouldn't go over the page limit.

People are sweating, red and squirmy. I guess I had an abnormally easy time with it. Easy might be overstating, but these people look like drinking poisoned Kool-Aid would be a relief.

Mr. Slater starts calling out names and making people walk the length of the classroom and hand him their paper. There's no hiding on this one.

Lucas has started sitting next to me. He's shaved his head for some unknown reason. When I heard I thought I'd miss his perfect hair, but he is still the most deliciousness boy in the world, even bald. He leans toward me. "How's your dad?"

"He's pretty much mended. Thanks for asking."

He nods. "You done?"

I nod. "You?"

"Barely. Tim helped." This last he drops to a whisper. "You going to prom?"

My heart races. My mouth gets dry. He's not asking me, he already has a date, but my body can't help but hope that was a nasty rumor. "I don't think so."

"You should come. Adam and Tim are getting tuxes later today. We're all going together."

Let's see, two couples and me. Let me consider. Ha, ha, that's so tempting. "I've already got plans with friends, kinda an anti-prom thing."

"That's cool."

My name is called and I scoot out of my seat, walk to Slater and hand him my paper.

"I'm looking forward to seeing what you have to say about yourself, Ms. Garibaldi." He checks off my name without looking up at me.

"Thanks." It's the closest thing to a compliment I've ever heard come out of his mouth. I almost ask if he's having chest pains or anything.

rave #10

working girls are wonderful

I got the job! I got the job! I love doctors! I love children! I got the job!

I'm a working girl again and I won't screw this up. I won't. I will duct tape my mouth. I will be demure, quiet, polite and competent. Besides, what could I possibly say to a sick kid that could get me fired?

twenty—two

I dump my bags, read the note Mom left. The parentals have gone to the grocery store for a short outing. Dad's clearly got cabin fever. Next to the note is a thick cream-colored envelope, one of those nine-by-twelve envelopes used so people don't have to fold pages or that college catalogs come in.

The return address grabs my attention. The Passport Program.

I slide into a chair. My stomach gets all clenched and excited. You know those moments when you think maybe something big is about to happen, but you're not sure quite what? This is one of those moments.

I close my eyes and picture myself in Piccadilly Circus, sailing down the Danube, climbing the ruins in Peru. I look happy. Relaxed. My teeth sparkle like in the catalog, my skin is flawless, my clothes are European chic.

I take a great gulp of air and rip into the envelope. I pull out a heavy pocket folder with a glossy blue cover. A letter slides out. My eyes scan it so fast I have no idea what it says. I read it out loud: " 'Dear Ms. Garibaldi: Congratulations. You've been selected to participate in the Passport Program for the upcoming fall term as a Traveler! The following spring, your family will host travelers from places you will visit on your trip.' "

I exhale and blink. I jump up and pace the kitchen, clutching the paperwork. " 'Because of your stellar academics, phenomenal teacher recommendations from Ms. DaVoe and Mr. Slater, and your personal essay, we are pleased to offer you the highest honor of Passport Reporter. If you accept this challenge, you will be the voice of the Passport Program on the Web and for our print publications. You will be expected to keep a weekly report updated via any electronic means. As a thank-you we will allocate a stipend to be paid as a scholarship for our program along with airfare.' "

I grope for the floor. A scholarship?

I get to travel the world and get paid to do it? " 'Your family will be expected to pay for your food, clothes and incidental expenses incurred on the trip. Please contact our offices right away to begin the paperwork. This package is only offered to a few select individuals, with all expenses paid by . . .' " I look over the list of Fortune 500 companies who support this exchange program. The motto is "One World, One Future." Which is catchy, if overly cute.

Do I want to go? Do I want to leave this behind? Am I ready for change with a capital "C"? Holy-Mother-of-Answered-Prayers, I am so ready. All I have to do is grab my toothbrush.

Then I see the bold print: **Must have parental permission.** There's always a catch. I haven't even told them I applied. Because let's face it, I didn't expect to get accepted, so why share? I should have prepared them for this eventuality. I am so screwed.

I scuttle the papers upstairs and grab the phone. There's only one person who might possibly know how to handle the parents. Mike.

"Oh, bestest brother in the whole world?" I ask.

Heather picks up an extension. "Hi, Gertie, what's up?"

"Do you have another tweezer emergency?" Mike drawls.

"Cute," I say, then spill my guts.

Mike and Heather help me decide to wait until this weekend to tell the parents, when they're here for a family dinner and can back me up. Mike doesn't think they'll have any problems at all; Heather's a little more reserved in her predictions. I don't know how Mom and Dad will react. They worry I'm not grown-up enough; will they let me fly off into the wild blue?

Mom is cooking. She says she's missed it. We're all popping precautionary Pepto. She manages to make pasta that is one clump, burns the sauce and leaves the salad on the stove so the lettuce is all wilted and runny.

Heather brings a heart-healthy cheesecake from the new bakery in town for dessert. I'm not sure the twelve-inch cake is going to be enough to feed all of us.

It is times like these I wish my parents were animal people and we had a dog. I've never been able to feed brussels sprouts and pasty pasta to a four-legged creature. I've always been expected to eat enough to sustain life.

Heather thinks they should lead with their news. I'm fine with this. I can't help but wonder if my news will cause Dad to have another cardiac episode.

"We've set the date," Mike throws into the conversation. His sense of timing is all wrong.

"That was my line." Heather pokes him and laughs.

"I couldn't wait." Mike looks sheepish and forks up a bite of cucumber.

"Oh, that's wonderful news." Mom claps her hands and does a little sitting dance. "When?"

"Memorial Day weekend next year. We want to make it a fun weekend, not just the wedding. A brunch, a laid-back barbeque, that kind of thing."

"How fun."

"Now your mother has something else to fuss over. Thank you." Dad chuckles.

"Bill," Mom scolds.

"I'm going to Timbuktu!" I shout. Yes, I shout, and yes, instead of saying Paris, Sydney, even Rome, I pick Timbuktu to break the news.

"What?" Dad's brow furrows.

"Is there such a place, dear?" Mom asks, picking up another slice of bread like I just told them I was showering in the morning.

I roll my eyes, but seriously I'm too nervous to make any sort of cogent thought come out of my mouth.

Mike jumps in. "Gert's been accepted into the Passport Program for secondary students. Isn't that great?"

Heather imitates Mom and claps with a chair dance.

"What is that?" Mom asks Mike.

This is not the excitement I'm hoping for.

"Don't worry, I checked it out through the college, it's completely legit. Gert, why don't you tell us about it." Mike emphasizes his command with his formidable unibrow.

"I go to many different places, I take American classes online so I don't get behind on school, even though while I'm in town I go with the host student to school. I stay with families and do local stuff." I glance at Dad, who is thoughtful and silent.

"Oh." Mom puts down her fork. "I didn't know you wanted to travel?"

"Yeah, well." How to say high school sucks without making my parents put me on suicide watch? "I'm ready to change the scenery. You know, school is the same and I'm ready for different. I want to stretch my wings and spread my leg—wings." Oh, hell, I almost butchered the metaphors and made myself into a hooker in one sentence. Priceless.

"I see. Is it expensive?" Mom's tone is worried.

Heather wades in. "That's the great part. Gert's working all summer to pay for herself."

I am? News to Gert.

"Gert, why don't you tell your parents about the best part?"

"What?"

"The scholar—"

"Oh, yeah, if I write a weekly thingy for their website and stuff, I get a scholarship for the program."

Dad holds up a hand. "Mike, you've checked this out? You knew about this?"

"I called him." I swallow. "I didn't know how to—" I break off.

"Did you tell us you'd applied?" Dad asks me.

I shake my head. "No, I didn't tell anyone and then stuff happened and I forgot about it."

"And you want to go?"

"I think so." I pause. "No. I mean yes, I'm sure I want to go."

"Well, that's . . . wow. This is so unexpected." Mom's got tears in her eyes. "Our little girl's going to travel the world and write about it."

Dad reaches over and squeezes my hand. "Congratulations. Sounds like this is an opportunity you shouldn't miss."

"Really?" I wasn't anticipating the caving or the enthusiasm.

He nods. "You've proven you're responsible and can handle a crisis. I see no reason why we shouldn't let you go."

Mom sniffles. "My little girl."

"It's only for a term. And then you have to let other kids come here," I say, wondering if this is the part they'll object to.

"That'll be fun." Mom beams. "I can introduce them to the Bunko girls."

That'll be a highlight, I'm sure. "Right."

"Who wants cheesecake?" Mom leaps to her feet, quite sprightly. "We have good news to celebrate!"

Dad laughs and shakes his head. I breathe.

With only finals and the last week of school left, it's prom night. "When are the guys coming by?" Clarice asks as she dumps two duffel bags, her sleeping bag and a grocery bag of snacks on the living room floor. The parentals are thrilled I've invited my friends over for a slumber party, and as long as the police aren't called for a noise disturbance, they've promised to give us plenty of space.

Adam and Tim are coming by to show off their outfits and get photos taken. Adam's parents pretty much want to ignore his orientation, so he keeps a very low profile at home. They're not what you'd call open-minded Catholics (the Pope is proud, I'm sure). In the meantime, they break Adam's heart all the time. "Between nine and ten. They want to be suitably late."

Maggie pokes through Clarice's bag. "Did you bring enough?"

"My sister thought we needed most of this. She's still worried that I'll, you know, never get over what happened."

"Did she really make you get a blood test and birth control pills?"

"Yes, and she checks to make sure I'm taking them. It's a little too helicopter."

"It's cool that she didn't freak out, though." Maggie shudders. "My mother would disown me if she thought I even knew the definition of sex."

According to her parents, Maggie is going to be a nun like Mother Teresa. If she ever works up the nerve to be okay liking a boy, Jesse is going to be toast.

"Did you hear Jenny dumped Stephen?"

"No!" I leap onto the couch. "How did I miss this?"

"I guess she told the entire cafeteria that the bathroom was right, he has a tiny dick and he doesn't know what to do with it."

"That's harsh." I cackle. I can't help it. I'm human.

"I know, but I heard she got tired of him groping and grinding without caring if she was having a good time."

"She's telling people that?"

"Yep."

I digest. Part of me feels bad for the guy. But part of me doesn't really feel bad at all. I think coffee may start tasting good again. "Mags, what did you bring for entertainment?"

"Prom movies!" Maggie pulls out discs with a flourish. "Keeping with the theme, we have *Carrie*, *Pretty in Pink*, *American Pie*, *Prom Night*, and *The World's Best Prom*."

"Eclectic and genre-fying. Nicely done!" Clarice gives Maggie a high five.

I trip over pillows and bags on my way to the CD player. "To start the party, I really think we need a little sing-along." I hit play and the Ramones' "Strength to Endure" comes belting out of the player. Clarice hasn't sung this, or Avril, in months, and I'm starting to worry that she's lost her love of music. It's like she decided she's outgrown it, or worse, doesn't deserve it. She's had a little self-hate going on that it's time to ditch.

I start yelling out the lyrics and Maggie joins me. We dance on the furniture, and after a second of indecision Clarice picks up the song and the tempo with her hips.

We've collapsed in a pile, and we're eating chips and Twizzlers, watching the cheesiest slasher movie ever and loving every minute of it when there's a knock on the door.

"I'll get it, honey," Mom yells.

"Adam and Tim." We all glance at each other. How is Mom going to react? She's not exactly "in the know." We scramble over each other and I grab the camera.

"Adam, Tim, nice to see you boys again." Mom is ushering them in. "And don't you just look dapper in your tuxes. Your dates will be quite honored for you to escort them," she's saying as the three of us girls arrive in the foyer.

There's an uncomfortable silence until Adam says, "Mrs. Garibaldi, Tim is my date for the evening. He's my boyfriend."

Tim beams. Totally glows. I know how hard it is for Adam to make this announcement and set himself up for more rejection.

"Then I hope you bought him a corsage." She giggles. "Maybe a boutonniere? What's the proper etiquette, I don't know." She straightens Adam's tie and smooths his lapels, then moves on to Tim.

Adam smiles at me. I've never seen him quite so happy. "We got each other boutonnieres."

"Yes, I see that. Orchids are a lovely choice. Very now, I've heard." Mom's not even acting like she's okay with this; she is okay with this. "Gert, you have the camera? We should have a photograph of these two gentlemen. Especially since you're boycotting the prom this year." She huffs at me.

I turn the camera over as Maggie and Clarice snicker behind their hands. The boyly-mans do look absolutely stunningly manly.

"We'd better get going." Adam hugs me. "Thanks," he whispers in my ear.

"Clueless," I whisper back.

"Have fun tonight, you guys!" Tim waves as they head back down the sidewalk holding hands.

"You too! Call me later with details!" I yell as I close the door.

Mom's standing there looking at me. "You could have told me, you know. I wouldn't have worried so much about the time you spent together."

"Sorry?" I say. I pegged my mom as a homophobe. My bad.

"I made a pan of brownies for you girls. Try to get at least a little sleep tonight."

"We will," we answer, fully intending to watch all the movies and sleep only if absolutely necessary.

"Your job starts Monday, Gert. You don't want to be too tired," Mom calls from the stairs.

"Yes, Mom."

"Oh, and Gert?" Mom stops. "There's a nice note from your English teacher and your paper on the kitchen table. We're very proud of you."

I race to the kitchen. "He *mails them home?*"

"The Who papers?" Clarice asks. "Yep, my sister's got mailed home with a big red F on it. He uses different envelopes and return addresses each year so parents are sure to see them."

I pick it up. An A. I got an A. "I got an A."

Maggie's jaw drops. "Nobody gets an A."

"I got an A," I repeat.

"Wow, look what he wrote." Clarice leans over my shoulder. " 'Congratulations and well done. I'll look forward to reading your thoughts on the world as you travel next year. Best of luck, Mr. Slater.' "

"Wow."

"Wow."

We stand there in awe. "Can I use yours as an outline for mine next year?" Clarice asks, and we giggle.

"Sure." I tap her head with the paper.

"What job was your mom talking about?" Maggie asks.

I shrug. "I'm going to be the file-office-greeter-phone-answering-person at a pediatrician's office for the summer. I need money for souvenirs, and a college fund."

Clarice nods. "You have to bring us presents, but I hear you on the college thing. I'm applying to Claire's in the mall."

We raise our brows at Maggie. She mutters, "Busing tables at Romano's."

"Do you get free food?" I ask. I love that place.

She brightens. "Orientation is Friday. Maybe."

We're all working this summer. It's odd really. So much change, so fast. It's mind-boggling when I slow down and think about it, so I don't think about it often. We still have finals, but the year is almost over.

I grab cold cans of Coke. "Let's get back to the prom from hell."

We settle and hit play. "Have you noticed the lead's resemblance to Jenny?" I ask, and they throw chips at me. "Kidding." Kinda.

the butt-cheek
philosophy of life:
an addendum

Okay, here's the deal: the pants change, the butt changes, but the process doesn't. The jeans of life don't always fit well: the crotch can be too short, the waist too binding, the legs too long or short. They can even have strange finishes or cuts that feel outdated or wrong. Like acid-washed, or skinny, or they might have sequins on them or little kitten appliqués. Sometimes it's about doing the best you can and wearing whatever pair you're dealt that day with confidence. Even if you have to fake it.

It's about squishing your butt into whatever jeans you have; then it's about accessorizing to make them work. Because life changes. There are crises and opportunities, unexpected obstacles and expectations from people around you that you can't control.

There's a point in all of this where your butt becomes coveted, where you go from butt to booty, childhood to quasi-adulthood. Where boys and men start seeing more and seeing less. Somewhere in the last few months I changed from butt cheeks to booty. To feeling and thinking more like a woman, even when I still fear things like a girl.

But here's what I do know. Pants are pants and you put them on the same way, no matter what they look like. It's all still one booty cheek at a time. One. At. A. Time. Try it! It's gotten me this far and it's gonna take me to Timbuktu.

About the Author

Amber Kizer is not one of those authors who wrote complete books at the age of three and always knew she wanted to be a writer. She merely enjoyed reading until a health challenge that began in college forced her to start living outside the box. After one writing workshop, she fell in love with telling stories; a million pages of prose later she still loves it. Her characters tend to be opinionated, outspoken, and stubborn—she has no idea where that comes from.

A food lover, she plans trips around menus, wishes cookbooks were scratch and sniff, and loves to make complicated recipes—especially desserts. When she's not reading from a huge stack, she's coaxing rosebushes to blossom, watching delightful teen angst on television, or quilting with more joy than skill. She takes her tea black, her custard frozen, and her men witty. She lives in the Seattle area on a veritable Noah's Ark: a pair of dogs, a pair of cats, fifteen pairs of chickens, and uncounted pairs of shoes—without the big boat and only some of the rain.

A celebrated speaker and teacher, Amber gives writing workshops for all ages. For more information about Amber, for a list of appearances, or to request a school visit, please see www.AmberKizer.com. For more from Gert, including original material and sneak peeks of upcoming Rants and Raves, visit www.OneButtCheek.com.